THEY WERE AS ONE

Their single goal now seemed attainable. To die in such an enterprise would be an honor bestowed on only a few fortunate men in the history of the world. An elite group.

Nadi Amur turned to face them. He'd made his decision.

"We are in position. We must act now. We will send the message. The Americans think they have felt pain." He laughed as he said it. "It is but a pinprick. Now they will truly feel the pain. Now they will understand. We will go forward. We will go home at last!"

The room was filled with the sound of cheers.

THE WARNING

THE
WARNING

HARRISON ARNSTON

ZEBRA BOOKS
KENSINGTON PUBLISHING CORP.

ZEBRA BOOKS

are published by

Kensington Publishing Corp.
475 Park Avenue South
New York, NY 10016

First printing: December 1987

Printed in the United States of America

For four fine people whose support was above and beyond the call of simple kindness:

Deborah Schneider
Judy Paris
Cynthia Ergenbright
Margaret Landry

Chapter One

The terrible sound the bullets made as they crashed into the ship took the captain completely by surprise. For a few moments, he just stood there, his hands on the wheel, trying to understand. The distinctive clatter could be heard even above the sound of the pounding waves, the howling wind, and the groans and shudders of the ancient ship itself. The French freighter *Armand Lavertue* continued lurching through the twenty-foot swells, her captain uncomprehending at first, then finally recognizing sounds he'd thought he'd never hear again.

Jean Leblanc clenched his jaw tightly, his teeth cutting into the stem of the pipe that seemed a part of him. The ship's position was some one hundred nautical miles east of the island of Malta, on a course that would take it to the Suez Canal, and eventually, Japan. Captain Leblanc had made the voyage many times, in seas much worse than this. But it had been forty-four years since he'd found himself on board a ship that was under attack. His head snapped to the starboard side of the ship and his eyes peered through the rain-covered window, straining to capture some sight of his attacker. It was an instinctive reaction, because there was nothing he could do. The ship was unarmed.

Just as the sounds of destruction behind and above him stopped, he saw it. A slate-grey submarine, without flags, bobbing in the sea not fifty yards distant, a fifty-caliber machine gun trained on the freighter.

The intercom sputtered.

"Captain, communications room. Our antennas have been destroyed. All of our electronics are out."

The captain acknowledged and trained his binoculars on the submarine. In addition to the machine gun, the front deck held a missile launcher equipped with four slender white missiles, also aimed at the freighter. Beside the missile launcher stood several men in black wet suits, one of them holding a crude cardboard sign. A simple message was scrawled on the cardboard. One word. *"Arrêt."*

The captain ordered the ship brought to a speed of ten knots. To come to a complete halt would be dangerous in these seas. He was sure those on the sub would know that. He wasn't sure they would care. By now, several of the freighter's crew, concern clearly etched in their faces, had entered the closed bridge area, all of them speaking at once, wanting to know what the hell was going on.

Captain Leblanc simply pointed to the submarine and shrugged his shoulders. He was attempting to appear nonchalant but he was anything but, his heart beating wildly and his mind filling with omi-

8

nous thoughts.

Whoever they were, they had shot his radio and radar antennas away first, an action that guaranteed no radio messages could be sent. Now, or later. Somehow, the captain had the feeling that these were no ordinary pirates. Of the crew members, only he was aware of the true contents of part of the manifest, a knowledge that he now felt was shared by those in the submarine.

A small black inflatable rubber dinghy was dispatched from the sub. The dinghy held four men in black wet suits carrying machine guns. A rope ladder was lowered from the freighter and the pirates made their way on board and to the bridge.

They stood there, the water dripping from their bodies, Uzi machine guns resting carelessly in their hands. The leader of the group seemed pleasant enough. He was tall and slender, the skin on his face olive-colored and heavily creased, as though he'd spent most of his life out-of-doors. Captain Leblanc had the feeling that somewhere, somehow, he'd seen this man before.

The tall man smiled at the crew, apologized for the inconvenience and seemed anxious to set their minds at ease. His smile and gracious manner seemed to offset the menace. His French was impeccable.

"Captain, we wish you no harm. Please order all of your crew to assemble on the bridge. We will retrieve what we are seeking and be on our way. Your cooperation will ensure that no harm comes to you or your crew."

The captain spread his hands and pointed to the

9

roiling seas. "Please, you must let us proceed. Take what you will, but if we don't get underway, we'll capsize in these seas."

The smile remained on the pirate's face. "In a moment," was the reply.

Captain Leblanc did as he was told and ordered all crew to come to the bridge. As they made their way, the captain glanced out the window and noticed another rubber dinghy coming toward the rusting freighter, this one holding two more men and a load of something bundled in tarpaulins and rope. The captain's sense of impending doom became stronger.

Finally, all of the crew was assembled. The man with the charm smiled, nodded once, and four Uzis opened fire.

For a split second, Leblanc thought it might be a dream, some terrible nightmare that would wash away in the clear light of wakefulness. But, as the slugs tore into his body and the pain reached his brain, he had the briefest of instants to realize that it was no dream, before his life ended and he crashed to the floor. The old sea captain and his entire crew were dead in seconds, forever unconcerned with the further activities of the men in the wet suits as they went about their business.

Moving quickly, they located sixteen crates in the hold marked "Tourneau Crystal Works," attached flotation devices to the crates, and then pushed them through an opened gangway into the sea. Another dinghy was waiting, and four men leaped into the water and attached ropes to each crate as it hit the water and then tied the ropes to the dinghy.

10

After all of the crates had been secured, the men still on board the ship opened up the bundles of plastic explosives, placed them in strategic locations around the ship, and set the timers. Then all of the attackers were in the water, headed back to the submarine. Once they reached it, they attached the crates to ropes from a block-and-tackle rigged to the railing, hauled the contraband aboard, and stowed it below. .

The tall one went below and into the radio room. He nodded to the young man seated at the controls, who began speaking in French into the microphone immediately in front of his lips. His voice sounded excited, then progressively more frantic as he read from the notes in front of him. Then, in midsentence, he pushed a switch, stopped talking, and leaned back in his chair.

The tall man, his black rubber suit still dripping, lit a cigarette and grinned in satisfaction. Then he picked up the intercom mouthpiece and barked, "All ahead full!"

The submarine was almost a mile away when the charges exploded and the *Armand Lavertue*, four massive holes in her hull, broke apart and slipped beneath the waves, heading for the bottom some twelve thousand feet below.

The entire operation had taken all of twenty-three minutes.

David Baxter rarely snored, but tonight was an exception. He was exhausted. He'd just spent the last week showing his vacationing sister and her husband the sights.

Bob and Barbara had left the kids at home and embarked on a second honeymoon of sorts. Since David was working in Paris, they chose France. After all, Bob and David were the best of friends, and who would know better where to see the "real" Paris.

Actually, David had looked forward to the visit. It had been almost three years since he'd laid eyes on either one of them, and their arrival brought a flood of warm feelings that washed away some of the many layers of disillusionment that had built up over the years.

The vacation was theirs, but it was David who really benefited from it, by forcing his mind to focus on something besides his work . . . and his life.

It was a tonic watching the two of them, their eyes widening like little children's as he took them to the usual tourist spots and some places far from the normal path.

David was fluent in French; in fact it was that ability that had caused the agency to assign him to Paris. He was supposedly working for the Department of Trade, attached to the State Department. At least, that was his officially stated position. In fact, he was a CIA agent; his assignment: counter-terrorism.

Showing Bob and Barb around had been pure fun. Like most Americans who'd never been abroad, they were astonished at how *old* everything seemed. Compared to Newport Beach, Paris was light-years away in age. And culture.

The three had enjoyed the reunion immensely. It was clear that almost six years of marriage had not dulled the couple's enthusiasm for each other, and there were fleeting moments when their happiness almost made David jealous, his own marriage having lasted less than a year.

But the moments were just that. Fleeting. Barbara and David were very close, and her obvious joy was a wonderful thing to witness.

And now, having returned from Orly where he had seen them off, heading back to Newport Beach, with their luggage stuffed with little knickknacks for the kids, he fell into bed and immediately started cranking out loud rumbles that woke him up from time to time.

The ringing of the bedside phone brought him awake instantly. This was going to be a very long night, he thought, as he reached for the black instrument on the bedside table.

He looked at the clock. It was almost one in the morning. What stupid fool!

He picked up the phone and barked into the mouthpiece. "Yes!"

It was Grant.

"David! I want you here . . . now!"

David knew better than to ask. He simply grunted his assent and hung up the phone.

Grant Talmage sat at his desk, a small film of perspiration glistening on his bald skull. His eyes were fixed on the report in his hands, a report that he'd read over and over again, as if by concentration he could produce words that were missing. Words that would give him the answers to questions that were burning in his brain. Questions that needed to be answered as quickly as possible.

He felt dreadful. It was now past one in the morning, and his mouth tasted foul from a combination of too many cigars and too little food. His body ached from a full day and night of tension, and the stale smoke from the cigars hung in layered wisps, giving the room a ghostly cast. The stink was terrible, even for Grant. He snubbed out the cigar in the large glass ashtray. He was simply getting too old for this crap.

There was a light rap on the door and David entered the room, his arms chopping at the smoke as though the blue-grey wisps were cobwebs spun by a thousand industrious spiders.

"Grant, you keep smoking those things, you'll never see fifty."

The bald man didn't smile. Instead, he turned and poured some scotch into two glasses and handed one to David. "Here," he said. "Have a drink. You'll need it. How did your relatives enjoy France?"

David didn't really feel like a drink . . . not now, in the middle of the night, but the look in Grant's eyes changed his mind. The question was purely rhetorical, as though Grant wanted somehow to delay getting down to business. He went along and answered. "They really had a great time. Wore me out. I was just catching up on some lost sleep when you called. You certainly don't like to give a man a chance to recover from the rigors of a week off."

Talmage grunted.

David sat in the old leather chair and sipped the drink, waiting for Grant to tell him why he'd been summoned in the middle of the night. He knew his boss well. The man was a consummate professional, but he did have a certain flair for the dramatic. The room was poorly lit, a single lamp on Grant's desk providing the only illumination. David wondered if Grant was deliberately setting a mood, or if the environment within the room had evolved naturally.

The older man slumped in his high-backed chair and tossed the blue-covered report into David's lap. David opened it and tried to read. The light was too weak. He got up and moved his chair closer to the lamp, then looked the report over carefully. It was a copy of an Urgent CIA report that had been forwarded to Langley. The report concerned the loss at sea of a French freighter, which had reported it was dead in the water and breaking up before communications were lost. A simple enough occurrence on the face of it, but when it was combined with other intelligence, something more sinister began to emerge.

Item: The constant surveillance of submarines carried out by the CIA and other intelligence agencies had revealed that the Libyan submarine *Al Fateh* was in the approximate area of the freighter at the time of the emergency. This had been confirmed by the fact that the submarine had reported picking up the distress signal from the stricken freighter and had claimed to have conducted an unsuccessful search for survivors before returning to its home port.

15

Item: Libyan submarines were normally staffed with Russian technicians, which was part of the deal made when the Soviets agreed to sell the vessels to Libya. This exercise, according to intelligence, had been conducted without the Russians, who, it was suggested, were more than a little upset.

Item: The *Armand Lavertue* had just undergone a refit. The seas were rough, but there was no clear explanation as to why the freighter would encounter such difficulty. Her captain was a man with many years of experience, and so were most of the crew.

Item: A key engineer by the name of Fazel Khan, who had been working at the supersecret Pakistani nuclear research facility in Kahuta, had been missing from Pakistan for six months. There had been one report that the man had been seen in Tripoli three weeks ago. Unsubstantiated.

Item: A new building, constructed less than two years ago and located about a mile from the Bab al Azzizia barracks near Tripoli, was rumored to be the headquarters for an intensive Libyan effort to develop a nuclear device. The building was the most heavily guarded building in all of Libya.

Item: The *Armand Lavertue* was carrying sixteen drums of plutonium to Japan for use in their nuclear generating stations. The shipment was supposed to have been top secret and done with a minimum of fanfare. The drums were concealed within crates marked as crystal. The French intelligence agencies were now involved in the questioning of every person remotely connected with the shipment. The shipping company was located in Marseilles. No reports as yet.

16

Possible conclusion: Libya had managed to get its hands on enough plutonium to develop a nuclear bomb. The ramifications of such a possibility were staggering.

There was more, but that was the main gist of it, and the obvious reason for the discomfort being felt by Grant Talmage.

David stood up and refilled his glass. He glanced at Grant and raised the glass as if to make a toast.

"I take it I'm off to Marseilles."

Grant nodded and handed him a plane ticket. "Your flight leaves at seven. That will give you time to pack a few things. I'll meet you at your flat at five-thirty and brief you on the way to Orly."

David watched the man light still another cigar. He said, in a voice that had a slight edge to it, "Why me? You have agents already in place down there."

Grant shot a glance at him with red-rimmed eyes. "Our information is that Pierre Query is heading up the investigation. He's an old friend of yours. We haven't got the time or the inclination to go through the regular bullshit. You know the French.

"So, you are to talk to Pierre and find out what the hell happened. We need to know whether or not that ship went down from natural causes or if it was something more sinister. Pierre, I'm sure, will tell you. He'll have finished his investigation by the time you get there. His outfit moves quickly, as you well know. That enough for you?"

David nodded, raised his glass, and said, "See you at five-thirty." Then he drained the scotch and left the office.

17

Grant looked terrible. Worse than David had ever seen him. The man worked too hard at the best of times, but this time he looked as though he was working himself into an early grave. In a way, David wasn't surprised.

For years, the United States had struggled with an enormous concern. The continual efforts of several groups of terrorist organizations to lay their hands on nuclear devices had created a blizzard of worst-case scenarios in the inventive minds of those in the intelligence community. Mental exercises were played out by people charged with the responsibility of dealing with the prevention of such a happenstance, or, in the event of its realization, creating an effective way to handle it. In every case, the scenarios ended in disasters of various proportions, ranging from a large loss of life to the ultimate disaster.

Although the conflict between the United States and Soviet Russia received the media attention, it was the terrifying sense of inevitability that occupied much of the time of these men in their almost desperate mission to prevent terrorists of whatever persuasion from gaining possession of nuclear devices or the capability of developing their own.

The ultimate terrorist act. A blackmail perpetrated by men without a history of rationality, but dedicated to the attainment of goals they considered worthy. Goals that must be reached no matter what the cost. The modern version of the kamikaze. Only the target was not a warship, but something larger. And just as vulnerable.

Grant Talmage set the alarm signal on his wristwatch, switched off the lamp on the desk, and leaned back in his chair. He was exhausted and hoped to catch a few minutes of much-needed sleep.

But his mind was filled with images that would form, disappear, and reform. Perhaps David was right. Maybe he would never see fifty. But it wouldn't be the cigars.

On the way to Orly, Grant brought David up to date. His voice was hoarse and his eyes were blood-shot as he tried to make sure he passed on every piece of information.

"As you know, there is a group inside Libya that is even crazier than Khadaffi. In fact, there are some who believe that Khadaffi is really only a figurehead, allowed to exist simply because he draws attention away from the group. The theory is that as soon as they are in a position to use the nuclear weapons they've been working so hard to get their hands on, they'll take the colonel out and assume full control. Right now, he serves their purposes. In any case, the French are being very tight-lipped about the freighter. They usually aren't too cooperative at the best of times, but in this case, they are really ticked. They were warned by everybody and his brother about shipping pluto-nium to Japan in such an open manner, but they were sure they were right. Now, with egg on their faces, they're probably bound to insist that the freighter had a natural accident. Pierre's been a friend of yours for some time. You're going to have to get at the truth. We simply can't afford to wait for the diplomatic approach. We have to know now! If that plutonium is in Libya, we'll have to take action immediately."

David glanced over at his boss and then snorted. "Action! What are we going to do? Attack?"

Grant didn't hesitate. His answer was a one-word rasp. "Exactly!"

David looked at his boss for a moment and decided that Grant was attempting to be dramatic again. It was unlikely that the United States would attack Libya at this point. There had been many opportunities in the past that had not been seized upon.

Grant's voice seemed to become even more hoarse. David could see that the knuckles on his hands were white from the tightness of his grip on the wheel.

"David . . . I can't tell you how important this is. If this group produces a nuclear bomb, they'll use it without batting an eye. And we have no idea where or how. These people are truly out of control. Unreachable. Untouchable. They have cells all over the Middle East and Europe. We'd have to kill twenty million people to be sure we got them. We're in an untenable position. If the plutonium is in Libya, we can make a strike. But if and when it becomes a weapon, and is moved somewhere else, we're done. You aren't alone. There'll be other people making other approaches to the problem. But your mission is very important. I can't stress enough how vital it is that we know about that ship. The people in Marseilles are the key. And Pierre has got to tell us. That's all there is to it."

Grant handed David a manilla envelope. David switched on the overhead lamp, opened the envelope, and pulled out the contents. There was a passport, some information regarding codes for the next four days, and a photograph of a woman, among other things. The picture on the passport was of David, and the name being used was David Bateman, of Los Angeles, California. It was a diplomatic passport, indicating that Mr. Bateman was with the United States Department of State.

David pulled out the little spotlight from the glove compartment and plugged it into the cigar lighter outlet. He looked at the picture of the woman.

'What am I doing in Marseilles?" he asked.

"You're on vacation. Also visiting an old girl friend who now lives there. Her picture and address are in the envelope. You're divorced. You'll be staying at the Sofitel Marseilles on Charles Livon Boulevard. So will she. She's French, but one of ours. There's a camera in the back seat. Take that with you and be the typical tourist. The girl will try and find out where Pierre is and you can take it from there."

David looked again at the picture of the woman. She was quite beautiful. Dark hair, slightly sloe-eyed, a small nose that turned up at the end, and full lips.

Grant continued. "She'll have a radio and a special unidirectional transmitting antenna. As soon as you have any information, you'll put it in code and transmit the message. You'll point the antenna at a hundred and two degrees. Your message will be picked up by one of our ships in the Med. Right now, because of all of the terrorist activity, the fleet is conducting exercises off the Libyan coast. Some of them will be keeping a watch on the entrance to the Med and one of them will be in a position to receive your messages. Depending on what you find out, those exercises may develop into a full-scale attack."

David looked at Grant sharply. "Jesus Christ! I thought you were just speculating, but you aren't, are you?"

Grant returned David's stare. "No. The rules, if indeed there really are any, are out the window. Whatever has to be done will be done. If we get the cooperation of our allies, great. If not . . . tough shit. I don't think they really understand what's at stake here."

Talmage went into a minor coughing fit. He recovered and continued with his discourse. "I told you. This is important. There are other factors involved. The President wants to make a clear statement regarding Libya's involvement in terrorism. A raid has been planned, and it is hoped that the information you contribute will allow another operation to be combined with the raid. Time is of the essence. Like I said, there are others involved. If you find out that an attack has commenced, that just means someone else got the information. Don't let that deter you. We still need to know whatever you can find out."

David put the material in his briefcase and hung the camera around his neck. "Anything else?"

Grant croaked, "No . . . not really. Everything I've told you is included in the file. There's some other stuff in there that you'll want to review before you arrive."

They reached the airport and David shook hands with Grant, hauled his suitcase from the back seat, and disappeared into the vastness of Orly. Grant put the car in gear and pulled away, heading back to downtown Paris and the American Embassy.

David wasn't the only agent being sent on this mission. There were probably a total of twenty agents involved in this, a most important undertaking. Grant rubbed his forehead as he considered the chances of success. They were better than fifty-fifty. Much better.

David Baxter was one of the good ones. He'd joined the agency six years ago, ostensibly because he was looking for action, but Grant knew that his real motive was to leave behind a bad marriage. Baxter had been a lawyer for a short time, and when he'd first joined the agency he'd been appalled to learn of some of the agency's more nefarious activities. The young ones always were. They didn't understand the stakes, imbued as they were with some fantasy image of the dirty business of intelligence gathering.

Baxter was fluent in French and had been assigned to the embassy in Paris, which he used as a base of operations to gather information on terrorist activities. France, with its typical laissez-faire attitude about activities not directly related to the Republic, was less than diligent about who was doing what to whom. Where it involved themselves, the French could be ruthless, but when the target was Britain, or, as was usually the case, America, they seemed simply to shrug their collective Gallic shoulders, as if to imply that nothing could be done. It was infuriating.

David Baxter was supposedly assigned to the Department of Trade, and his easy manner and good humor had resulted in his ingratiating himself with many of France's business community. He had a way of making connections that had been extremely useful in determining the origin of groups sympathetic to terrorist causes. He was a careful man, and this kind of work was something that he believed in. So much so, that when called upon, he was also capable of ruthlessness. As long as he believed in the cause. His primary fault was his inability to accept orders without question. He was always probing, asking questions that were not his concern, as though he had some right to determine which assignments he would accept and which he would not. He had the arrogant attitude that he was entitled to make a judgment about certain tasks assigned him.

This had created problems large enough that the agency had seriously considered ending his employment. But after some discussion it was determined that he would be kept on, and assigned to those missions where it was predetermined that his and the agency's interests were in tandem. An accommodation, to be sure, but it was the bottom line that was important. At least in Grant Talmage's section, it was. There were other sections where Baxter would have been cashiered in thirty minutes.

This time, it was clear that David Baxter understood the importance of the mission. There had been no hesitation. At least none that Talmage could perceive.

As he drove the car through the ever-increasing traffic, Grant Talmage felt the tiredness attack his body, fighting his consciousness. He pulled the car over to the side of the road and stopped, letting his head lean back on the headrest. He was asleep in seconds.

Chapter Two

David Baxter had just arrived in his room and removed his jacket when there was a light rap at the door. He walked over and asked who was there.

"Michele Dumont."

He opened the door and the woman whose picture he had examined in Grant's car entered the room. She was even more beautiful than her photograph.

The dark hair was longer, piling up around her shoulders after falling in seeming disarray. Her eyes had little makeup, nor did they need it, being large and dark and instantly the center of attention. She was short, but her body was full, and wrapped as it was in a skin-tight red jersey dress, was another attention grabber. Low profile, she was not.

She held out her hand. "Mr. Bateman, I am pleased to meet you."

Her English wasn't bad, either. David took her hand and felt the dry warmth.

"And I you, mam'zel. It didn't take you long."

She smiled, the open mouth revealing perfect white teeth. "I've been expecting you. I have some information."

It was David's turn to smile. At six-three, he towered over this woman, who couldn't have been more than five-two, even in the high heels she was wearing. "OK, let's hear it," he said.

She got right down to business, not even taking the time to sit down. She pulled a small notebook from her handbag and began reading.

"The *Armand Lavertue* left Marseilles on schedule. It belonged to the Latour Shipping Company, an old company with many government contracts. Within hours of its disappearance, the Special Services people arrived at the shipping company in droves and took several people away. Your old friend, Pierre Query is handling the investigation, and the interrogation of suspects is taking place at a building near the Cantini Museum. The building is surrounded by police and no one has been released as yet. As far as I can tell, the men are living in the building. All meals are being brought in. There have been several other men coming and going who I think are from the government, but I can't be sure. As I said, none of the Special Services men that I was able to identify have left as yet, at least not to my knowledge."

David looked distressed. "Who's watching the place now?"

She looked up at him and smiled again. "I have six people working in shifts around the clock. We'll know of anyone who comes or goes. We have the back and the front covered."

28

David put his hands in his pockets and paced the floor. "Describe the building for me."

"It's a two-story office building. Very old. It was scheduled to be demolished and a new one built. The windows on the lower floor are boarded up, but the windows on the second floor are not. There are lights inside at night, so they have restored the electricity."

David shook his head. He had to get to Pierre, but it wasn't going to be easy. He turned to Michele and asked, "Is there any news on the street? What about the shipping company? Is it still operating?"

She shook her head. "The shipping company is closed. Nobody knows anything for sure, at least not that I can determine. There were nine people taken away and the rest were told to go home. They have no idea as to why. Only those who could possibly have known about the shipment were taken away. The press is beginning to speculate, because shipments such as these have taken place before. In the past, they used different shipping companies. Never the same one twice. And the plutonium was always from different interim vendors. They thought that the avoidance of any sort of pattern was enough security, I guess."

David sat in the chair and digested what Michele had told him. It was a typical Special Services operation. They would take people to a place that was divorced from any normal authority, so that questioning could take place away from the eyes of people who might have some legal objection to the methods used. When Special Services talked to people, they used the traditional concept of Napoleonic Law, guilty until proven innocent.

Their methods of interrogation, developed over the years, gave the lie to the idea that a human being could resist attempts to gain information against his will. In these days of modern chemistry, it was simply impossible. Those fools who tried to prevent it from happening were subjected to unneccessary pain and suffering before they spilled their guts. It wouldn't be long before Pierre would have the answers, if he didn't already have them.

And then David began to wonder about something that had been nagging at him ever since he'd met with Grant at the embassy.

The sinking of the freighter had been monitored by American intelligence. They knew that a Libyan sub was in the area. He wondered if they knew that there was plutonium on board the freighter. It wasn't mentioned in the report that Grant had given him, nor had Grant mentioned the possibility.

The Libyan sub had to get past the American Sixth Fleet to return to its home port. Why had they waited? Why hadn't they intercepted the sub before it reached Libya? They were considering a strike against Libyan land targets. What would be the problem with attacking a sub?

It had been almost sixteen hours between the time when the freighter went down and when Grant called him. A lot of time. They should have acted sooner. If they were at all convinced that the plutonium was on its way to Libya, they should have taken immediate steps. Why the delay?

The report had said that the Russians who would normally be aboard the sub had missed this trip.

Had the Americans thought that the Russians were aboard? Was that why they hadn't taken action? Were the Russians not on board because they knew of the mission? Or had they simply been left at the dock?

"Mr. Bateman?"

It was Michele. David had been sitting there totally ignoring her. She was still standing in the middle of the room, her notebook clutched in her hand.

"Sorry, Michele. I was just thinking about something. I appreciate the information. Well done. I've got to find a way to talk to Pierre. Drive me over there, so I can have a look at the place."

Michele smiled and handed him his jacket. Her cheerfulness was becoming a pain in the ass.

Pierre Query put his arms on the table and rested his head on them. He was exhausted. The interrogation was finished. Marcel Lacoste, a director of the shipping firm, had been the one to sell the information. Not to the Libyans, but to a woman known to be connected to Nadi Amur's group of Palestinian terrorists.

Stupid man. What did he take them for? Did he think they wouldn't find out? Did he think that they would accept this idiot story of a freighter sinking at sea without question? Did he think they would simply come and ask politely if anyone had spilled the beans?

Marcel Lacoste. A man of fifty-seven who still thought of himself as a thirty-year-old. A man who

31

loved to go to Monte Carlo and gamble the night away. An ugly little man who thought he was possessed of a charm that women found irresistible, when in fact it was the money he so carelessly pissed away that they found irresistible.

The son of one of the founders of the shipping company. A stupid, stupid man, whose life was now over.

Finding himself unable to pay his gambling debts, he'd leaped at the chance to sell the information to his newfound girlfriend, who was never seen again after gaining the information on the shipment.

From the description of the woman, Pierre figured she could have been Hana Azzuz, one of Nadi Amur's most trusted associates, a dazzler who was an expert in the art of trading sex for information. In this case, she'd used sex first and money second.

Pierre lifted his head and stared out the grimy window of the old building. He thought about Nadi Amur. Almost a phantom. A Syrian who'd spent six years in the United States attending college, graduating with a Master's in Mechanical Engineering. Fluent in three languages and imbued with a hatred of America and Israel so intense that the others seemed almost rational by comparison.

A man dedicated to the destruction of Israel, and, if possible, the United States. The object of a worldwide hunt for nine long years. Nine long, unsuccessful years.

He traveled the world freely, using a variety of disguises and papers. By the time there was a line on him, he'd vanished and left another hideous act of wanton murder in his wake.

Pierre's thoughts turned back to Lacoste. Lacoste had said that the woman had made his acquaintance in Monte Carlo a week ago. That the deal had been struck three days ago, and that the final information had been given to her by telephone less than twenty-four hours before the shipment left Marseilles.

All border stations had been alerted, all airports, all train and bus stations. A rendering of the woman and a photograph of Amur had been distributed. The hunt was on, but Pierre doubted that either would be found. The photo of Amur, one that was constantly being printed in newspapers all over the world, was eleven years old. It was unlikely that he looked anything like that photo today.

As for the woman, Hana Azzuz had never been photographed, although she had been apparently seen in many countries of the world at various times. They both would have left the country long before the attack on the freighter even began.

It now looked as though Amur was preparing for his most ambitious act of terrorism. The information secured by Hana Azzuz had been turned over to Amur. He had, in turn, passed it along to people capable of making use of a Libyan submarine. Khadaffi? Doubtful. No, it was probably "the group." The cadre of unknowns rumored to be the real power in Libya. Was Amur working for the group, or was it the other way around? Or was it a joint effort?

Pierre got up and walked into the next room. The information gained from Lacoste was being transmitted by radio back to Paris. It was up to them now. His work was finished.

A seasoned veteran with the Special Service, Pierre Query was five feet, five inches tall. On that shortened frame he packed a muscled 165 pounds. As a child, when he realized that he would never be tall, he had determined that he would be the toughest short man in the history of the world. At the age of fifteen, he began working out with weights, studying three of the ancient Chinese martial arts, becoming highly proficient in all of them.

Even boxing. At the age of eighteen, he had been the odds-on favorite to win an Olympic Gold Medal for France in boxing, but had been kept out by an attack of appendicitis. Upon his recovery, he had decided to become a professional boxer. In his third fight, the man he'd knocked out in the first round died of a brain hemorrhage, and Pierre quit the ring.

At loose ends, he became a policeman, but not without some difficulty. The requirements excluded Pierre because of his height. Pierre proposed a simple test. Take the toughest man in the department, place him in a ring with Pierre, no holds barred, and see what happened. If Pierre won the battle, he would be accepted. If he lost, he would go quietly.

The offer was rejected until Pierre offered to place a wager on the outcome.

It was no contest. The big man never knew what hit him. And the story of Pierre's big fight became a legend. A legend that reached those responsible for recruitment in the Special Services branch.

That had been sixteen years ago. It seemed like a hundred.

He needed some air. The dust in the old building had been aggravating his sinus condition. He looked at his watch, then told the others he would be back in an hour, and headed down the stairs and out into the street. There was a restaurant across from the museum and he headed toward it, waving at the policeman ringing the building.

David and Michele were walking up the street when the unmistakable form of Pierre Query striding away from the building, alone, caught David's eye. An unbelievable stroke of luck. David had been trying to figure out how to make contact, and there he was, out in the open.

Pierre crossed the cobblestone street, the leather soles of his shoes sliding on the wet pavement so much so that he almost fell. Marseilles . . . he hated the place. It was so . . . old. Over twenty-five hundred years old. As far as Pierre was concerned, the Greeks could have it back.

Out of the corner of his eye, Pierre noticed a man and a woman approaching from the other direction. As usual, Pierre's eyes focused first on the woman. He recognized her immediately. Then his attention turned to the man, and he smiled to himself. He continued walking up the street away from them, giving no sign of recognition, until he heard the familiar voice call out to him.

"Bonjour, Pierre."

At first, Pierre seemed surprised, and then he reared back and burst out laughing. "I might have known they'd send you. Come, we better get out of the streets. There are people here who won't appreciate me talking to you."

As the three made their way to the restaurant, Pierre's gaze never left Michele.

"And you, my love. Why have our paths never crossed before? A woman of your incredible beauty would surely have burned an indelible image into my brain. Don't tell me that you are working for the Americans . . . it would break my heart."

Michele giggled. "Mr. Bateman and I are old . . . friends. We met in Paris two years ago. At a party at the embassy. We just happened to bump into each other here in Marseille. Fate . . . *n'est-ce pas?*"

Pierre's grin grew wider, his pencil-thin mustache wrinkling across his upper lip. "Of course."

Michele smiled at him. "How do you know Mr. Bateman? For that matter, who are you? What is your name?"

Pierre laughed aloud again. "Not bad. I almost believe you. Look . . . you're French. The French should be working for France, not the Americans. The pay is not as good, but the benefits are tremendous. You know that Americans are lousy lovers. There's more to life than work."

David looked at the two of them and had to admit they made the perfect couple. They were both short. He made the introductions. "Michele, allow me to introduce an old friend, Pierre Query. Pierre is a government official. A customs officer, no less. Pierre, I have the pleasure of introducing Michele Dumont. Mam'zel Dumont is a translater at the American Embassy in Paris. And just so that everyone knows everything they should, I can tell you,

Michele, that Pierre is married and has eight children."

Pierre laughed again. "And three mistresses. But there's always room for one more. Especially one as delightful as you, my love."

They reached the restaurant and took a booth. Michele immediately rose, mumbled something about forgetting to turn off a hair curler at the hotel, and left.

Pierre watched her leave and then turned his attention to David. "She's very good for someone so young. Especially the eyes. I've learned to watch the eyes when people lie. It takes years to learn how to control the eyes. She's a natural. The eyes are hard to read. I'm impressed."

David shrugged and said, "That's because she's telling you the truth. She really is a translator. She's just here on a holiday."

Pierre laughed. "David, your eyes are the eyes of an experienced liar, but I spotted Michele yesterday, as soon as I arrived in Marseilles. She's been watching the building along with some friends ever since. We knew someone would be coming, but not who. I'm glad it was you."

David grinned. The waiter arrived and they both ordered dinner. Pierre asked for some wine and the waiter brought a carafe and left it on the table.

David got right to it. "So . . . what did you find out?"

Pierre sipped the wine and shook his head. "The ship was attacked and sunk. No question about it. The submarine must have taken the plutonium. The information on the shipment was obtained from one of the directors of the shipping company. It was given to a woman we believe was Hana Azzuz, one of Amur's people."

David felt a sharp intake of breath. That was bad news. Very bad news. The combination of Amur's manpower and cunning with "the group's" money was a frightening situation.

"Anything else?"

Pierre shook his head. "Not much. We think the plutonium is now in Libya, but we don't know as yet. Your people are working on that."

He sighed. "This is a bad business, my friend. I doubt if the information we've gathered together will be relayed to your people officially."

"Why not?"

Pierre's gaze left David for a moment. He looked around the room and then lowered his voice. "You know as well as I. The government was asked many times to find another way to make shipments of plutonium to Japan. For reasons which are now obvious. Unfortunately, they took it as an affront, because they have a certain . . . attitude about American suggestions . . . now they look like fools. It is an embarrassment. It has already caused problems."

David's curiosity was intense. "What problems?"

Once again, Pierre's eyes seemed to have a furtiveness. "We are aware of certain problems between your government and ours."

David was losing his patience. "Quit dancing around, for Christ's sake. Give!"

Pierre looked worried. "David, I think there's trouble brewing. I understand the Sixth Fleet is

38

preparing to attack Libya within days."

David's eyebrows rose. "Really?"

Pierre's expression was serious. "Yes. Your people asked our government for permission to fly over France from England. Permission was refused. You understand. We still do a lot of business with Libya. It wouldn't look too good."

The waiter arrived with their food. They talked about old times, the weather, and a few other things while the waiter served the food with a flourish. Left alone, Pierre continued.

"There is going to be a real stink. The Europeans think you Americans all have a Rambo complex. This attack is going to turn many against you. It is ill-advised."

David shrugged. "Pierre, I don't make policy. I just carry out assignments. They must have their reasons. In any case, I appreciate the information. Tell me, how do you know about the United States asking France for permission to fly over French soil?"

The normally twinkling eyes of the Frenchman grew cold. "There are certain things I cannot discuss, David. I've told you more than I should. If I was ever discovered even talking to you about the weather, my children would mourn the death of their father. It goes without saying that they are aware we are friends. I'd appreciate it if you didn't follow me out of the restaurant. Gaston is here. That ass-kisser would spot you right off. As soon as your people make a move, I could be in trouble if it was known you were here."

David nodded. "I understand. I'll be careful. I'm

only here to learn about the sub. I'll be leaving today."

Pierre nodded. "Good. This makes us even, *mon ami*. My debt is paid."

David took another sip of the wine and smiled at the little man. "You're wrong, Pierre. There never was a debt. You owed me nothing."

David left the restaurant alone and took a taxi back to the hotel. It was two in the afternoon. Michele was waiting in his room. She set up the radio and positioned the unidirectional antenna, while David transposed the message into code. With the small computer, it took but moments. Then he tapped the series of numbers out on the key, waited for an acknowledgment, and turned the set off.

"Did you eat?" he asked Michele.

"Yes."

"You really didn't need to leave. Pierre knew who you were. He spotted you tailing him yesterday."

She turned up her nose as though she'd just encountered a foul smell. David grinned at her. "Don't let it bother you. Pierre's a pro. He has a particular eye for women who are shorter than he is. He could pick one out of a crowd in a football stadium. He was impressed. Said your eyes never gave you away. You've got a lot of talent for one so young."

She smiled again and lay on the bed. "I thank you for the compliment."

"Don't thank me, I'm just repeating what Pierre said. Tell me, where did you develop this talent of yours?"

She smiled sweetly, licked her lips, and in a voice that seemed suddenly husky, said, "I was a whore for five years."

David simply stared at her. She seemed amused by his expression.

"I see that shocks you. You're a typical American, David Bateman. You like to classify your women, don't you? All very neat and tidy. Once a whore, always a whore. A woman who couldn't possibly have intelligence because, after all, why would an intelligent women become a whore?"

There was no reason for David to be shocked. He knew the agency used whores . . . but they were usually assigned to projects that capitalized on their primary talents. Michele was being used in a capacity that didn't fit the pattern.

She smiled and sat on the edge of the bed. "Pierre was right about one thing, you know. Americans are lousy lovers. Always in a hurry, as though making love was something to be endured rather than enjoyed. They're always so anxious to get a woman into bed, and as soon as they do, they're anxious again to have it over with."

She couldn't hide the bitterness in her voice.

"A Frenchman likes to savor the experience. Americans don't know how to please a woman. Not at all. Nor are they willing to learn. They pretend to know it all, when in fact they know very little."

David had heard enough. Now his voice had an edge to it. "If you're so unimpressed with American men, why are you working for the CIA?"

The smile grew larger. "What has that got to do

41

with anything? I just said that American men were lousy lovers. They do have other qualities. There is more to life than making love."

Indeed, there was.

On Tuesday, April 15, at two in the morning Tripoli time, America attacked Libya. U.S. Air Force F-111s from bases in England, along with A-6s, A-7s, and F/A-18s from the Navy carriers *Coral Sea* and *America* attacked targets in Tripoli and Benghazi. At the height of the attack, two C-5A transport planes landed at Tripoli International Airport, disgorged a cargo of troops, tanks, and armored personnel carriers, then waited, surrounded by heavily armed troops.

The convoy rushed to the secret facility near the Bab al Azzizia Barracks and smashed their way inside. As a diversion, a ground attack was made on Khadaffi's home near the barracks, which, combined with the attack from the air, kept the Libyan defenders busy.

After ten minutes inside, the special force started back to the airport. During their absence, the airport had been attacked from the air, an effort that destroyed several military aircraft on the ground. It also kept Libyan troops away from the C-5s, sitting on the other side of the airport.

In the confused aftermath of the air attack, the force made its way back to the airport, where anti-aircraft guns were still firing at the now empty skies. Once the troops and equipment were back on board, the C-5s took off without incident. The defenders had been given the information that the aircraft taking off were their own, that they were on their way to attack the American fleet in reprisal. Unable to see any markings in the darkness, some of the troops actually cheered as the C-5s lumbered into the blackness.

The attack was twofold. One purpose was to impress upon the world in general and Libya in particular, that terrorism would no longer be handled in strictly diplomatic terms. The United States had declared war on terrorism, not with words, but with deeds.

The second purpose of the raid was to recover the plutonium that was suspected of being kept in the secret research center located near the barracks complex.

Four hours after the raid, David Baxter was seated in the old leather chair in the office of Grant Talmage as they reviewed together the information now trickling in. As each piece of intelligence was decoded and brought into the office, the looks on their faces got longer.

On the other hand, the raid had been successful. The Libyans, even though suspecting an attack might be forthcoming, had seemed ill prepared. American losses were light, with only one F-111 reported as missing. Damage to the targets in Libya had been substantial.

On the other hand, nothing had been found in the research facility. Well, not exactly nothing, but no plutonium.

They couldn't understand it. The Russians had been advised of the raid beforehand and had made sure they were out of danger. Obviously, they had not warned the Libyans. In return, the Russians had passed along the information that the Libyan submarine suspected of sinking the *Armand Lavertue,* had slipped anchor on that fateful day and left port without their knowledge or approval. In fact, they advised, not even Khadaffi had been aware of its mission.

Trucks had reportedly been seen at the dock as the submarine returned. Crates had been seen being placed in the trucks. Crates whose description matched the crates missing from the freighter. Everything fit. The plutonium had to be in the research center.

But it wasn't.

Along with the troops who attacked the center were twelve men skilled in the science of nuclear weaponry, armed with sophisticated equipment. They had raced through the building as fast as they could. They had checked every nook and cranny, looking for the lethal material.

They'd found a very small quantity of enriched uranium 235, not enough to make even a very small device if the other technology was state-of-the-art, which was doubtful. But the plutonium was not in the building. There was no evidence that it had ever been in that building.

There were no people in the building, either. Although the guards were in place, they were protecting a shell. An empty building. The crude equipment found inside was, without question, there for only one purpose; the production of nuclear devices. But the scientists were gone. The plutonium was gone.

David Baxter read the report again and set it aside. His eyes locked onto Grant Talmage's, and together they nodded their heads. They both had the same thought at the same time.

Something was terribly amiss.

There was no evidence that Libya had been ready for an attack by the Americans, but the evidence was clear that those in the research center had been aware something was going to happen. The fact that there were no people in the center could be explained by the hour. But there was no explanation for the fact that certain equipment had been moved prior to the raid. That the plutonium had been moved.

David rubbed his forehead. "Grant . . . it doesn't fit."

"No kidding."

"No . . . I mean, the distress signal from the freighter. Our people picked that up, right?"

"Yes." Grant grabbed the file and leafed through it quickly. "The signal was picked up by one of the communications ships. The nearest Sixth Fleet ship was about a hundred thirty nautical miles away."

"And our people knew the Libyan sub was in the general area."

"Of course."

"Why didn't they try to intercept it?"

Grant shrugged. "Because the whole picture wasn't clear until sometime after the sub was back in Tripoli. As a matter of fact, we didn't even know that the freighter was carrying plutonium. We started asking questions after we learned that the

Special Services people were interrogating those working for the shipping company."

David started pacing the floor. For a while he didn't speak, and then he stopped in the middle of the floor and whirled to face Grant. "It was a setup, Grant."

The bald man looked up and lit another cigar. "I'm listening."

David walked as he talked, his arms cutting through the air. "OK. The Russians are very cooperative. The report says that they passed along the information on the arrival of the sub. That the crates were seen being removed. The crates we assumed contained the plutonium. That information came from the Russians, didn't it?"

"Yes, but so what? You know the Soviet attitude on Libya is ambivalent. They have no desire to see Khadaffi or 'the group' get their hands on any nuclear device. Sure, the Russians have poured a lot of money in there and supported terrorists activities, but the line stops at atomic weapons. That scares the hell out of them. As a matter of fact, there are some who think that one of the reasons the Russians are so tight with the Libyans, besides the obvious, is so they can make sure they don't get their hands on any nuclear devices."

David grunted. "If that's the case, why would the Russians even allow the facility to be built in the first place?"

"There could be a number of reasons. They could keep an eye on it . . . or possibly . . . they simply weren't in a position to interfere . . . we don't really know."

David nodded. "Maybe there's another reason. The Russians pass other little bits of information along to us from time to time, but . . . only when it suits their purposes. They had advance warning of the raid, which we gave to them, right?"

"Right."

"And Pierre knew all about the fact that the United States had sought France's permission to overfly and that it had been turned down. He never got that from us. Pierre is a member of the Special Services branch . . . there's no reason he should have that kind of information. That's cabinet-level stuff. Unless the French government wanted that information leaked prior to the raid, or immediately afterwards. Pierre knew it before the raid, so we have to assume others did as well."

He rubbed his chin as he continued to think out loud. "Tell me, would we have attacked Libya if we'd known for sure that the plutonium wasn't there?"

Grant coughed and shook his head. "I don't see what you're driving at. In answer to your question, I'd probably guess that the raid would have taken place regardless. What is it you're trying to say?"

David stopped pacing. "I think the submarine took the plutonium and then transferred the crates to another ship before returning to Libya. There are hundreds of ships in the Med at any given moment. I think that the crates seen in Tripoli were fake. We were told about their existence by the Russians. None of our people actually saw the offloading. I think somebody wanted to make sure the raid took place, so they used the attack on the freighter as another carrot. I don't think the plutonium ever made it to Libya. I think that so-called research facility is a blind. A red herring. And I think the Russians know that."

Grant grunted. "You're making a hell of a lot of assumptions."

David sighed. "Yeah . . . but something's out of kilter here. Pierre said he expected me down in Marseilles. If not me, somebody from the agency. There was no hesistation on his part about filling me in. It's as though he wanted us to know everything they found out. Or, at least, to think that we know. I'm not sure whether Pierre did that on his own or had other reasons. Maybe the French wanted to make sure we carried out the raid, while appearing to be opposed to it."

David paused and started pacing again. "It's too pat, Grant. Take the attack on the research center. Complete success. Three wounded soldiers and that's it. That place is the most heavily guarded building in the country. It just doesn't make any sense."

Grant puffed on his cigar. "So you're saying that the French manipulated us?"

David shook his head. "No . . . I think they're being played for fools, just like we are. They're being manipulated, we're being manipulated, and so, for that matter, are the Russians."

Grant sighed. "And you think it's Amur."

"Damn right. The whole thing was a giant smoke screen so he could get the plutonium to wherever the hell his *real* factory is. Look . . . the Berlin nightclub attack is just the kind of thing Amur would pull. The statement by the President said that the Berlin nightclub attack was the final straw. That Khadaffi had to be convinced we meant business. "You know, it wouldn't surprise me if it turned out that Khadaffi knew nothing about the Berlin attack."

Grant Talmage snubbed out his cigar, stood up, and stretched. He looked at David and smiled weakly. "David, our intelligence says otherwise. Look . . . you're tired. I'm tired. I think you're letting your imagination run away with you. Amur is a man just like you and me. He's no superman. Just because we've been unable to track him down, he's becoming larger than life. Making out like the guy is some sort of master manipulator of anyone and everyone is just serving his purposes. Give it a rest. Maybe we'll have a better idea of things once we've had a little sleep."

David started to protest, but Grant held up his hand. "That's it for tonight. Go home. I'll see you in . . ." he looked at his watch, "eight hours. OK?"

David nodded reluctantly and headed out the door, down the stairs and out of the building. It was raining. He'd forgotten his umbrella again. The hell with it. The rain ran down his neck and started soaking his clothes, but his pace never quickened. Maybe it would wash away some of the cobwebs in his mind.

Chapter Three

Michele Dumont had been soaking in the tub for almost a half hour. Each time the water began to cool, she would add some hot water along with more oil, until now, the silky water threatened to overflow. Her skin was becoming wrinkled, but the warmth that enveloped her body felt so good, she hesitated to end the bath. She grabbed a towel and wiped her hands, then reached for a cigarette.

She was back in her flat in Lyons, a rather small one-bedroom place that failed to reflect the true nature of the occupant. The furnishings were bland, the walls were unadorned, the colors muted. It might have been the residence of a simple woman employed as a maid by one of the wealthy Lyons families.

It certainly didn't look like the home of a woman who had earned a considerable amount of money in the world's oldest profession, not to mention the money the Americans had given her. And the Russians.

Someday she would spend it. Someday soon, she would start taking the money out of her account in Zurich and travel the world. But for now, she was content to earn it. To pile it up to the point where she would never have to work again. She was almost there.

She heard a key turn in the door. Instinctively, she stubbed out the cigarette and reached for the pistol on the chair beside the tub. And then she heard his voice.

"Michele . . . are you there?"

She put the gun down and felt a shiver go down her spine. It was he! He hadn't sent one of his people, as he normally did, he'd come himself!

There was a musical sound to her voice as she called to him. "In here! I'm in the bath!"

When he entered the room she broke out laughing. He was hunched over, the bulge on his back pushing against the fabric of the old and dirty jacket. The face was covered with some sort of makeup that gave his skin a whitish look. The false strawlike hair hung lifelessly below an old beret, the eyebrows and beard white and streaked with dirt.

He was walking with a cane and looked as though he was close to eighty. It was a masterpiece of disguise.

She couldn't stop laughing. It was infectious, and he started to laugh as well while he carefully extricated himself from the elaborate disguise and stood before her, nude.

"I think I should join you. I feel the need of a bath," he said.

He climbed into the tub and immediately the

room was awash. The soapy water spilled out into the bedroom, its wetness darkening the thin carpet that covered much of the floor. Michele didn't even bother to look, instead, her eyes were riveted on the man as he washed the makeup from his face, leaned forward, and kissed her on the lips. Then his tongue slid slowly down her body until his entire head was submerged and she felt him between her legs, the sensations strong even through the water.

She pulled him away and stood up in the tub. She reached for the towel and began to dry herself off.

"You took a chance coming here, you know?"

He smiled, the deep creases in his olive-colored face becoming deeper. "Life is not without risk."

She was standing in the tub and he was on his knees, his hands on her buttocks, pulling her toward him. Almost involuntarily, she felt her legs sliding apart, giving him access.

She placed her hands on the top of his head and pushed him away, gently.

"Come to bed," she said.

He looked up at her. "In a minute."

She laughed again. "You don't make love like an Arab, Nadi."

He didn't answer. Instead, he pulled her down, back into the slippery water, his arms encircling her, his lips pressing against hers.

And then, in one quick motion, his hand was on her mouth and both arms were around her neck. A sharp twist and it was over.

Nadi Amur stood up and stepped from the tub. He dried his body with a towel as he gazed at the lifeless body of Michele Dumont, now almost fully submerged in the fragrant bathwater. Carefully, he reapplied the disguise, wiped the tub clean of any fingerprints and left the flat as he had come. A lone figure with a cane, leaning forward, the body deformed and ugly. A disguise that, in its own way, announced the true contents of the soul that lay within.

David Baxter and Grant Talmage were reviewing the latest intelligence that had come in during the night. Agents throughout the Middle East and Europe had reinterviewed contacts, and it was now clear that much of what had been given them was false information. There was no other explanation. Too many answers failed to lead to logical conclusions.

David threw a file folder on the floor and stood up. He rubbed his forehead as he paced the floor.

Talmage watched him pace. It was a habit David had, as though he was incapable of thought while sitting still. He'd pace the floor, his head down, his arms moving in all directions, blurting out whatever came into his mind.

He was an American, but he seemed to have the disposition of a Frenchman at times. Animated, excitable, full of ideas. But he didn't look like a Frenchman. Tall and athletic, with that tight curly hair, the clear, dark eyes that seemed sharply focused. The nose that should have been repaired, a testament to his college football days.

Grant had asked David once why he didn't have it

fixed and David had contended it would make him look too pretty. That was the word he'd used. Pretty. He certainly didn't want to look pretty.

"Grant, where did we find Michele Dumont?"

Grant placed the cigar in the ashtray and leaned back in his chair.

"Actually, she came to us. Right here to the embassy. She walked in one day, said she was a whore and that one of her customers had blabbed something about blowing up the embassy. We took it seriously, considering that her customer was a Libyan. Sure enough, the next day our power went out and the electrical truck sent out to fix things up was a moving bomb. They'd placed C-4 in thin sheets between false walls inside the truck. If we hadn't been looking for it, we'd never have found it."

David put his hands in his pockets and stopped pacing. "Michele told you what to look for?"

"Not exactly . . . she gave a complete description of the man, and he was spotted driving the truck. He was shot as soon as he made a move to detonate the explosive, as was his partner, so we never were able to question him. Without the information from Michele . . . I wouldn't be here today. Our investigation pointed to Amur, but that's where we got blocked out. As usual. As for Michele, we checked her out thoroughly and she seems to be what she claims. We asked her to work for us as an informant. She moves in some interesting circles."

David had a puzzled look on his face. "Did she ever undergo training?"

Grant nodded. "Yes. We sent her to Honduras

55

for a month."

"And she's still operating as a prostitute?"

"Yes, of course."

David resumed his seat. "She told me she *used* to be a whore. As though that was in the past. She also had some harsh words to say about American men in general. What else do you know about her?"

Grant got up and moved to the file cabinet, opened a drawer and pulled out a file, which he handed to David. "Here, read for yourself."

David looked over the material. Michele Dumont was twenty-six years old. She'd been born in Bordeaux, one of three children born to a wealthy wine-making family. At the age of sixteen, she'd been raped by a house guest who was also an important distributor of the family's products. The parents had implored her to keep the matter quiet, which she had. But the experience had destroyed her relationship with her parents and she'd moved to Paris shortly thereafter.

She'd worked at a series of meaningless jobs for a number of years, until the age of twenty, when she caught the eye of a man named George Gastien. Gastien, a man in his forties, nurtured her need for a replacement father and eventually persuaded her to become a whore. She worked for him for three years as one of his stable of expensive prostitutes, then moved to Lyons, where she worked for herself. The parting with Gastien was amicable, a rarity in the business.

She maintained a small flat in Lyons, traveled a lot throughout France, and had a regular customer list of men located all over the country. She made visits to her clients according to arrangements made during previous encounters, and the only new clients she accepted were through referrals.

After being hired by the CIA, she passed along any and all information she collected, important or not. Some of it had proven useful and well worth the $2,000 being paid to her each month.

The file made no mention of the nationality of the man who had raped her when she was sixteen.

David asked, "This rape thing. Was there ever any confirmation of this?"

Grant shook his head. "No. Well, not really. We did interview some friends of the family and they alluded to some problem that caused her to leave the home, but we were never able to verify it completely."

Grant puffed on his cigar. "What's bothering you?"

David waved at the cigar smoke and sighed. "I don't know. It was just too easy. As soon as I got to Marseilles she had Pierre staked out. Then, when I talked to Pierre, he told me that he'd spotted her the day before. And . . . as soon as I showed up at the building, Pierre was out in the open where I could talk to him. Then . . . when I asked Pierre how he knew about the raid before it happened, he got really chilly with me. Something isn't right."

They both grew silent, then David slapped his knees and stood up again. "I'm going to have a chat with Pierre. I know where he lives and I'll just wait there for him. He's got to show up sometime. In the meantime, I'd suggest you put some people on Michele's ass."

Grant shrugged. "All right. But what makes you think Pierre will tell you anything?"

"Nothing. I've just got to give it a try."

David Baxter hadn't lied when he'd told Michele that Pierre had a wife and eight children. They ranged in age from two to eleven. Madame Query had been kept occupied for some time, but it seemed to suit her. She ran the household without domestic help and knew just where each child was at any given moment.

She offered David some tea. "Pierre didn't say when he'd be back, Daveed . . . I don't know . . . it could be some time."

David smiled at the buxom woman. "Well, Madame Query, it wouldn't be the first time I've sat here and waited for him, would it?"

She yelled at one of the children as she poured the tea. "My, no. That seems such a long time ago. We don't see you anymore, Daveed . . . why don't you come by?"

It had been over a year. "You know how it is, Madame Query, we get very busy and we . . . never have time to do the things we should."

It was a weak explanation, but the look in Madame Query's eyes indicated that she understood. Her husband never discussed his work with her. And all she knew about David Baxter was that he was an American involved in something that connected with what Pierre did. He'd spent two nights at the home outside Paris a year ago. She didn't know why, but she knew that something important

58

had happened, because Pierre had seemed so happy. Happy to be alive.

Pierre walked through the front door three hours later, the children swarming over him like flies, grabbing legs and arms and pulling him down to the ground. It was a ritual, and they went through it almost every time he entered the house, whether he'd been away for weeks or just hours.

He gave each one some personal attention and they returned to their various activities.

Pierre eyed David with a hint of suspicion. "And you, my friend . . . to what do I owe this honor?"

David motioned toward the window. "I think we should talk outside."

Pierre poured himself some tea. "As you wish."

They stepped onto the stone driveway and then walked toward the rear of the house. The house was new, and large by European standards. Much like a typical American suburban five-bedroom two-story. It stood at the end of a small road, the rear yard backing onto open farmland used as grazing land for a small herd of cattle.

Pierre walked to the wooden fence and leaned against it. "Ah . . . it's quiet here. Peaceful. When we first moved here, the farmer raised sheep. When the wind was from the east we would almost expire. Then he switched to beef, thank God. Otherwise I think we might have moved."

Then, without skipping a beat, he said, "Did you know Michele is dead?"

He said it with such little fanfare that David was stunned. All he could say was, "What?"

Pierre's expression was impassive. As though he

were some television newsman delivering the day's collection of bad news. "Michele. Your friend in Marseilles. They found her about two hours ago. Her neck was broken while she took a bath. There are no clues other than the person who killed her was someone she knew. Probably had a key to her flat. Perhaps it was one of her customers."

David could feel a tingle at the back of his neck. It was a familiar warning signal that he was getting close to losing his temper. His voice betrayed his anger. "Pierre, I'm really getting tired of this game we seem to be playing. How did you know Michele was a whore?"

The little man's expression remained impassive. "When I spotted her tailing me in Marseilles, I had her checked out. I knew she was CIA within hours, so I didn't get too upset. The next day we had the whole package."

David stared at his friend, and there was a hint of sadness in his eyes as he said, "Pierre . . . you aren't being straight with me. I know it, and you know it. You're saying things to me that you know I can't accept. You're trying to tell me something without telling me. For God's sake, cut the bullshit and level with me!"

Pierre looked away. "I don't know what you mean."

David's face was beginning to redden. "Crap! You just said that a customer might have killed Michele. You know damn well that whores don't give keys to their customers. You know that and yet you tell me that. Why the game? This isn't you!"

They stood there, looking at each other, neither

60

man saying a word, listening to the sound of gentle winds brushing green grass and tall pines. Then Pierre sighed and looked away again. "David, you don't understand."

The tingle in the neck was becoming a throb. "For Christ's sake, try me!"

Pierre hesitated for a moment and then cursed. "All right! All right!" He almost spit out the words. "Your precious CIA! Nobody trusts them anymore! Information gets tossed around like so much confetti. You have so many morons in your midst, a secret stays a secret for days at best. You're riddled with double agents, and you don't even know it!

"If I tell you what you want to know, you'll tell your superior and people will be assigned. They'll be clumsy and stupid and another opportunity will be lost. We've been after Amur for years, and so have you. But every time we get close, one of your people screws up and the whole effort is wasted. We're tired of wasting our time. We're tired of cooperating with you! You'll just get us all killed!"

He stopped and took a deep breath. "David, you don't belong in this business. You're a . . . decent sort of man. This job requires men who have little decency. Men who are as ruthless as Amur. Men without feelings. Robots without souls."

David scraped his foot in the rich soil. "And you, Pierre? That's you? A robot without a soul? Is that why you have eight children?"

Pierre laughed. "No . . . the reason I have eight children is because of my schedule. The rhythm method is fine for a man who's home each night. Not so fine for a man who travels a lot."

David snorted. "So, a man without a soul who follows the doctrines of a church. Come on, Pierre, forget the speeches, forget the bullshit, just give me the damn facts. The agency has its problems, but so does every other agency, including your own. Unless we get our hands on that plutonium, this discussion may become redundant. Just help me do my job."

The little man leaned against the fence and his body sagged. "Very well . . . but hear me, David Baxter. If this gets screwed up, I'll hold you personally responsible. I mean it. If you really want to know, I'll tell you, but what happens from this moment forward is on your shoulders. We are tired of it, David. This is the last time. You understand?"

David watched the man's eyes, hesitated, and then nodded.

"Michele Dumont was a triple agent. She worked for you . . . she worked for the Russians . . . but most important, she worked for Nadi Amur."

Baxter took a step backward, as though he'd been hit in the face. "How do you know this?"

"Six days ago, before the attack on the freighter, we had a lead on one of Amur's people. We followed him to Marseilles and observed him talking with Michele. Later, we intercepted him and managed to get out of him all that he knew. It wasn't much, because Amur is very careful, but it was enough to confirm that Michele was working for Amur. And you probably know that she tipped your embassy to a planned attack."

David was still stunned. He managed a meek "Yes."

"Well, doesn't it strike you as odd that one of Amur's people would tell a whore about a planned attack on an American embassy? That's one of Amur's favorite tricks. He'll sacrifice any number of his own people to achieve his goals. You Americans have difficulty in understanding pure ruthlessness, and Amur knows it. Therefore, he exploits it. Michele was placed in position by Amur so he'd know how close you were to determining the real fate of the *Armand Lavertue*. Once he realized that we had one of his people, he had to get rid of Michele. It was Michele who gave your agency the information about the facility in Tripoli, wasn't it?"

David shrugged. "I don't know."

"Well, check it out. I think you'll find out that it was her information. That whole thing is a blind. The facility has been a fake from the beginning. Oh, there's a real facility somewhere, with perhaps a hundred men working feverishly to develop nuclear weapons. But it's not in Libya. Perhaps Pakistan, perhaps . . . anywhere."

David suddenly felt very cold. "Are you sure about this?"

Pierre shook his head. "Unlike you, when we seek information, we find information. We're not thwarted by some old-fashioned rules that went out of style the moment you unleashed the atom. Michele was in it for the money. That's all. She had no particular loyalty to any cause. I'm not sure, but I think she planted the story about seeing the crates coming off the sub in Tripoli. If not her, then another of Amur's people. The bastard has us all running in circles."

David wanted to hit him. "Why, Pierre? Why the hell didn't you tell me this before? If you knew in Marseilles that Michele was working for Amur, why the hell didn't you let me know? And why not grab Michele? You talk about us screwing up, missing opportunities . . . you just blew a big one."

Pierre's face was becoming flushed. "In the first place, I didn't tell you because I wanted Michele on a string. I had no idea what you'd do if you knew. I simply couldn't take the chance. In the second place, we intended to question Michele, but we were hoping she'd give us another lead to Amur. We followed her back to Lyons, and staked out the place. But the bastard got by us somehow. It was either Amur or one of his people. We're not sure. All we know is that we finally decided to pay her a visit and found her body."

David's expression turned into a sneer. "You sanctimonious son of a bitch! You talk about the CIA like we're a bunch of rookies, and then you stake out a place and fail to prevent a murder! Once you questioned her contact, you knew Amur would kill her. You should have grabbed her then!"

Pierre's fist came up fast and landed flush on the jaw of David Baxter. Instinctively, Baxter tried to respond, but he felt his legs giving out from under him. They felt like rubber. He pitched forward, the taste of dirt and blood mixing in his mouth before everything turned black.

When consciousness returned, he was lying on a soft bed, a cold towel pressed against his forehead, a thoroughly chagrined Pierre Query standing by the bed, a glass of brandy in his hand.

Pierre handed the glass of brandy to David. "Here, drink this . . . and please . . . forgive me, David. I simply didn't need to hear the truth. We missed a golden opportunity. We might have had him . . . I had to strike out. I'm sorry, you were just handy."

David drank the brandy and smiled. The effort hurt. His jaw was swollen and sore. Fortunately, it wasn't broken. All of the teeth seemed to be there.

"There'll be no forgiveness, Pierre. Now that I've got you feeling guilty, I intend to press my advantage." He grimaced. "I haven't been hit that hard in a long time."

Baxter rubbed his jaw. He could see why Pierre had such a fearsome reputation. It was the first time in his life that anyone had ever knocked him out with one punch. He asked, "The information about the raid. You got a little hostile with me when I asked how you knew about the raid. You got a little hostile with me when I asked how you knew about our asking permission to overfly France. What about that?"

Pierre sighed. "I got a little hostile, as you put it, because I was ashamed. The answer is simple. One of our people is a member of the cabinet."

"I know that. But they normally don't discuss those kinds of things with the men in the trenches. Why this time?"

Pierre shrugged. "I don't know. The word came down, that's all. Perhaps our man was upset and wanted the information leaked . . . I don't know."

David tried to sort it all out in his mind. It didn't make sense. If they wanted it leaked, they'd go to the press, not tell Pierre's people. Pierre seemed anxious to change the subject. His voice softened as he said, "David, there's no question. Amur has the plutonium. He has the money, the people, and the talent to make a bomb. Perhaps more than one. And there's no question that he'll use it. This is no game, my friend. This is a contest that you must win. The man is capable of destroying the world. And he'll do it with a smile on his face. Perhaps he's the devil himself."

David looked into the eyes of his friend. For the first time, he saw something he'd never seen in those eyes before. Fear. It was then that David realized the purpose of the speech Pierre had made about ruthlessness. How it wasn't a business for decent people. It wasn't David Baxter he was trying to convince. It was himself.

In a customs warehouse located at the Port of Montreal, a young man in a business suit handed a sheaf of papers to a uniformed customs official. The papers were import documents for a shipment of wine destined for a distributor in Medicine Hat, Alberta.

There were two hundred cases of the wine, each case containing twelve twenty-five-ounce bottles. Since this was the first shipment of goods to this particular distributor, the representative from the customs broker had attended to the matter personally. Future shipments would require less attention.

The man in the uniform looked over the documents and waved at the young man in the suit.

"OK, let's have a look."

They walked together through the large warehouse until they located the shipment, the cases of wine sitting on wooden skids and strapped securely. The customs inspector smiled and nudged the young man. "Tell your client that if he's smart, he'll containerize in the future. He's liable to lose a few cases if he continues to ship this way. Maybe more than a few, if the wine is any good."

The young man grinned. "Yeah, I'll tell them. I think they're a little new at this. Medicine Hat! Christ! Why anybody would set up there is beyond me. The market is Quebec and Ontario. Who can figure it?"

The inspector cut the straps on one of the skids and pulled three cases down to the floor. He opened each case and took out one bottle. Then he opened the three bottles with a corkscrew and poured some of the wine into a paper cup. First he sniffed and then he tasted.

"A little sweet, but . . . not bad. OK, pay the cashier and I'll clear the shipment."

The young man smiled and headed toward the cashier's window.

Chapter Four

Three years later. . . .

John Campbell was tired. He'd been driving for almost ten hours straight and his entire body ached. As a young salesman traveling the four western provinces of Canada, he found himself on the road a lot, the distance between accounts anywhere from sixty to two hundred miles. So he was used to it. But last night, when he'd talked to Irene on the telephone, she'd seemed even sicker than when he'd left on this trip.

She kept insisting that it was just the flu, but she *sounded* different. She seemed disoriented, really down, and it scared him.

What with the baby coming and all, she'd insisted that she take a job, and for the last month had worked at the Stevens Implement Repair Shop, a new business that had just opened up in the old tannery building. Jobs were scarce on the prairies, like everywhere else, and although it was a dirty job, she was grateful for it.

John wasn't. He didn't like the idea of his wife's

working, especially in greasy overalls, but she'd insisted, so he gave in.

She'd been sick for four days now. She'd refused, in that stubborn way of hers, to go to the doctor, even though it wouldn't cost a thing. She just didn't like doctors, she said, and anyway, it was the flu. Everybody got the flu.

He'd called her from Winnipeg, and after listening to her on the phone, had begged her to see the doctor, if not for her sake, then for the sake of the baby. She finally agreed to go over to the hospital. John had jumped into his car and headed for home, without sleep. Along the way he'd made several phone calls and had discovered that Irene had been admitted. The doctor wouldn't say what it was, but it certainly wasn't the flu.

The hospital was now in sight. Six blocks from the blue frame house on a short street two blocks off the main artery that John and Irene called home. He pulled into the parking lot and entered the hospital.

There were two RCMP officers there and Dr. Perkins, who looked very upset. The doctor took the two officers and John into an office and offered coffee.

John wasn't interested in coffee. He was concerned about his wife. His young face seemed older as he asked, "Dr. Perkins, what's wrong? What's the matter with Irene? And what are the Mounties doing here?"

When Irene Campbell stumbled into the emer-

70

gency room of the Medicine Hat Community Hospital, she could hardly walk. Dr. Robert Perkins, who, like most of the area doctors, took turns working a shift at the hospital, was appalled at what he saw. Her body was covered with open blisters and she was burning up.

As he ordered various tests to be done, treatments to be started, his gut diagnosis kept coming back to something that was impossible.

He knew the woman. While he was not her regular doctor, it was a small town and almost everyone knew everyone else. Irene Campbell had recently started working at an implement repair shop in the old tannery building on the outskirts of Medicine Hat. It was inconceivable that she would be suffering from severe radiation poisoning, but that was exactly what it looked like.

When the tests results were available, there was no longer any question. The doctor was stunned.

Irene was almost incoherent, drifting in and out of consciousness. The doctor asked her several questions and made careful notes. Then, when she slipped into unconsciousness once more, he ordered medications to make her as comfortable as possible and walked down the hall to the common office shared by the doctors. The doctor called the RCMP.

RCMP Sergeant Jack Feller arrived within minutes and was shown to the office. As he took a seat across from the doctor's desk, he sensed that something very serious was afoot. Dr. Perkins was a longtime resident of the town and was known to almost everyone. His reputation was that of a thoroughly competent professional, not far from retire-

71

ment, who was not easily frightened. But he looked frightened now.

The doctor ran his fingers through his white hair and collected his thoughts. He looked at the Mountie sitting in the chair and seemed to have difficulty finding the words.

Sergeant Feller was a tall, heavily built man, with short sandy hair and a large bushy mustache. In Medicine Hat, like many areas in western Canada, the RCMP acted both as a national police force, equivalent to the FBI, and as a state police force. Sergeant Feller, although new to the area, had quickly become a fixture in Medicine Hat, because of his rollicking sense of humor and good nature. A bachelor, he was eagerly sought after by the single women of the town, even though he was a cop.

Though he sensed the problem, whatever it was, was serious, he tried to keep it light. He could see the doctor's reluctance to speak, so he grinned and asked, almost offhandedly, "Well, Dr. Perkins, what seems to be the problem?"

Perkins took off his glasses and rubbed his temples. There was no use trying to pussy-foot around it, so he didn't bother. His voice was filled with sadness. "Sergeant . . . I've got a woman in the examination room who's about to die from radiation poisoning."

The burly sergeant bolted upright in the chair, his gaze boring into those of the doctor. "Radiation poisoning! Are you certain?"

"I'm certain. She'll be dead in hours. Her husband is a salesman and is on his way here. I expect it'll be a few hours because he's driving. He's phoned twice and I talked to him the second time. He thought she had the flu . . . I haven't told him. But I did learn that *he's* feeling fine . . . which would indicate that the radiation source is not their home. Judging from her condition, she's been exposed to a heavy dose. I've been able to talk with her a little, and all I can tell you is that she works at Roberts Implement Repair. You know . . . the old tannery. She told me that she started feeling sick about ten days ago and it just got worse. She's a stubborn woman and didn't go to her doctor because she . . . just doesn't like doctors.

"Four days ago her husband went off on a sales trip, and she decided to stay in bed. He's been calling her, and I guess he finally convinced her to come in. In any case, she's been nowhere except her job and her home. We haven't had any other cases at the hospital, but I do know that Mrs. Campbell is the only woman working in the back of the implement repair shop. Because of her smaller size, she'd probably be the first to exhibit signs of poisoning."

Sergeant Feller played with his mustache. "Are you saying that you think the tannery is the cause of this?"

Dr. Perkins nodded. "Yes, I do. I want to check everyone who's been working there. I could be wrong, but I can't think of anywhere else she could have come in contact with radioactivity . . . I mean, there's no reason why there should be any there. . . ."

The doctor's voice trailed off, and Sergeant Feller

realized exactly what was on the doctor's mind.

The tannery!

The old building had been there for almost a hundred years. For twenty of the last twenty-three, it had stood empty, until . . . a group of Arabs had bought the place, which they used as a warehouse for some French wine.

They were a strange lot, keeping to themselves, living in the old house beside the place, as though it was a commune. They rarely came into town, except to buy necessities, and everybody said that it was impossible for them to be making any money, because they hardly ever made any shipments of wine.

Sergeant Brooks, Feller's predecessor, had paid them two visits, been shown through the place, all except for their quality control lab, which, they explained, was off limits. But, they'd been friendly enough, and the sergeant had seen the many stacks of wine cases.

Canada was a nation of people from many lands, and no one was unusually suspicious of these quiet Arabs. There was no reason to be concerned. Oh, there was the usual gossip, but nothing untoward. They paid their bills and caused no trouble.

And then, after three years . . . they had left. They'd turned the place over to Bray's Real Estate for sale or rent and simply took off.

When Elmer Bray looked over the place, it was empty, and the rent being asked was extremely low. So, it was only a month before Jim Roberts decided to rent the place for his implement repair shop.

During the time the Arabs had occupied the place, there'd been talk of strange comings and goings at night, but nobody had really bothered to look into things, because, after all, people in the prairies had a live-and-let-live attitude. They went out of their way to be gracious to new arrivals.

Jack Feller stood up. He was still putting it all together. Arabs . . . radiation . . . he put on his cap and started toward the door. "Doctor, I'll round them up and get those people down here so you can look them over. Then, I'll get in touch with Calgary and have the place checked out. In the meantime, let's keep this between us. Until we know what's really going on."

Dr. Perkins nodded. "Fine. The sooner the better."

It was the middle of the night, but within two hours, every employee had been tested, and all but one was found to be suffering from radiation sickness in varying degrees. Most had assumed they had the flu, just like Irene.

Sergeant Feller had asked for a team of scientists from Calgary to come and check the place over, and they arrived in the morning, almost at the same time as Irene Campbell breathed her last, her hand held by her husband, who, exhausted from the lack of sleep and worn down by the anguish of his wife's illness, collapsed to the floor.

Irene Campbell was three months pregnant. Even if she had been eight months pregnant, attempts to save the child would have been futile. John Campbell had begged his wife not to take a job. The injustice of it all was more than he could bear.

Along with the scientists came a number of RCMP officers, who began an immediate investigation into the affairs of a small group of Arabs engaged in the business of distributing French wine. It wasn't long before several discoveries were made.

The radioactivity was in the form of a small amount of black dust clinging to bricks in a corner of the old tannery. The scientists quickly determined that the dust was plutonium, and equipment was brought in to decontaminate the place.

Unfortunately, Irene Campbell had worked closest to the corner containing the dust, and it was for this reason that her sickness proved fatal. The other employees were ill, but short-term recovery prospects were good. Long-term prospects were less assured.

The building was roped off, and the news, despite the best efforts of everyone, spread through Medicine Hat like a raging brushfire. By noon, the Canadian media broke the story, and minutes later the wire services were sending it throughout the world.

An old building occupied by a group of now suspicious wine distributors had been found contaminated with plutonium. The radioactive material had caused the death of one pregnant woman, and illness in eight others, all men. There was a lot of speculation about the fact that the wine distributors were all Arabs, and while the RCMP was still investigating, initial indications were that none of the names appearing on the registration for the business was legitimate.

Social Insurance numbers were being checked,

and while there was no comment from officials, unnamed sources were contending that the numbers were phony.

Conclusions were being drawn quickly. The mixture of unknown Arabs and plutonium seemed to spell out one thing. One terrifying, impossible thing.

By midnight, Eastern time, a hurriedly prepared analysis was dropped on the desk of Deputy Director Frank Brown of the CIA. He read it over carefully and felt his heartbeat quickening.

For over three years, the agency had focused much attention on the search for the plutonium missing from the French freighter, and on some other thefts, which had occurred all over the world, including the United States.

In addition, the extensive search for Nadi Amur had continued, with nothing to show for it. The man was like a phantom, frustrating the best efforts of the most powerful nation on earth. One man. Driving them all nuts.

And now, a bunch of Arabs had disappeared from an old brick building in Canada, leaving in their wake some plutonium dust. Was this the secret facility they had been searching for all this time? According to the preliminary report, it seemed likely. After years of searching, they might well have found it. Too late. And only by accident.

The Arabs had abandoned the place. That seemed to indicate only one thing, according to the report. The work on the bomb was finished. The

Amur group had succeeded in producing the bomb they'd been trying to manufacture for over a decade.

The report contained other conjectures. It was possible that the plutonium had not been left by accident, but by design. Whoever they were, the people responsible had wanted the place to be discovered. There was simply no other explanation. Either a bomb had been produced and the plutonium left to bear witness to the fact ... or no bomb had been produced and the plutonium had been left to make it appear that one had.

As the deputy director hurried to the office of the director, he pondered the question. Already a team of agents was on its way to Medicine Hat, armed with pictures of men suspected of being part of Amur's group. If any of the faces were recognized, that would provide the link. He prayed he was all wrong. That there was another explanation. But, for once, he felt the dread of being right.

In the small Syrian village of An-Nakhi, about thirty-five miles south of Damascus, Nadi Amur sat on a chair, smoking American cigarettes and rubbing the stubble on his chin.

He was surrounded by eight of his followers, who were sitting patiently awaiting his reaction to the news that had just arrived by courier. There was a silence in the room broken only by the sound of the flies that buzzed noisily as they flitted from sweaty body to sweaty body. All eyes were focused on Amur, a legend, leading them on this, the greatest of missions.

They were as one. A single goal that now seemed attainable. To die in such an enterprise would be an honor bestowed on only a few fortunate men in the history of the world. An elite group.

Amur took a deep drag of the cigarette and let it out of his lungs slowly. Little rivulets of sweat dropped off his forehead and made tiny wet spots on his worn khaki pants. He looked at each man in turn and then stood up and stared out the window of the small two-room concrete house.

Then he turned to face them. He'd made his decision.

"They have found the building in Canada. Right on schedule. We are in position. We must act now. We will send the message. The Americans think they have felt pain." He laughed as he said it. "It is but a pinprick. Now they will truly feel pain. Now they will understand. We will go forward. We will go home at last!"

The room was filled with the sound of cheers.

Chapter Five

For years they'd looked and found nothing. Lead after lead had surfaced, only to be followed down another blind alley. Frustration mounted on top of frustration, until the search for Nadi Amur had become almost an obsession within the agency.

The limitations of manpower and resources had dictated that a task force of six men, led by David Baxter, would devote their full time to the hunt, with the full support of other agency personnel. But after a year, the force was narrowed to three men. After another year, the force was reduced to two, then, finally, the force was abandoned altogether. There were other problems, other situations, and until a break in the case came, it was determined that a lower priority would be placed on the project. That seemed counter to everything the men involved believed in, but the conventional wisdom was that they were simply getting nowhere. The search would continue, but it would be an ongoing project, like the FBI's, "Most Wanted" list.

And then, the news of the discovery of plutonium in a little town in Canada galvanized the agency into renewed action. It was quickly determined that two known Amur associates had been positively identified, through photographs, as having been seen in Medicine Hat. Working with a group of Arabs engaged in the business of distributing French wine. Using a building where the deadliest of all materials had been found.

It seemed highly likely that the long-sought facility had finally been found. It was possible that at least one nuclear device had been produced, in a building that was hours away from an unprotected border of the United States. It was possible that Nadi Amur now had what he wanted, a nuclear device in place somewhere inside America. At least that was what the report circulated to specific government agencies contended.

David Baxter sat across from Grant Talmage in the familiar office of the American Embassy in Paris and read the entire report in silence. The task force had been hastily reassembled, this time with more men and a top priority. The discovery of the Canadian building had come right out of nowhere.

There hadn't been the slightest hint where the plutonium stolen from the French freighter three years ago might show up. People had been interrogated, thousands of computer hours had been logged . . . and nothing. Now, something so conspicuous as loose plutonium dust had put them on the trail again. It didn't make sense. As David finished reading the report, he shook his head.

Grant smiled. "I thought you'd find that interesting. Are you thinking what I'm thinking?"

David grunted. "If you're thinking that the report's conclusions that we were supposed to find the place are right, then . . . yes." There was anger in the voice. "He's such a diabolical bastard. Leaves a little plutonium dust in a corner, knowing that somebody will get sick, maybe die. Knowing we'll follow up, show some pictures around, find out that two of his people were there.

"He's so careful, there's no way it could have happened by accident. The man is a master of disguise. He'd have taken steps to make sure his people were unrecognizable unless he wanted them identified. He throws away people like used toilet paper. God!"

Talmage ran his hand over his skull and then lit a cigar. "I agree with you. The question is, why? Why would he want to tip us off? Why take the chance? What's the purpose?"

David leafed through some papers in the report and tapped his finger on one of the pages. "The answer is here. The psychological profile. The man is a supreme egotist. Perhaps insane. No . . . make that *definitely* insane. It's a game with him. He loves dropping clues, large and small. Some mean something and some mean nothing. Only he knows which is which, and that knowledge is power to him. He's got us running around, and he loves it. Revels in it. Which, in a way, gives us a break. The first break we've had."

Grant looked surprised. "Break? You call that a break? I'm afraid I don't share your optimism."

David jumped to his feet and started pacing the

83

floor. "Read this profile over carefully and you'll see it. Like I said, it's a game to him. Once the game is over, the whole meaning is over! His whole reason for being is over! Therefore, the game is the thing. Not the end result! Don't you see? That gives us time! He won't do anything drastic until the last possible moment. Until he's drained every ounce of pleasure he can from this power trip he's on. As long as we play by his rules, nothing bad will happen. As long as we look like fools, he'll have his enjoyment. We can, if we're smart, use it to our advantage."

Talmage didn't agree. "You forget. He's insane. Which means he's unpredictable. Totally unpredictable. You start thinking you can match wits with someone who's crazy and you're in deep trouble. You'll do this by the book, David. Try and get tricky and you'll blow it."

David grimaced. "I'm not stupid enough to think I could ever match wits with Nadi Amur. I agree that he's unpredictable. But think about it. These kinds of people have a history of making mistakes. Look at Hitler. If he'd played his cards a little better, Europe could still be Nazi to this day." He paused for a moment and then continued. "They all screw up sometime, Grant. Even the most brilliant ones. Nobody's that smart. Amur's need to gloat will be his undoing."

Talmage shook his head. "David, so far, the man hasn't made too many mistakes . . . I wouldn't hold my breath waiting for it."

David smiled. "I won't. But . . . it's different now. Look, it follows a sort of pattern. Amur's always followed a regular pattern. Everything he's done up to this point has been carried out in total secrecy. He's planted bombs, killed people, whatever . . . but always made sure he never left a clue. Only afterwards, when he would send a message, would he reveal his inner knowledge of what had happened, so we'd know it was him. He's always delighted in challenging us. Giving us little tidbits of information that had us running in different directions. Remember the investigation three years ago? How he used Michele Dumont? It's hard to know whether or not he ever really intended to blow up the embassy. But, by making sure it looked like it, he managed to insert Michele into position. We went for that one in a big way.

"But this is different. He's bragging *before* the fact. He wants us to know he's got the bomb. Instead of simply telling us, he goes through this elaborate charade, letting us find the building, the plutonium . . . identifying two of his people . . . before whatever he has in mind takes place. That's a switch. A change in the game plan. He wants to savor this for a while before he does whatever he plans to do. That's what the shrinks think, and I agree with them. In the beginning, he didn't have the power. The bomb. Now he does have the power. The power will bring him down. He'll get crazier and crazier. And if he doesn't kill us all first, we'll finally have a good chance at him."

The thought sent a shudder down David's spine. The thought that if Amur followed his old pattern, he'd explode the bomb . . . or bombs . . . and then send his message. The thought caused the enthusiasm to leave David as fast as it had arrived. "We better hope they're right."

"The shrinks?"

"Yes . . . because if they aren't . . ."

They both looked away from each other for a moment. Then David said, "You're right about one thing, Grant. The man is on another wavelength. A very dangerous situation. But, he's still human. That means he's got to make mistakes."

Grant said nothing for a moment and then asked, "You haven't said what you think about the other question. The big question. Did he produce a bomb or didn't he?"

Their eyes locked for a moment and neither man said anything. Then David said, "You know the answer to that as well as I do. Just look at the facts. Aside from the attack on the French ship, there have been several other thefts of plutonium, some right here in the States, according to the FBI, and many of them were pulled off by Amur's people. This is something he's been after for years. Every terrorist outfit in the world has been trying to get their hands on nuclear weapons. It's been an open secret that it's the administration's biggest single fear. Amur just decided to get the raw materials and make his own. Takes longer that way, but now . . . he's got what he wanted.

"You remember the flap five . . . six months ago, when that reporter for the *Washington Globe* did the article on terrorist groups' efforts to produce nuclear weapons? She had it all, Grant. She'd researched practically every plutonium theft in the world. According to her, there's enough of that stuff floating around to make fifty bombs. She showed how it could be done, outlined the information available in libraries. In fact, she had some college students design a five hundred-kiloton bomb! She said it was just a matter of time before it happened. So they made her look bad. Real bad. They wanted to disqualify her article, so they attacked her. Printed all sorts of bullshit about her. But you and I both know she was right. Right as hell! Instead of taking her seriously, they just took after her. Assholes! So now . . . Amur has done it."

He looked at Grant with eyes that were now thin slits. "He's got the damn thing, Grant. It won't be long before the other shoe drops. Anyone who thinks that Amur is bluffing on this one needs their head examined. He's got a bomb, all right. Maybe more than one. The question is where and what . . . he intends to do with it. Or them."

The room seemed colder somehow.

Grant grunted and opened another file folder, looked at it, and handed it to David. "Well . . . you're outta here, David. They want you back in the States. Langley . . . for a briefing, then Medicine Hat. They want you to have a look at that place. You'll be working for Deputy Director Brown. I wish you . . . good luck, my friend. For all of us."

David took the folder and shook the hand of Grant Talmage. As he did so, a strange thought entered his mind. He wondered if they'd ever see each other again.

Brian Carter parked the cruiser in front of the rundown frame house in West Hollywood, picked up his nightstick and his cap, and left the car.

This was a crock. The city had just passed an ordinance outlawing the placement of satellite receiver dishes on front lawns, and the police department had been instructed to serve notices on all those people with dishes. They had thirty days to move them to backyards, out of sight, or get rid of them altogether.

He was a cop. He was supposed to be out there catching criminals. Instead, he'd spent the morning taking abuse from people who'd spent thousands of dollars on their electronic gadgets and were fighting mad. It wasn't his fault, he'd told them. Bitch to the city, not him. He was just doing his job.

Most of the people considered him a representative of the city, and he'd been getting an earful all morning.

He rapped on the door and steeled himself for another outburst. The little man who answered the door took a look at the uniform and became instantly frightened. The fear in his eyes was impossible to miss.

Carter looked at his notes. "Mr. Khamil, is it? Did I say that right?"

The little man nodded his head nervously. "Yes . . . what is it? What do you want?"

"Mr. Khamil, I'm here on behalf of the city of West Hollywood." He handed the olive-skinned man a folder. "This folder will advise you of the new ordinance just passed regarding satellite receiving dishes, like the one in your front yard. I'm sorry, but you'll have to get rid of it. They've been banned from front lawns and roofs. They can only be placed in rear yards, and since you don't have a rear yard, I'm afraid you're out of luck."

Khamil reached for the folder and nodded again. "Yes, I see. Well, I'll sell it. Would you know where I could sell it?"

The cop shook his head. "I'm sorry, Mr. Khamil, I don't. Right now, those things are kind of a drag on the market, y'know. Ever since all the TV companies scrambled the signals, at least in the big cities, anyway."

The little man nodded again. "Yes . . . well, I'll take care of it. Thank you."

The door closed quietly and Carter went back to the cruiser. Funny little guy, he thought. A raghead who didn't bitch and scream about his rights being abused. Most of them were a real pain in the ass, bringing their odd-ball religious beliefs over to America and expecting everyone to kiss their asses.

This guy just nodded his head and said he'd take care of it. Weird! The satellite dish was a twelve-footer that must have cost the guy a bundle. And not a peep! People who lived in this neighborhood didn't usually have a bundle.

He turned the key in the ignition and put the car in gear. People were strange, he thought, as he headed for the next house on the list.

The man known as Agmar Khamil watched the police car leave and then scurried back to his bedroom. He opened the closet door and pulled a black shortwave radio from the upper shelf and placed it on the bed. He ran a wire to the thin wire antenna that circled the eaves of the house and connected it. He then opened his code book and began to prepare a message.

He stopped halfway through. His instructions were clear. He was to stay off the radio, except for the regular acknowledgment, unless it was an emergency.

Was it an emergency? Nadi had said that this would all be over soon. When Khamil had bought the satellite dish, the salesman had warned him this might happen. That he might have to remove the dish.

But Nadi had said it didn't matter. That the Americans were notoriously lethargic about enforcing unpopular laws. That it would be months before they got around to forcing him to remove the dish. And this mission would not take months.

On the other hand, if there was a delay . . . the Americans might negotiate . . . they had in the past, even though they denied it, more attention might be paid to the house. He didn't want to attract attention. That was why he left the house only once a week to get supplies, and only in the middle of the night. In Los Angeles, the grocery stores were open twenty-four hours a day.

He looked at his watch. He was to send the acknowledgment of the regular signal in another two hours. But it simply meant that everything was fine. That he hadn't been discovered. His next regular communication was not for two days.

Two days. The policeman had looked at him strangely. They always looked at Arabs strangely in Los Angeles. Unless they were driving Rolls Royces and shopping in the stores on Rodeo Drive. The policeman might come back and ask some other questions.

It was too dangerous. The situation made him nervous. He finished the message. Amur would have to be advised. Perhaps the bomb buried under the old house would have to be dug up and placed somewhere else. Someplace that allowed the installation of a satellite receiver dish. Otherwise, the message from Amur could never be received. The message that would tell him to detonate the bomb and obliterate everything within a six-mile radius of the house.

Los Angeles would be turned into ashes in a millisecond. And so would the man known as Agmar Khamil. Willingly. But first, they would have to find a new location. Amur would know what to do.

Chapter Six

President Brandon Taylor sat in his chair behind the big oak desk, his hands fingering the document he'd just read, his handsome face reflecting the emotions that roiled within him.

It had finally happened. The nightmare that many inside and outside government had feared was inevitable, no matter what the precautions, was now a reality. The ultimate extortion. A nation held hostage by people who were beyond all reason or, for that matter, retaliation.

The most powerful nation on earth struck helpless and impotent by a small cadre of dedicated terrorists with a singleminded passion that would not be dimmed even if it meant the total destruction of human life on earth.

A hundred contingency plans had been drawn up, discarded, and drawn up again, for just this horrible eventuality, which no one believed could ever really happen and all feared just might.

And now it was upon them.

They had all agreed that the message was genuine. The record of Nadi Amur was a bloody and consistent one. The man had never bluffed in the past. Capable of violence of whatever sort, he rarely gave warnings but rather killed first and sent messages later. This time, he had veered from that policy.

Along with the message had come the proof. A copy of the real manifest of a French freighter lost at sea three years ago. It had taken six months before a remote deep-sea exploration vehicle had located the sunken wreck and confirmed that it had, indeed, been blown up. The manifest included with the documents now in the hands of the President showed that a shipment of plutonium to Japan had been part of the cargo. It proved that Amur had known the plutonium was on board the vessel.

There were other thefts of plutonium that had been verified, some of them within the borders of the United States. Documentation supporting the theft of high-speed precision switches known as Krytons was also included. There was a photograph of a smiling, blindfolded Arab with six of the small devices in his hands.

There was a scientifically accurate blueprint of the actual bomb that had been constructed. The message said that twelve bombs had been built. They had been placed somewhere within the twelve largest cities in the United States, ready to be detonated by an electronic signal sent from half a world away.

Another photograph showed the same blindfolded man standing beside twelve bombs sitting on wooden platforms. Each bomb was inscribed with a legend written in chalk. The legend read: "Death to America!"

According to the signed message, unless the United States took the necessary steps to return the nation of Israel to the Palestinians within thirty days, the bombs would be detonated and thirty-three million Americans would be instantly vaporized.

Thirty-three million Americans.

Any attempt to warn the people or take preventative action would result in immediate detonation of all bombs. Any attempt to seek out the signers of the message would result in immediate detonation of all bombs. Any attempt to destroy or alter the position of any of the satellites circling the earth at a height of twenty-two thousand three hundred miles would result in immediate detonation of all bombs.

The message said that there would be no further contact. Either Israel ceased to exist as a nation by Oct. 6, or thirty-three million Americans would die instantly.

Perhaps as many as fifty million more would die later.

The design of the bomb was crude but effective. It was a particularly "dirty" bomb, capable of unleashing immense quantities of radioactivity, the effects of which would be felt for centuries.

Each bomb was rated at two megatons, a hundred times the power of the Hiroshima bomb.

President Taylor leafed through the report again,

his eyes stopping at a reproduction of the actual message, signed by six men, the first of which was Nadi Amur. He stared at the message—obscenely designed to emulate the Declaration of Independence—as if by some miracle he could make it disappear by pure concentration.

After a few minutes, he put the report down and noticed for the first time that his hand was shaking. He looked out into the faces of four men sitting stiffly, seemingly holding their collective breath.

President Taylor tried to control his emotions. "There's no doubt in your minds?"

CIA Director Fred Briggs shook his head. "Mr. President, we've gone over every single item on the list. They've provided solid proof. There are things in there that could not possibly be known unless they were a party to the theft. The biggest single plutonium theft was the French freighter. We've been trying for three years to track that down. The diagram for the bomb is accurate. The total amount of plutonium known to be lost is more than enough to produce the twelve bombs." The director's voice started to crack. He paused and then continued, with some effort. "There's no question, sir. No question at all."

President Taylor glanced at the blue-edged document and leaned back in his chair. He hoped they couldn't hear the pounding of his heart. "Well . . . it's finally happened. All of the warnings . . . now they'll know we were right. Too damn late!"

He slammed his hand on the table. "Assholes! We warned the Europeans and the Japanese to stop using plutonium for their reactors. We especially warned them about their shipping methods. But they kept telling us that the real threat lay with us. That terrorists would get their hands on one of our nuclear weapons. There was no way they could get their hands on plutonium from them. No way! Goddamn arrogant bastards! They never listen to us. It's as though they take some special pleasure in thumbing their noses at us. Especially the damn Japs! Screwing up our industries for years and bowing and scraping and saying, 'Sure, we'll open up our markets, no problem. . . .' We put those assholes back on their feet! We built their damn industries for them! Might as well have shot ourselves in the foot! So now it's happened. And they'll all turn to us and say, 'It's your problem!' "

His tirade was over. The frustration had boiled over into unaccustomed anger. President Taylor rarely lost his aplomb, especially in the presense of others. But he seemed unembarrassed by the outburst.

He turned to face the group. "First impressions? Anyone?"

The four looked at each other and then NSA Director Ashton White spoke. "Mr. President, I'm sure we're all agreed that Amur means what he says. His record speaks for itself. He's quite capable of such . . . an act. Every shred of intelligence we've been able to gather over the years points out the fact that the man is totally unreachable. As difficult as this may be, I'm afraid we have no choice . . . but to do as he says. Any attempt to locate the weapons would, I'm afraid, be met with . . . disaster. In fact, I fear that the man may almost *want* us to try to stop him. He may be looking for an excuse to detonate the bombs."

President Taylor leaned forward. "Ashton, you know as well as I that we have no legal or moral right to encourage or cajole Israel into an action they would fight to the death. Even to consider such a possibility is out of the question. The only question that we must face is how do we stop this from happening?"

"But Amur? He's obviously got the bombs . . . and he'll use them! We have to save America!"

"And capitulation is your answer? Is that what you're saying."

Before he could answer, Presidential Security Advisor Richard Douglas jumped to his feet. "That's ridiculous! Amur knows that would serve no purpose! What would be the point? He wants Israel destroyed, not us! That's what he's been fighting for all these years. He's simply holding a gun to our heads, and there's little we can do about it. But we certainly can't go along with it! No matter what the threat, we can't have some terrorist dictating foreign policy!"

Warren Tate, the secretary of defense, nodded his head. "Mr. President, for once, Richard is correct. Besides, Amur isn't looking for an excuse. He doesn't need an excuse! If he wanted to blow us up, he'd just go ahead and do it. No message . . . no warning . . . nothing! In the past, he's always killed without any warning whatsoever. It's Israel he wants. I'm sure of it."

The voices were beginning to rise, the tension in the room was palpable. The President held up his hand. "Take it easy. I'm asking for first impressions here, not something chiseled in stone. Why not blow up Israel?"

Fred Briggs answered that one quickly. "There's no point to it. The land would be uninhabitable for years. Israel would be destroyed, but so would the Palestinian homeland. It would be like destroying your own land. If Amur were successful in forcing us to bend to his will, he would accomplish two things. They get the land back, and they humiliate Israel and the United States as well."

The President bristled. "So . . . we have one opinion suggesting we have no choice . . . but to surrender . . . and two others suggesting surrender is unthinkable. George, what about you?"

The director of the FBI shook his head. "Mr. President, this is outside my area of expertise. I can only say this: almost all of the plutonium thefts in the United States over the past few years can now be tied to Nadi Amur, based on the evidence he's provided. In my opinion, he has what he says he has: twelve nuclear bombs. There's no question in my mind. As for our response . . . I simply couldn't say."

The President's lips hinted at a smile. "George, forget the diplomacy. I want your opinion as a man, not as the director of the FBI."

The FBI man gave it. "Very well. Experience with domestic situations, coupled with the experience of other countries, has taught us that while each situation is different in many respects, there is a common thread. You can negotiate . . . provided the negotiations lead to a solution of the problem. An end to the threat. But in this case, I don't think that holds true. While it might look, on the surface, as though some sort of negotiations should take place, if only to give us more time, I think that the man we're dealing with, this Amur . . . is insane. I'm afraid that any attempt by us to negotiate would be leaked . . . by Amur. The Israelis would have only one response. And you all know what that would be. We're between a rock and a hard place. I think we have to take the high road. Ignore the threat, go after Amur, find the weapons, and disarm them. I know it sounds simple, but I'm convinced that any attempt at negotiation would be used by Amur as a way to publicize his position. I'm concerned that he may announce to the world the same information he's provided to us. If he does, the panic in this country would be of staggering proportions. In fact, I think we need to alert all civil defense organizations right now . . . just in case."

The President turned his attention to Fred Briggs. "Well, Fred? Do you agree?"

Briggs shook his head. "Not as far as alerting anyone at this time. We still have a lot of brain-busting to do before we take action. But George has a point. Amur has been jerking us around for years. There's no reason to assume he won't do it now."

The President's voice was starting to betray his anxiety. "Ashton, am I to understand that you feel that we have no choice? That we are supposed to go to Israel and tell them that we'd appreciate it if they'd get lost? What then? Amur picks up his bombs and takes them home?"

White was wringing his hands. "Sir, our position is untenable. We've done countless case studies on this possibility. We've never been able to develop a workable plan. I don't think we'll be successful now. If we don't do as Amur says, this country will be destroyed! There simply is no choice!"

Fred Briggs held up his hand. "Ashton, that's bullshit, and you know it. There are many choices. Surrender happens to be one of them. But you know as well as I do that to surrender means total surrender. It won't stop with Israel. It will mean that we are going to let Nadi Amur dictate to this country from now on. That's not acceptable."

White seemed genuinely frightened. "But . . . don't you understand? The man has placed twelve bombs in twelve cities. You want to kill half of America? Is that what you want?"

Fred Briggs stared at the man. You never knew how people would react to a certain situation until it was there, right in front of them. The man was not thinking clearly, his mind was clouded with undisguised fear. Briggs wondered how many others would react in exactly the same way. He also wondered what would happen if a man like Ashton White had somehow managed to become President of the United States.

The room was quiet, save for the labored breathing of five men who were having difficulty understanding the horror of the moment. Five men who were confronted with a situation that was excruciatingly painful. Five men who could feel the lives of millions of Americans slipping through their fingers.

President Taylor sighed and stared at the ceiling. To no one in particular, he asked, "What about the theory that Amur is insane? Where does that leave us? According to this report, he's been leading us around by the nose, up one dark alley and down another. Is there any possibility that he doesn't, in fact, have a bomb at all? That it's all a gigantic hoax?"

Fred Briggs, the author of much of the report, took it upon himself to speak to the question. "Sir, I would place that possibility in a very low order. Amur has the money, that we're sure of. His people have been responsible for countless robberies throughout Europe and the Middle East for years. And we're sure he's been getting healthy amounts of cash from 'the group' in Libya, along with some other Arab states. We're sure he's got the plutonium he needs. We're convinced he has the people capable of producing the bomb. The blueprints are accurate. He may be crazy, but with opportunity, the means, and the motive, I see no reason why he would *not* go ahead and produce the bomb. It wouldn't make any sense."

The President tapped a pencil on the desk as he continued to stare at the ceiling. "The building in

Canada. You're *sure* it's the place where the bombs were produced?"

Briggs hesitated, cleared his throat, and then answered. "We won't be absolutely sure until we've completed the search of the pond in back of the building. We think that's where the equipment was dumped. Then we'll know. The water in the pond is radioactive and progress is slow. There's been a little problem with the Canadian authorities."

The President jerked around in his chair and stared at Briggs. "Problem? What sort of problem?"

"Well, they're a little miffed. They don't like the idea that our people are in charge of the investigation. They feel that since this place is on Canadian soil, the investigation should be headed up by their own people."

President Taylor grimaced. "So, you have some heavy-handed agents pushing people around again. Terrific!"

Briggs protested, "Sir . . . we don't have any choice. We have to move fast. If a few noses get bent out of shape in the process, that's too bad. This situation calls for some quick action. We need to know exactly what went on there, as soon as possible."

Taylor shook his head. "Amur won't give you much. The bastard will let you see only what he wants you to see." He picked up the report again. "Incredible! Absolutely incredible! It's almost impossible to believe that one sick psychopath can place the entire earth in mortal danger. What the hell is the matter with us? Are we all that incompetent?"

Nobody answered.

President Taylor sighed. "I'll talk to Sanford and get his cooperation."

Briggs asked, "Do you plan to tell him the truth?"

"Of course not. The fewer people that know about this, the better. Fred, I'll need some recommendations. You'll work with George and Richard and some others I'll assign. As of the moment, I'll keep an open mind . . . except for one thing. There is no way on God's earth that we give in to Amur. You'll need to provide me with several possible directions to take. Quickly. In the meantime, I want a full investigation begun, and I want it done in such a way that Amur hasn't got the foggiest notion of what we're doing. Understand?"

Fred Briggs gulped and nodded. "Yes, sir. I'll get right on it."

Taylor slammed his hand on the desk, then pushed a button on the phone on his desk. He practically yelled into the speaker beside the telephone. "Get me Prime Minister Sanford."

"Yes, sir. Mr. President?"

"What!"

"Tim is here. He says he needs to see you. He says the *Post* is about to print a story claiming that a group of Arabs are blackmailing us. He's begging to see you, sir."

President Taylor slumped in his chair and in a low voice, almost a moan, said, "Send Tim in."

The press secretary entered the room just as the

president's secretary announced that she had Prime Minister Sanford on the telephone. President Taylor talked to the Canadian as five sets of eyes watched him, and gave thanks.

Gave thanks that it was he, and not they, sitting in the big leather chair.

Deputy Director Frank Brown was still at his desk, even though it was approaching two in the morning. Lately, this had become the rule rather than the exception. There had been so much work, in fact, that he'd taken to sleeping on the couch in his office on some evenings.

Not that it mattered much. Mary, his wife of thirty years, hardly spoke to him anymore. There was nothing nasty or spiteful about her attitude. No overt effort to express dissatisfaction or displeasure. Simply indifference.

She was always there when he needed her, for social obligations or other official functions where the presence of the dutiful wife was expected. And she was always the perfect role model. Smiling, articulate, witty. Pleasant company.

But when they were alone, she treated him as she might treat a casual acquaintance. The bond between them had started to erode slowly some fifteen years ago. A gradual but inexorable change that turned what once was a partnership into two separate existences. His, a world of intrigue and mystery, hers, a world of art shows, benefit concerts, and women's clubs.

She seemed happy enough. At fifty-two, she was still a very attractive woman. The fact that they hadn't shared a bed in three years seemed not to bother her one wit.

Once, on a whim, he'd had her followed, suspecting she might have a secret lover. But if she did, she'd found a way to handle it that would make the KGB envious.

The blue telephone rang.

"Brown."

"Sir, this is Bennett. I wonder if I might see you for a moment."

"Sure."

Bennett wasn't working late. This was his normal working hour. Down in the bowels of the building just outside Washington, down where the communications equipment hummed twenty-four hours a day, three hundred sixty-five days a year.

He was there in minutes, his face flushed with excitement. "Sir, we've intercepted a coded message that might be interesting. It originated in Los Angeles, on a very low-watt low-wave frequency. But, the interesting thing is that we cross-checked with the NSA and they picked up the same message."

Brown raised his eyebrows. "Let me see it."

The message had been decoded, and it read: "Must find new location within thirty days. Send assistance. Thirty-four."

Brown looked at Bennett with some irritation. "That's it?"

The tall, thin communications expert licked his

lips. "Not quite, sir. In the first place, the code used is one commonly used by Nadi Amur's people. It's an unusual code. Quite distinctive, really. Actually, it's a variation of the one-write. . . ."

Brown cut him off. "Spare me. What else?"

"Well . . . using the info from the NSA and our own direction-finding equipment, we've been able to locate the source to within a six-block area of West Hollywood."

Brown was staring at him intently. "Go on."

"We did some checking and it turns out that West Hollywood has just passed a city ordinance that bans those big television dishes from front lawns. They gave everyone thirty days to move them. We think the message refers to that. We think that whoever 'thirty-four' is, he wants Amur to know that he has to move his satellite dish within thirty days."

Brown rubbed a thick hand over his face. "Have there been any other intercepts on this frequency, or this . . . thirty-four?"

Bennett nodded. "One. About three weeks ago. It just said, 'In position.' " The thin man handed the report to Frank Brown.

"That it?"

"Yes, sir."

"OK. Leave it with me. Nice work."

"Thank you sir."

The deputy director chewed on a pencil as he studied the yellow sheet of paper. What the hell would Amur have to do with a man and a satellite dish? Satellite dishes were used to receive television stations from space. Why would Amur be broadcasting television signals?

He picked up the green phone and pushed two buttons. "This is Brown. I want the following message sent to Los Angeles. Priority One. Message follows."

He dictated the message and hung up the phone. Then he picked up his suitcoat and headed for the door. He suddenly felt a wave of tiredness come over him. Tonight he'd sleep in the big bed at home.

He was almost out the door when the black phone rang. He turned and picked it up. It was a call from Walter Stewart in Medicine Hat.

"Yes, Walter."

"Sir, I've pretty well finished up here, but I've received instructions that I'm to wait around for some turd from the State Department. I've got some men here. Is it really necessary for me to hang around? The place is crawling with media types and every politician in Canada is after my ass. I'd like to get the hell out, if it's all right."

Frank Brown practically exploded. "Stewart! Your heavy-handedness is the very thing that's pissing off the Canadians. Canada isn't some dinky little tin-pot republic, you asshole! The man who's on his way is an experienced diplomat. He's there to smooth things over. You'll give him your full cooperation, you understand that?"

"Yes, sir."

Brown slammed the telephone back on its cradle, then punched a button on his desk.

"Sir?"

"Get me the director at his home."

"He's not at home, sir."

"Where is he?"

"At the White House, sir."

Brown looked at his watch. It was two in the morning. They were having a meeting at two in the morning? Jesus Christ!

"Has Baxter arrived yet?"

"His plane landed about fifteen minutes ago, sir. He should be here within a half hour."

"Have him brought directly to my office."

"Yes, sir."

He had intended to have someone else brief Baxter and send him on his way. After listening to Stewart and finding out that the director was meeting with the President, he decided to hold off. Something very big was brewing.

He lay down on the couch and closed his eyes. Immediately, the intercom buzzed. Slowly, he pulled himself up from the couch and answered the page.

"Sir, the director has returned and would like to see you."

Brown practically dragged himself to the director's office. He was immediately ushered in, and the look on the director's face told him that there was very big trouble ahead. The man looked as though he'd aged five years in one day. He seemed grateful that Frank Brown was still there.

"Sit down, Frank. Have a drink?"

"No thanks, Fred. One drink and it'll be all over."

The director poured one for himself and sat

behind the desk. He pulled a report from his brief-case and handed it to his deputy. "Don't read it now. I'll give you the lowlights. Amur has sent a message to the President. Israel is to go out of business in thirty days or twelve two-megaton nuclear bombs go off all over the country."

The air seemed to leave Frank Brown's lungs in a rush. He felt dizzy, his face felt hot, and for a moment, he thought he might faint. He decided to have that drink after all. As he poured it, the director continued, his voice a flat monotone, devoid of emotion. "The Medicine Hat building appears to be where the bombs were constructed, although there are other schools of thought on that. In any case, Stewart has certainly angered the Canadians. You still planning on sending Baxter up there?"

Frank Brown held the report in his hands and stared at it. The shock had begun to pass and now he was becoming angry. "Sir . . . this report was prepared by us. I'd like to know why I wasn't involved in its preparation. I'm a deputy director and I've been kept in the dark until now. Why?"

Fred Briggs sighed. "Frank . . . take it easy. The message from Amur was delivered to the President, sealed, by the Syrian ambassador, who claims he thought it was a message from the PLO. Our first job was to verify the authenticity. You were working on the Canadian thing and I didn't want to burden you with this until I was sure it was genuine. You've had a heavy load these past few months, and I was trying to give you a break.

"Now that we know it *is* real, I'm placing it in your hands."

The white-haired director's voice was soft and soothing. Unlike Frank Brown, he was an appointee, a man whose experience lay in administration, not in intelligence. There was always resentment within the agency when the director was a man who hadn't come up through the ranks, which was usually the case.

The anger left Frank Brown as quickly as it had come. "I'm sorry, sir. I'm afraid this hasn't been a very good day."

"When does Baxter get in?"

Brown answered him, but his own voice seemed to be coming from somewhere else, not from his own larynx. It even sounded different. Thin, uncertain, tentative. "He should be here any minute."

"Good. You can fill him in. He seems to be more familiar with Amur than any of us. Perhaps he can determine if the Canadian building is really the place, or if it's just another one of Amur's games. In any case, Stewart is to be pulled out of there immediately. You still intend to have Baxter going there as a member of the State Department?"

Brown nodded. The director paced the floor as he thought out loud. "Good. Aside from assessing the situation, he's to smooth some feathers. The key thing is this: Amur has threatened to blow up the bombs if it appears that we're trying to track him down. Baxter has to know this. The investigation has to be carried out with the utmost discretion."

Frank Brown nodded again.

The director stopped pacing. "Frank, try to read as much of that as you can before you send Baxter off. Then, get some sleep. You look like hell."

A small grin played over Brown's lips. "Looked in a mirror lately?"

"Afraid to."

"Sir . . . we may have located one of the bombs." Fred Briggs looked stunned. "Where? How?"

Frank Brown handed him the yellow sheet of paper. "Just a fluke, really. We monitored a short radio transmission and so did the NSA. It could be tied in, and then again, it may be nothing. But I have a team of men checking it out right now."

The director's eyes scanned the report as he sat on the edge of the desk. "Jesus Christ! This could be a break! A real break!"

Frank Brown rubbed his forehead. "Maybe . . . we'll know in a few hours."

Chapter Seven

The long flight back to the States seemed to take forever to David Baxter. His mind wouldn't stop working, the thoughts bursting like little bubbles in his brain, one after the other. After encountering nothing but failure for so long, they now had a lead — granted, one that had been planted, but a lead nevertheless, and Baxter wanted to get on with it.

For over three years, Baxter had allowed Nadi Amur to become almost an obsession. He'd spent many a sleepness night going over psychiatric profiles of the man, trying, in some way, to get inside Amur's head. It hadn't worked. Not really. While Baxter understood the motivation and the total ruthlessness, he still found it impossible to predict the man's actions, or to feel comfortable with any judgments he might make as to the reasons for such actions.

Judgments *had* to be made. Like the one regarding the plutonium left in the old tannery. There had to be a starting point. But David wasn't comfortable with it.

When he finally arrived at the office of Frank Brown, his discomfort had become acute, even though some things were starting to make sense.

Frank Brown looked sicker than Grant had looked. The former marine, with the crew-cut hair and fireplug body, seemed almost fragile, his motions slow, his speech tentative, as though he were completely unsure of himself. As David read the report, the reasons for Brown's appearance became obvious. It was the worst possible news.

David finished reading and felt a numbing sense of coldness. He looked at Brown and shook his head. "Jesus Christ, Frank. It's worse than I could have imagined."

Brown ran a beefy hand over his face and slowly nodded. "Now it becomes clear why the bastard left the plutonium lying around. He wanted to make sure we believed him."

David cursed. "He didn't need to do that. The stuff he gave us is convincing enough! God! Twelve bombs!"

Brown's eyelids flickered for a moment, and then he asked, "Do you believe it?"

David answered without hesitation. "Absolutely! There's no question in my mind at all. What does the President think?"

"He's convinced. He wants us to start the investigation immediately," Brown stopped and took a drink of water. "And we have to make sure that Amur never finds out."

Baxter started pacing the floor. He didn't speak

for a moment as he tried to sort out his thoughts. Then he shook his head. "It's impossible, Frank," he said. "There's no way we can conduct any sort of investigation without tipping Amur. Just the sheer numbers are enough to screw it up."

"David . . . we don't have a choice. The decision has already been made."

Baxter continued to pace. "What about the FBI?" he asked.

"The President has made this a joint effort, under the direction of Briggs."

"They must love that."

Brown snorted. "Actually, I think George is relieved. This is a responsibility nobody in their right mind wants."

They both remained silent for a moment, the enormity of the problem pressing like a great weight. Brown picked up a file folder and handed it to David.

"There may be a lead in Los Angeles. I'm going out there now. I want you to go to Medicine Hat, check things out, and then meet me in L.A. Stewart's up in Canada now, screwing things up in his normal fashion. The Canadian press is making a big deal out of this, and we have to dampen those fires. We're working on a cover story and the information will be relayed to you while you're in the air. Once you get to Canada, you'll have to move fast."

David glanced at the file and felt a sudden burst of adrenaline. Something in the report had caught his eye. The satellite dish. Amur. The man with the incredible ego. There had to be a connection.

"Frank . . . this report. What's happening?"

"I've got a team on it now. I should have some answers for you when you get to L.A."

The rush left and the tiredness returned. It was draining his strength. He could understand why Grant Talmage and Frank Brown looked the way they did. It wouldn't be long, he thought, before he too looked like an old man.

"OK, Frank. I'll get to work."

They shook hands, and David headed for the airport and the State Department plane that would take him on another long journey. Another long, sleepless journey.

Chapter Eight

Cynthia Green awoke slowly, her mind clouded by the hangover, her body shaking slightly from the cold. She'd forgotten to turn on the heat last night, and the early-in-the-season cold snap had made the whole apartment feel like a giant refrigerator. As she pulled the covers back to get out of bed, she saw him, his head burrowed into the pillow, and she swore under her breath.

She'd promised herself it wouldn't happen again, and she'd let it. Stupid, stupid.

She padded quietly to the bathroom and closed the door behind her as quietly as possible. The face that stared back at her in the mirror seemed stern and reproving. She scowled at her own image and turned on the shower.

She let the needle spray pound her body, as though punishing herself for being such an idiot.

Her head was aching and her stomach felt uneasy.

As she soaped herself, she wondered if she'd ever really be free of him. He always knew just where to find her — usually at Flanigan's after the paper had gone to press and the reporters were having a few drinks to calm the flow of adrenaline that coursed through their veins as deadline approached.

She'd never see him at first. But he'd be there, once a month or so, hanging back in the shadows, waiting until she'd had two drinks, and then he'd be standing there beside her, that stupid grin on his face, being charming and attentive, as though their three years together had never happened.

The bastard knew he still turned her on, and that after a couple of drinks she was vulnerable. The sex had always been great.

But Gary was such a loser, such a rebel, never making the effort needed to achieve the things he was capable of, that she'd finally given up and thrown him out. The shock of that had straightened him out for about six months, and for a while she'd thought it might work out after all, that'd he'd finally grown up and decided to become a responsible citizen . . . but it was not to be. He'd quit his job on some minor point of principle, as though he had some, and took a "vacation."

And when he'd come back, he'd started with the once-a-month routine at Flanigan's. He'd stand there beside her, she'd see the warmness in the eyes and feel the magnetic attraction to his body, and she'd forget the arguments, the pain of it all, and she'd bring him back to the apartment and make love for an hour.

And every morning after it happened, she'd hate herself all over again.

This morning was no exception.

The shower door opened and he was standing there, that idiot smile back in place, his hands fondling her breasts.

"Knock it off, Gary," she said as she slapped his hands away and stepped past him, grabbing a towel and drying herself off.

He continued to shower, and she rushed through her morning ritual. The hair would just have to be tied in a bun. She didn't have time to fool with it this morning. She wanted out of the apartment as quickly as possible.

She put the coffee on and then got dressed. She was almost finished by the time he came out, a towel wrapped around his middle, his arms reaching out for her again.

She moved away from him, grabbed her purse, and then stopped and glared at him. Her voice was hard. She wanted him to understand.

"Gary, I simply can't take this shit. We're divorced. And it's for a good reason. I keep trying to put you out of my mind and you keep coming after me when my defenses are down, because you know me too damn well.

"I want you to leave me alone. I mean it. I never want to see you again. I want to start a new life, and you aren't included in any way, shape, or form." She could feel her voice rising. "If you don't leave me alone, I'll get a court order. So help me, I will. You've got to leave me alone. It's over, Gary, and you've got to accept that. You've got to let me accept that. Do you understand?"

He continued to grin at her. "Come off it, Cynthia. You still care for me, I know it. You couldn't make love to me the way you do if you didn't. Why the big deal? What's the matter with having sex once in a while? You like it as much as I do."

She looked away. "That's what got me into this mess, Gary. I do like sex, and you're a great lover. But that's all you are. That's all you'll ever be good at. That's all you'll ever want out of life . . . sex. There's no substance, no character . . . no depth. You're a dreamer. Just a little boy dreamer. Sure, you still turn me on. I can't deny that. But, I have to get over that. I have to get over caring about you. I have to get over worrying about hurting your sensitive feelings. I have to grow up. And if you won't help me, than I'll just have to become a bitch. You won't like it, Gary. You won't like it at all."

She was finally dressed. "You've got lots of girlfriends. Hell, you had lots of them when we were married. You don't care about me one little bit . . . so leave me the hell alone!"

She looked at him one more time, turned, and left the apartment. She felt like death itself, but she just had to get out of there. She'd get a coffee at the deli and put on her makeup in the john. Damn that man! Damn her own feelings!

In an hour she was at her desk. There was a note from Frank that simply said, "See me as soon as you come in."

120

She took out her compact and checked the makeup. It would have to do. She left her desk and strode to his office.

He had coffee waiting for her. Thank God.

She could see he was upset. He was pacing the floor, his hands pointing at her as he spoke, a habit of his that most people found annoying. "Cynthia . . . you did a story six months ago about a possible terrorist attack on the United States that was a really crackerjack job. How'd you like to follow up on that?" He had a strange expression on his face. Like he was holding something back.

Even the mention of it brought back bitter memories. She didn't hesitate a second. It was almost a scream.

"No!"

Frank sat down at his desk and played with an unsharpened pencil while he collected his thoughts. "Look, I know how you feel . . . but supposing . . . just supposing . . . the very thing you warned them about . . . is actually happening right this minute?"

She stared at him in total shock. Normally, she watched the television news before she came in, but this morning, what with Gary and everything . . .

"Tell me! What's happening?"

He smiled at her. "You look a little tired. Gary again?"

She blushed. Flanigan's wasn't exactly an out-of-the-way place. "Frank . . . please . . . I feel lousy enough as it is. Stop teasing and tell me!"

The managing editor of the *Washington Globe* nodded and reached for a large manilla envelope. "During the night, the wire services have been reporting on a plutonium discovery in a little place in Canada. The place was being used by some Arabs who were supposedly in the wine business. After they folded up, another outfit took over the building and one of their employees died from radiation poisoning. They found some plutonium dust in the corner during the resulting investigation. The speculation is that a nuclear weapon was produced there by the Arabs. I want you to check it out."

The words hit her like a slap in the face. "What?"

The smile left his lips. "Yes . . . it's possible. The envelope contains the research you did on your story, plus some additional information we've put together overnight. You'll have plenty of time to go over it, because you'll be in the air for four hours or so. I've written down some key questions that I'd like answered, and I want you to catch the noon shuttle from National. You're booked on a flight from New York to Toronto and from there to Calgary. You're headed for a town named Medicine Hat that's not too far from Calgary. You don't have time to pack, so pick up some stuff when you get there."

"What about my passport?"

"You don't need a passport to go to Canada. Just show 'em your press pass and your driver's license."

He leaned on the desk and stared directly into her green eyes. "This could be very, very big. I want you there now and I want to hear from you tonight. Some of the research in that envelope is very . . . sensitive. Nobody else has it, so be careful who you talk to and what you say. I've marked the ones to watch out for."

She took the envelope from his hands and put it in her lap. He reached down and took a small package from his desk drawer. "Here. There's a couple of recorders in there, some batteries and extra tapes. Get as many interviews as you can. I've contacted a stringer named Roberts in Seattle. Freelance. He'll meet you there. He's a good photo man. The place will be crawling with media people, so I'd suggest you rent a van and a sleeping bag in Calgary before you go to Medicine Hat. I don't expect there'll be any hotel rooms available."

She could hardly catch her breath. "How long have you been working on this?"

He looked at his watch. "About six hours."

"You've hardly slept at all!"

He grinned at her. "Now that I know this is in the hands of Cynthia Green, ace reporter, I can go home and sleep like a baby." He said it without sarcasm. Ever since she'd first started with the newspaper, he'd been supportive and helpful. Frank Bertram was a man who genuinely liked people, particularly those who worked for him. And what set him apart from other men was that he never tried to hide the fact.

The full impact of what he had just told her hit her for the first time. She felt a little dizzy. She looked at Frank, her face contorted by the unreality of it all. "Do you really think . . . I mean . . . is there a chance that there really was a nuclear bomb produced in this place?"

Frank Bertram rubbed his chin. His eyes projected the concern he felt. "I think it's a certainty, Cynthia. It's happening. Just like you and others predicted it might, if we didn't shape up. I still say you should have gotten the Pulitzer for that feature you did. You had the facts, the threat was real . . . it wasn't sensationalism. It was a well-done piece that deserved . . . well, that's water under the bridge. The administration didn't listen to you. Why should they? After all, you're just a smart-assed female reporter, who happens to be beautiful. We all know that beautiful women are stupid. Right?"

She was astonished at the bitterness in his voice. And he'd never told her she was beautiful before. She sat there silently as he continued. "Now, it looks like we'll pay the price, one way or another."

He sighed. "Cynthia, I know you'll resist the temptation to gloat. We have to be careful with this one. Really careful. You can imagine the ramifications if it's true. So . . . I want you to really dig. Dig hard. And don't be upset when I edit your copy."

Still stunned, she picked up the envelope, the package, her purse, and headed for the door. She could feel her heart pounding wildly, and it wasn't from the hangover.

Eight hours later, Cynthia Green was sitting in a hastily set-up press tent that had been erected about a quarter mile from the tannery. The immediate area of the tannery had been blocked off, and the only information available was from the hourly handouts and updates from a young government type.

The tent was jammed with reporters from Canada and the United States. Others were arriving almost hourly from all over the world. It was chaos.

According to the latest release, the Canadian Government was fairly certain that a nuclear device had been produced in the tannery. The people responsible were being sought, but identification was sketchy and there were few additional facts from those already known.

Roberts had arrived before her and had taken pictures of everything he could, although he wasn't allowed at the site. There were some photos included in the press handout, mainly of the building, and of the employees of the implement dealer who had radiation poisoning. There was also a wedding picture of Mr. and Mrs. John Campbell. The late Mrs. Campbell. None of the people were available for interviews.

It was getting late and it was getting cold. Winter came early in this part of the world.

She left the press tent and headed for the van. she'd phone in what she had, which wasn't much, and in the morning she'd start talking to people in the town. There was much more to this story than what was being handed out. What was surprising was that the Canadians were practically admitting that a bomb had been produced right under their noses. It seemed unusual.

Normally, great steps would be taken to cover up something as incredibly terrifying as that news. But they were being very matter-of-fact about it. Almost blasé. It didn't make any sense.

She found a pay phone downtown and called the paper. Normally, she would have talked to a rewrite editor, but in this case, Frank took the phone. She gave him what she had. He listened and then sighed.

"OK . . . we've got all of that already. Including the pictures. I've some other news for you. The White House is saying that the Canadians are jumping to conclusions. They are refuting the official Canadian Government position."

Cynthia smiled to herself. It figured.

Frank continued. "I've been going over some other stuff here. There seems to be a conflict between the Canadians and some CIA types who are up there. I think the Canadians are a little touchy about the American approach. In any case, there's a guy headed out there by the name of David Baxter. He's listed as a member of the Trade Department, but he's really CIA. He was . . . and is . . . very involved in the search for Nadi Amur. I think this is connected to Amur. Show those photos around. Some of them are old, but you might get lucky. And keep an eye out for Baxter. Try to get to him. He's about six-three, black curly hair, has a beat-up nose. Ex-football player. He's posing as a guy from State, but I think he's there to tie this to Amur. If it turns out that way, we're really in trouble."

She knew better than to ask where he got the information. They talked some more and then Cynthia hung up the phone. She got into the van and unrolled the sleeping bag. She was exhausted. In the morning, she'd go to work. Right now, she needed some sleep.

She crawled inside the sleeping bag and closed her eyes. Even though she was exhausted, sleep wouldn't come. Her mind kept replaying events that had taken place six months ago. The time she'd written what was probably the best piece she'd ever done.

It had been a warning. Terrorism was a global blot on civilization. Plutonium was being stolen all over the world. The knowledge required to produce nuclear weapons was available to far too many people. She'd done her research, put it all together, and had it reviewed by mathematical wizards, who had concluded that the odds of a group of terrorists' getting their hands on a nuclear device within the next five years were fifty to one.

In their favor.

Countries that used plutonium in their energy-producing reactors had been asked to convert to other materials. Materials that were less easily converted into weapons-grade plutonium. They had refused.

American manufacturers had suffered thefts of quantities of plutonium, had tightened security, and still . . . they had thefts.

She'd had two college science majors design a nuclear bomb, then she took it to the Pentagon and had it classified Top Secret. But not before she'd had confirmation that the design would indeed work.

When the article was published, she was arrested and held for almost ten hours before the *Globe* lawyers got her out. In the meantime, stories had been planted that accused her of being, in no particular order of importance, a communist, an alcoholic, a lesbian, a drug addict, a former mental patient, and the mistress of one of the Soviet embassy employees . . . a cook.

None of it was remotely true.

But it had served to deflect the import of her article. Instead of the focus being on the threat that existed, the focus became Cynthia Green.

The newspaper never wavered in their support, and assigned several investigative reporters to the task of finding the source of the planted smears. But they were unsuccessful — to a point. They were sure the stories had originated within the Pentagon, but that was where the trail ended. In any case, it gradually became yesterday's news, and a very bitter Cynthia Green resumed her normal activities.

But every time she attended a press conference, she'd be aware of strange looks from peers who still wondered . . . if maybe. . . .

And it had made her a much more empathetic reporter. Now, before she'd write anything that might damage a career, or a life, for that matter, she'd double-check and triple-check her facts to ensure that what she wrote was as close to the truth as was humanly possible.

As she tossed and turned inside the sleeping bag, she had a malicious thought that scurried around her mind for some time before she was finally able to excise it. It was that, in a way, she hoped it was all true. That Nadi Amur *was* in possession of a nuclear device. For one horrible moment, she even hoped that it would blow up . . . maybe in the middle of Times Square.

What would they say about her then?

She forced the thought out of her mind. It was sick. She wouldn't allow the bitterness to make her sick.

In the morning, she awoke with a pounding headache. She pulled her aching body out of the sleeping bag and headed for a service station, got some coffee, availed herself of their somewhat grubby washroom, and then started asking questions.

Most of the merchants were still closed, but by nine, they were open. At the second supermarket, she hit pay dirt. A very young assistant manager, excited about all of the attention the town was getting, was at first reticient, saying that he'd been told to keep his mouth shut.

Cynthia turned on the charm. "I appreciate that, Fred." She rubbed her fingers along his name badge, "and I don't want to compromise your commitment. Let's do this . . . I'll just show you some photographs of people and you tell me if you've ever seen any of them here in town."

He wanted to pull away from her, but the penetrating green eyes seemed to hold him fast. "I don't . . . think I should. Really . . . you know, I'm really not supposed to talk to anybody, eh?"

Cynthia nodded. "Fred, I understand. You don't have to say anything. Not a word. Just look at the pictures and if you recognize anyone, just nod your head. That's not saying anything."

"Yes, it is."

"OK, then don't nod. Don't do anything. Just let me show you the pictures and don't say a word."

"What good will that do?"

"Nothing. It just lets me do my job. If I don't show these pictures around, my boss will fire me. You don't want me fired, do you?"

He shook his head. "No . . . but I can't say anything."

"I understand."

She showed him the photographs quickly and watched carefully as he glanced first at the picture and then at her and then back at the photo. The sixth one she showed him got the reaction she was hoping for. His eyes widened involuntarily and he looked away.

She said nothing and carried on. There were no other reactions. She asked, "Did anyone else show you these pictures?"

He looked around before he answered. "Yes. Some Americans, eh? Like you. They said they were from the government."

"Did you recognize any of the pictures they showed you?"

He was getting very nervous. He kept looking at the ground and then all around the store. His voice got a bit thin. "Look . . . I told you. I promised not to say . . . but they had pictures of two of the Arabs. That's all I can say. I gotta go."

Cynthia gave him a kiss on the cheek. "Thanks, Fred. You probably saved my job for me. I won't forget it. You've been a real friend."

He blushed dramatically. "It's OK."

She patted his cheek and turned to leave. Then

she stopped, flashed the photo that he'd reacted to, and asked, "Did they have a picture of this guy?"

His gaze darted around the store again and then he nodded once and walked away.

Two hours later, she had five other confirmations of the one Arab. None of the other pictures she had shown seemed to draw any response. The CIA had done their job well. The town had been blanketed and everyone told to keep quiet. But, people were people.

The photo was of one of Amur's people. A known terrorist named Fhalih Jabbah. She headed for a telephone.

Chapter Nine

•

David Baxter's State Department jet was at a height of thirty-seven thousand feet, high over the Minnesota wilderness, when the onboard computers started clacking and spewing out paper.

The cover story was coming in, automatically being decoded and printed in plain English, page by page. David rubbed his tired eyes and started reading each page as it fanned out from the machine.

The story was a concoction had been hastily prepared in an effort to counter the growing speculation in the press that a group of Arabs in Canada had produced a nuclear device, present whereabouts unknown. If the speculation was allowed to build, it wouldn't be long before a sense of panic would set in, to remain and build until a satisfactory conclusion was reached.

The speculation had to be stopped fast. They hadn't a clue where the Arabs or the bombs were. There was no information on where Nadi Amur might be, nor was there a definite plan to counter

133

his hideous threat. All that could be done was to follow whatever leads were available and see where they led. So a completely false story had been developed that was supposed to calm things down while they went about their task. As David looked over the data, he shook his head. This one was going to be difficult to sell. It would take the considerable skills of many people to make it come off.

There was other information.

The house in Los Angeles was being monitored. Not much was known so far, except that the house was being occupied by an unidentified Arab.

A house with a large satellite receiving dish on the front lawn.

A single Arab, as yet unidentified.

More would come later.

The machine stopped and David stared out at the deep blue of the infinite sky.

His thoughts drifted.

What was the purpose of this? Was there really a God? If so, why was He allowing this to happen? There were enough problems in the world. Why would God give some demented genius the means to destroy the lives of so many people? Why? Was this some sort of test? Or was God simply abandoning the human race? A write-off. One small experiment in the vastness of the universe that had failed. Try again. Something else. Some other form of life that was more worthy of existence.

Baxter blinked hard and rubbed his temples.

The tiredness clawed at him like some rabid animal, trying to bring him down, trying to stop his mind from working. He fought it hard, because he wanted answers to the questions that nagged him. Questions that couldn't be answered. He wanted to sleep but was afraid to. He had a horrible sensation of immediacy.

There was no time.

Everything was wrong.

Sleep would have to wait.

But he couldn't fight it anymore. Against his will, the eyelids dropped, his arms went slack, and he fell asleep.

As the unconsciousness deepened, the images in his brain continued without a break. Horrible, frightening images that would sear his soul right up to the moment when the wheels of the jet smoked the runway at Lethbridge Airport.

Nadi Amur sat at the window of the small house south of Damascus and stared out at the dusty streets of the village. A stiff wind was sending clouds of sand streaming across the street, streets filled with women either coming from or going to the market in the square.

He smiled, a facial movement that emphasized the hundreds of creases in a handsome face. To those who didn't know the man, it seemed a most pleasant face, the eyes alive, seeming to sparkle with good humor and warmth.

He was a tall man, and thin. Small-boned, but muscular. The diet kept him thin. His hair was tightly curled and black, and even though he was now past his fortieth birthday, not a speck of grey appeared on his head, although several strands could be found in the thick, full, false beard.

Here in this village, he was known as Muhammed Farzi. Outside of a small group, none knew he was, in truth, the legendary Nadi Amur. If it had become known, they would have thrown themselves at his feet in supplication. Their adoration would have become bothersome, a hindrance requiring immediate movement to another location.

But there were times when he wanted to tell them. Tell them that soon, their suffering would be over. That victory would be theirs. He, Nadi Amur, had created the means by which Israel would be destroyed. Destroyed by the United States of America. At the command of Nadi Amur.

He felt a tremendous sense of satisfaction. Ever since the death of his father in the abortive attack on October 6, 1973, he had sworn his vengeance.

They had laughed at him, there in the quad in the middle of the campus in Ann Arbor. Crazy Arab, they'd said. One man against the strength of the United States and Israel. They'd taunted him, until one of them spoke up and told them that Amur was just expressing his grief over the death of his father.

Ann Arbor. A world away. He'd spent six years in Ann Arbor at a time when the United States was attempting to make some accommodation with the Arab States. It had been the most grueling six years of his life.

They were such spoiled children. Anything they didn't understand they made fun of. He didn't drink? He was forbidden to drink? Attend univer-

136

sity and not drink? Was he mad?

They were so rich! They had cars and money and all they ever did was have fun. They studied subjects that were of little importance and made brave sounds about the war in Viet Nam. They protested! And while they protested, they smoked grass, as they called it, and made love like animals in the Arboretum.

In the beginning of the year 1972, the football team had lost a contest in California by a single point, and they had wandered around as though their world had suddenly come to an end. *A football game!* Millions were dying around the world and they shed tears over a game!

They respected nothing. Not their professors, not their government, not their friends dying in the stupid struggle in Asia.

And yet they saw fit to ridicule him. He had worked hard to acquire the money to attend an American university. It had been his father's fondest wish that he go to an American school and learn how to be an engineer. What was left of the family's life savings had been added to Amur's own meager savings, and arrangements had been made.

When he had first arrived, they'd thought him strange. He had tried to explain Islam to them. Aside from a few black men, who had their own version, no one listened, or wished to understand why he must pray five times a day. He was simply some crazy Arab, and the sooner he returned to wherever he came from, the better.

He had been patient. He had carefully explained to them why the United Nations decision of 1947 had been wrong. Why Israel should never have been allowed to exist. Why it had been unfair to the Palestinians. Why the United States was every bit as much a dictatorship as their alleged enemy, Soviet Russia. Why their culture was morally bankrupt. Why they were headed for a life in hell, unless they took stock and realized the terrible mistakes they were making.

But they'd refused to listen. They stared at him, their eyes vacant, their bodies full of drugs, and accused *him* of being the one who was headed to hell.

Because of the war, he'd been unable to come home to honor his father. Not right away, anyway. There had been a delay. Arrangements had to be made. There was no money for an unexpected trip. And so it was that when the Arab countries stopped shipping oil to the United States, there was panic.

The campus had been full of people screaming and yelling obscenities at him. He was an Arab. The Arabs were trying to screw the United States.

He'd tried to explain that Syria was not a party to the oil embargo. That Syria was not a member of OPEC. But, again, they hadn't listened. Instead, they had taken their frustrations out on him. They'd beaten him senseless.

And the next day, the Americans had found a way to get him home to honor his father. To give him his certificate. To suggest he never return to Ann Arbor.

It had been a long time ago.

He wondered how they'd feel now. How they'd react when their government made the announcement that Israel must give back all of the lands to

138

the Palestinians. Not just the Palestinians, but to Nadi Amur personally on the anniverary of the death of his father. He wondered if any of them would remember him.

Probably not.

There was a light tap on the door. "Nadi! It is Abdel!"

Amur went to the door and opened it. One of his followers, his clothes covered with dust from the wind, entered and sat down. "I have news. The American press is saying that you have placed a bomb in their midst! They know it is you! They were ordered to keep quiet! They thumb their noses at us, Nadi!"

Amur placed his arm around the man's shoulder and smiled knowingly. "Abdel, my friend, you must pay attention. Here I am known as Muhammed, not Nadi. I have told you this before. Why do you not follow your instructions?"

The man was instantly mortified. His hand flew to his mouth as though he wanted to tear out his tongue. Then he nodded, his eyes staring at the ground. "Forgive me, Muhammed. It shall not happen again."

"Good. Now listen to me. The Americans know what we want them to know. That is why we left the plutonium for them to find. It is only natural that the American press will draw conclusions. Conclusions that only strengthen our hand."

The man seemed unconvinced.

"But this means they search for you. They search for the bombs! They refuse to meet the demands!"

"Calm yourself, my friend. It is all unfolding as

we planned. The Americans will know fear. Then they will panic. There will be rioting in the streets. They will demand that their leaders do what we ask. They will demand it! To trade Israel for their lives is an easy decision to make. The Americans have never really liked the Zionists. They are weak, and stupid, but most of all, they are greedy. It is the greed that will force them to bend to our will. The will of Allah!"

The man was still concerned. "But what if they find the bombs?"

"Do not worry yourself. They will search for us, but they will not find us. They have tried and failed many times. And even if, by some stroke of luck, they do find the bombs, they can do nothing. They will discover this soon enough." His grin grew larger. "Come, my friend. Have you lost faith in Nadi Amur? Have you lost faith in the power of Allah? Trust me, Abdel. The road ahead is short. We are almost at the end of our journey. This is no time for doubts! This is a time for rejoicing! To sit and watch as they squirm like lizards placed on a desert fire."

The calmness in the eyes and the smoothness of the voice was almost hypnotic. The man in the dusty clothes relaxed and sat on a wooden chair. The look in his face was one of reverence.

Chapter Ten

Walter Stewart was waiting at the Prairie Schooner Motel when David Baxter arrived in Medicine Hat. The same helicopter that had brought David to Medicine Hat would take Walter Stewart back to Lethbridge for the trip back to Washington and a transfer to some remote Pacific island.

David listened as Stewart gave him the latest details and then sent him on his way. He took the car that Stewart had rented and headed for the tannery.

The place was on the outskirts of town and was surrounded by an army of police and news reporters. It seemed as though the little building in a small town in western Canada had become the focal point of the world's attention.

David parked the car as close to the scene as possible and walked toward the roped-off area. He showed his credentials to three uniformed policemen and asked where he could find Robert Tines, the Canadian minister of national defense, who was the man in charge. He was directed to the press tent, where he found the politician standing in front of a bank of microphones, answering questions being thrown at him by a frantic corps of reporters.

According to Tines, certain pieces of equipment had been found in the pond and had been recovered. The equipment seemed to confirm that nuclear devices had been produced in the building.

There was to be an official "White Paper," a government inquiry into how a group of Arabs could enter the country illegally and set up shop without anyone's knowing what was really going on. In the meantime, the Canadian Government was completely in charge of the investigation and would, if it saw fit, pass on whatever information it obtained to the United States. They were, after all, the best of friends.

The politician seemed young for such an important post, perhaps late thirties, rather handsome, with long brown hair and a good speaking voice. He seemed the calmest person in the group.

David watched him carefully, and when he finished speaking headed over and introduced himself.

Tines smiled. "Ah yes . . . Mr. Baxter. The prime minister advised me that you'd be coming. I imagine you'd like to have a chat."

David smiled as he shook hands with the man. "That I would, sir."

"Fine . . . let's sit in my car. It's just over here."

They walked over to a long black limo that was surrounded by policemen, placed there to keep the press at bay. They sat in the back of the car, alone. Tines wasted no time in getting something off his chest.

"First, let me say this, Mr. Baxter. I am a member of the cabinet. I don't appreciate having to deal with some lower-echelon flunky from the State Department. I would have expected the United States would have enough respect for my position to send someone whose position more closely equal to my own. At the very least, an assistant secretary of state. This is an insult!"

David chose his words carefully. The affair had already been grossly mismanaged. "Sir, I can understand your attitude. You're quite right. The only reason that someone more senior is not here is because the President, the secretary of state, and two assistant secretaries are at this moment engaged in calming the fears of hundreds of diplomats around the world, not to mention our own citizens, who are besieging them with questions. Questions that have been raised by, with all due respect, your constant references to the existence of a nuclear bomb in the hands of terrorists. A reference that is totally incorrect."

The man's eyes widened and his jaw dropped open. David continued.

"I apologize, on behalf of the United States government, for the rather ignorant behavior of some of our people, who have overreacted to this hoax."

Tines was thunderstruck. "Hoax?"

"Yes . . . a hoax. Even as we speak, the facts surrounding this incident are being brought to light, and as they are, information is being passed along to the media. The President has a press conference planned for this evening. The plutonium and the equipment are all part of a cleverly conceived extortion plot that has proved unsuccessful in one sense . . . the ringleaders are in custody . . . no money was paid . . . but was successful in another sense. The country is in a state of some anxiety."

Tines recovered quickly. "I don't believe you! Not a bloody word of it! Our people have looked over this place thoroughly, and everything found so far is certainly in keeping with the theory that a bomb was indeed produced. Some of these Arabs have been identified as being members of Nadi Amur's group. They were here for three years, for God's sake! They wouldn't spend that kind of time pretending to be wine merchants! You're attempting a coverup of this entire matter. Well, it won't work. We don't manage the press in Canada, Mr. Baxter."

David could feel the tingle in the back of his neck begin to throb. He controlled his temper and his voice as he carried on with this necessary idiocy. "Sir, in the first place, the identifications were made from photographs, some of them old, and they are, I can assure you, in error. We've been able to identify five of the men as being members of another group, not directly connected with Amur. We have absolute proof, and the President will present it tonight. I can't say anything else . . . except that you must believe me. The important

144

thing now, and I'm sure you'll agree, sir, is to put out these fires of speculation."

The man took it as a put-down. "I don't need a lecture on how to do my job, Mr. Baxter. There is *no* speculation. There are facts! And the facts are that a bomb was built here in this town. Built by some Arabs who have a bone to pick with the United States and Israel. The only reason they chose this location was because of its proximity to your border. The people have a right to know what is going on. I'm sure the prime minister will agree with me that we will not be a party to this charade you're cooking up."

David practically bit his tongue. There were twelve nuclear devices hidden somewhere in the United States ready to be detonated on the whim of some insane terrorist, and this asshole was ready to tell the world. The throb in the back of his neck was becoming a living thing. He fought it with all his will. And changed the subject.

"Sir, I apologize for the behavior of Walter Stewart. He overstepped his bounds and there's simply no excuse for that. But you know the CIA. A bunch of looney tunes, if ever there was one."

The young politician's face softened slightly. "Yes, indeed. It's beyond me how a country capable of producing the talent the United States is famous for can allow an agency to function like the CIA. I've never seen such arrogance! The reputation is well earned, I can assure you."

David smiled. "I agree. I'm afraid there needs to be a complete overhaul. I understand, just between us, that it won't be long in coming."

"Really?"

"Yes. As a matter of fact, I was talking to the director just last evening."

"Well, it's long overdue."

David smiled again. "Indeed. Now, about this situation. The media are having a field day. The speculation is creating problems, not just in diplomatic circles, but for Joe Q. Public. To be candid . . . a lot of people are scared witless. I say again, we have absolute proof that the situation is not as serious as first feared. That was the reason for the President's telephone call to Prime Minister Sanford. I'm not at liberty to discuss the matter. . . ."

The man responded as though stuck with a pin. "Now, just a minute! If you know something relative to this situation, you damn well better share it with me here and now. This is a Canadian matter first. The tannery is located in Alberta, not Montana. If you have *any* information pertinent to this matter, you had better damn well tell me!"

David hesitated, sighed, and then, in a low voice, as though others were listening, told him.

"Very well. As I've already stated, through our contacts in the Middle East, we've learned that the Arabs who were here in Medicine Hat were sent here to play out an elaborate ruse. As you know, there has been concern for some time that terrorists might get their hands on nuclear weapons and use them to blackmail the United States or other countries. The terrorists are well aware of that concern, and a splinter group of former Amur followers was able to get its hands on a small quantity of plutonium. Not enough to produce a bomb, but enough

146

to give that impression. We've been assured that the plutonium found here was used for that purpose. The two men identified have been located and picked up in Greece. They were taken out of Greece and are now being interviewed in London. So far, they have confirmed that no bomb was built. A letter demanding payment of a hundred million dollars was received in Washington, and the finger-prints of one of the men captured was on that letter.

"I'm sure there'll be more information shortly, but for now, I think you can rest easy. In fact, we all can rest easy. As to why they took so long to set up this extortion plot, I can only speculate, but my guess is that the hoax was intended to be pulled off much earlier and was delayed because a theft of plutonium was prevented. They had to wait until they had their hands on the stuff. Or . . . it could simply be that staying here for such a length of time would give more credence to their original claim. The Arabs are like the Chinese in certain respects. Their sense of time differs from ours considerably. Years to them are like minutes to us. . . . The President is making a televised speech tonight that will explain the entire matter. I hope you'll keep this to yourself until that time. If word gets out that I told you, it could mean my job."

Tines leaned back in the seat and eyed David suspiciously. He thought about it for a moment and then sighed. "OK, I get the picture. You people have cooked up this whole story to prevent a possible panic. I can understand that, but it's terribly wrong. Look . . . you're about to tell everyone that they have nothing to worry about. The whole thing was a hoax, the men captured, let's get on with our lives. Great . . . except . . . what if something goes wrong, and the bomb blows up? Nothing President Taylor says again will ever be believed. The mistrust of the United States by the nations of the world will just grow deeper. You're taking a terrible risk. Have you forgotten Watergate already?"

The Canadian grabbed David's arm. "Baxter, I know damn well that those sonsabitches produced a bomb here. Trying to cover it up isn't going to help anything. . . ."

There was a rap on the car window. One of Tines's aides was motioning to him. He lowered the window.

"Yes?"

"It's the prime minister, sir. On the telephone. He wants to talk to you."

Tines excused himself and walked over to another tent that the Canadian scientists were using as a makeshift headquarters. When he returned, the expression on his face was grim. He resumed his seat and glowered at David.

"Well . . . the prime minister is going along with the story. My instructions are to do the same. I suspect you and I have nothing else to discuss."

Then he left the car again, without a good-bye or a handshake.

As David Baxter walked back to his car, he was chased by a woman, dressed in fatigues, her long black hair a mess, her face devoid of makeup . . . a small tape recorder in her hand.

She grabbed his arm and moved around in front

148

of him, a glint of triumph in her green eyes.

"Mr. Baxter, I'm Cynthia Green, the *Washington Globe*. I'd like to ask you a few questions."

David kept walking. "I'm sorry Mizz Green, but I have to get back to Washington. I have no comment at this time."

She was about five-six, and even without the makeup and in the crazy guerrilla outfit she was wearing, quite beautiful. Her voice had a certain musical quality to it, and there was genuine merriness in the twinkle in her eye. "Well, I really only have one question. Why they sent a member of the Trade Department assigned to the embassy in Paris all the way here to discuss something that has little to do with American dealings with France? Unless, of course, you're really with the CIA and part of the task force that's been chasing Nadi Amur all these years. Without success."

David was stunned, but continued walking and tried to bluff it out. "I don't know what you're talking about, Mizz Green. I'm with the State Department. In Washington. I was sent here because the biggies were all tied up. Perhaps there's another Baxter in France. I wouldn't know."

She grabbed his arm and forced him to stop walking. The merriness was gone from the eyes, replaced by a look of hostility. "Look, Mr. Baxter . . . I'm really tired of the bullshit. When I learned that a David Baxter from the State Department was coming here, I checked it out. There are two David Baxters listed as employees of the State Department. One is the guy in Paris. The other is a minor bureaucrat in the State Department. They wouldn't send him up here in a million years.

. The grin returned as she warmed to her story. "Look . . . I know who you are. You're here because this is tied in to Nadi Amur. There's a rumor flying around Washington that an extortion note has been received by the White House. That this whole thing was a hoax. You and I both know that's a load of bullshit. The only man capable of putting this all together is Nadi Amur. I interviewed some of the same people your guys interviewed. From the description of the men they identified, I'm sure that one of them was Fhalih Jabbah, a man who has positively been identified as one of Amur's people. Now, unless you cooperate with me, I'm gonna print the story and watch the shit hit the fan."

David didn't doubt her for a moment. He put his hands in his pockets and leaned against a truck. He pointed to the tape recorder. "Could you turn that thing off?"

"Are you prepared to make a statement?"

David turned and walked away. She shouted after him. "All right! I've turned it off . . . look!" She handed the small black box to him. It was off.

He handed it back to her and sighed. This was not what he needed right now. He tried to make it sound as though it really didn't matter, that he was just going through the motions. "Off the record . . . think about it for a moment. Just for the sake of discussion, let's say that Nadi Amur has produced a bomb and is now using it to blackmail the United States. So you print the story. What the hell good is that going to do? Nothing. If . . . just if

. . . negotiations were being conducted, it would screw them up. In the meantime, you'd have succeeded in scaring the living shit out of most of the world. There would be panic the likes of which you'd never seen. You would also have destroyed the faith of the American people. Faith that their government is capable of dealing with terrorism and protecting them. Is that what you want?"

She actually smirked. "Oh, come now, Mr. Baxter. I'm a big girl. So are most Americans. If we're in for it, we have a right to know. Not to be snowed by a bunch of Washington bullshit artists. If the people of America lose faith in their government, it's when they try to bullshit their way out of a serious situation. So spare me the phony concern. I've got a job to do. Print the truth. No matter what the consequences."

His voice took on an edge. "Print the truth? And what is the truth? How would you possibly know what the truth really is? Are you absolutely certain that one of the men is Jabbah, or whatever his name is? Are you absolutely certain that a bomb was produced here, or is it possible that things were designed to make it appear that a bomb was produced here? Are you certain that I'm CIA? Are you certain that your list of people in Washington is accurate? That maybe lists of government employees are sometimes inaccurate? Do you know for a fact what really went on here? Are you convinced that what you print will be beneficial to the country and the people? Or . . . are you just another hard-assed bitch out to make a name for herself? Do you really give a shit one way or the other?"

They stared at each other for a moment and then David turned away again. His car was less than fifty feet away and he wanted to get back to the motel. He had people to debrief before he headed for L.A. But she wouldn't let him alone. Her voice was softer this time, her words more measured. "Mr. Baxter . . . please. . . ."

She was standing in front of him, blocking his way again. But it wasn't a gesture of defiance. The expression on her face was one of genuine concern. "Mr. Baxter . . . please. Off the record . . . I'm just scared. This thing terrifies me."

David stared into her green eyes. And then he remembered who she was. Cynthia Green! Sure! She was the reporter who'd done the piece about the sloppy security surrounding most things nuclear. A well-researched article that pointed out the very real possibilities that had now been actualized.

When the article had been published, the administration had reacted stupidly, accepting the Pentagon plan to discredit the woman, instead of dealing with the real problems she had outlined in her story. And she'd been right. The proof was here in Medicine Hat. And it was obvious from the look in her eyes that she knew she was right.

His voice softened. "Mizz Green, I don't think you're terrified at all. I remember the article you did about six months ago. A good piece. Most of us in the State Department were duly impressed. So . . . I imagine that you'd like nothing better than to create the impression that your story was prophetic. I can understand that. But . . . don't let your imagination carry you away. The President is making a speech tonight that will clear up everything. We've got a lot of people engaged in counter-terrorism inside and outside this country. It's a much larger force than has been publicly revealed. At least until now, because the President is going to announce their existence tonight. They do their work well. They've prevented a lot of tragedies. In this case, we're even more fortunate. There was no tragedy to prevent. Just a sick operation by a small group of greedy men. You'll see."

Her face reddened. "Look . . . you can hand that bullshit to whomever you like, but I'm not buying it. I'm going ahead with the story."

David could feel the throb returning in the back of his neck. He was fighting to keep control of his temper, but his voice was rising again.

"Go ahead! Write the damn story! The one you wrote before was accurate. And they tore you apart! This one isn't. They'll tear it apart again! Then what! They'll grind you up into little pieces! Anything you write from then on will have about as much impact as a marshmallow!

"Look . . . you're a good reporter. You've written some things that needed to be written. Even though you were chewed up publicly, there were those who took it seriously. Actions were taken . . . actions that may have prevented something from happening. But you're wrong on this! The man you've identified as Jabbah is not Jabbah! Jabbah has been dead for almost a year. You know as well as I do that identification of people from photographs is not always accurate. Especially when people are trying to identify someone of another race. All

Arabs look alike to some people."

He paused and tried to get his emotions under control. His face broke into a grin. "Look ... Cynthia ... give me a break ... give us all a break. We've got a serious situation here, but it isn't what you think. The President will explain it all tonight. In the meantime, don't print something that'll scare the hell out of everyone and make you ... your paper ... and everyone else look bad."

She wanted to believe him. She really did. He seemed so sincere. But she sensed he was lying through his teeth. And that *did* terrify her.

"Tell me this," she commanded, "and tell me straight. Just who the hell are you ... really?"

He grinned again. "I'm David Baxter from the State Department. Really. The David Baxter in France is my cousin. There are actually four David Baxters working in the service of their country. The other two aren't related. The government doesn't print the names of everyone, you know."

She smiled at him. "Thanks again. I feel much better."

"Good. Then I can count on you?"

Her smile grew wider. "Sure!"

She turned and started walking away from David Baxter, her heart beating wildly. He was smooth, but not smooth enough. He was lying. She was certain that Jabbah had been identified. She was certain that David Baxter was CIA. Frank Bertram didn't make mistakes on those kinds of things. The government was engaged in a coverup. That meant that the story was big. Bigger even than they imagined. She had to get to a phone. Frank would want to hear it all. Especially the tape she'd made on the second recorder. The small one she'd kept in her pocket. Off the record? No way, Jose. The stress analyzer would confirm that David Baxter was lying through his pretty teeth.

Baxter watched her moving away from him and made an instant decision. She was good. Too good. The carefully constructed facade would crumble under her relentless pressure. The kind of decision he'd just made was really outside his authority. Media people were like snakes in some regards. They had to be handled very carefully.

Baxter mulled it over in his mind and then sprinted toward her. By the time he caught up to her, she had her hand on the door handle of the van. He was breathless.

She turned and looked at him, her eyes expressing a tiny bit of fear. "What is it?" she said.

He paused to catch his breath. "I was just thinking. Maybe . . . we owe you something."

"What are you talking about?"

"The story about you. It was a low blow. Really low. Maybe I can make it up to you."

"How?"

"Well, I have to get approval, but there's a possibility that the State Department may allow a single pool reporter to follow us around on this. It wouldn't be an exclusive, in the sense that the story would belong to the State Department. But, on the other hand, there'd be a certain amount of prestige attached."

She lit up like a Christmas tree. "So, I'm right! I am right, aren't I?"

Baxter shook his head. "No, you're wrong. But, if I can swing it, you'll find out the entire story, and it will be almost as interesting as the one you think you have. Look, I have to see some people, and then I'm taking a State Department plane down to L.A. If you want in on this, you'll have to come with me now. Right now."

The brightness dimmed and the expression became suspicious. "How do I know you aren't conning me?"

Baxter laughed. "You don't. But, I'm going back to my car right this minute. I'm leaving. It's up to you. You can come with me or stay here. No problem."

Her eyes seemed to search his face for a moment, and she broke into another grin.

"OK. You've got a deal."

Baxter turned away while she retrieved some things from the van and wrote out a note for the photographer. He let out the air he'd been holding in his lungs for the past few seconds. Then, as they started toward his car, he motioned to one of the agents standing by, who nodded and moved toward the van, reached it, and destroyed the note.

156

Chapter Eleven

Brian Carter was back on patrol. All of the owners of satellite dishes in his area had been given their folders. All of the ones who were home, at least. He'd just put the folder in the mailbox in some cases. Without regret. It saved him from getting more abuse.

Now he was back on patrol. There'd still be abuse, but he didn't have to sit and take it from the sleazes on the street. With the citizens, you had to take whatever they dished out. With the sleazes you could give more than you took. And then some.

As he drove down the street the van caught his eye. He'd been by twice already, and the thing was still parked two doors away from the little raghead's place. He'd almost written a ticket the first two times, but he'd had other things to do. This time, there was no excuse. He was almost ready for code seven.

He pulled the car over to the curb, put it in park, and grabbed his nightstick and cap. He picked up his ticket book from the dash and headed back toward the van.

It was blue and looked new. The windows in the front were almost blacked-out, another violation. And then a little warning bell went off in his head.

They'd been warned about vehicles with blacked-out front windows. You couldn't see what was inside. Cops, with the new rules requiring one-man patrol cars, were very vulnerable when approach such vehicles. Only last week, a cop in Long Beach had been blown away while trying to give a ticket to a car with blacked-out windows. Two junkies who blew away a cop and then crashed into a bridge trying to leave the scene. Neither one of them had been hurt. Not then, at least.

He wrote down the plate number and returned to the patrol car, got inside, and grabbed the radio mike.

"This is Three Adam Six. I'd like wants and warrants on a blue Chevy van, California six, Charlie, Charlie, Foxtrot, four, seven, four."

"Ten-four."

He waited while they ran it through the computer. In a moment, they were back on.

"Three Adam Six, Go to tac four."

He switched the radio to the special frequency. "This is Three Adam Six."

"Three Adam Six, this is Captain Towers. Disregard blue van. They're on the job. It's the feds."

"Ten-four, captain."

The feds. He looked in the rearview mirror. For the first time he noticed the strange-looking black bulge on the roof. It was supposed to look like an air conditioner, but it was too big.

What the hell were the feds doing here? Was it the little raghead they were after? He remembered how fearful the man had looked when Brian had knocked on the door. Maybe the feds didn't know that. He decided to tell them. What the hell, you never knew when a favor would be repaid.

He got out of the patrol car and walked back to the van and rapped on the window. It opened a crack and a voice yelled, "Fuck off, you asshole! Check with your precinct!"

Brian was momentarily stunned. More abuse! He was getting a little fed up. "Look, I've got some information for you, if it's the raghead you're after."

There was silence and then the voice said, "Come around to the other side."

Brian did. Another voice asked, "So what's the information?"

Brian cleared his throat. "Well, I was here yesterday. I had to tell the guy to move his satellite dish. As soon as he saw me, he seemed scared shitless. I talked to about twenty people yesterday, and he's the only one who didn't chew me out. I thought it was kinda funny."

"You saw him?" The voice sounded interested.

"Yes."

"Describe him."

Brian took off his cap and scratched his head. "Well, he's a little shit. An Arab, like I said. Maybe five-six. About forty. Thin . . . probably no more than one-twenty or so. Very nervous."

"Just a minute."

159

Brian waited and then the window opened a little more and a sheaf of photographs appeared. "Take a look and see if any of these is the guy."

Brian looked through the photos carefully. The seventh one was the raghead. A little younger, wearing a suit and tie, but it was him. The eyes looked scared, even in the photo. He handed the photos back through the crack in the window. "The guy on top, that's him."

"You sure?"

"Yeah. That's him."

"OK . . . you've been a big help. We'll see you get a commendation. Now, get the fuck lost, will ya."

Ungrateful bastards. Brian Carter had a sour look on his face as he headed back to the patrol car.

Inside the van, Ronald Wilson pushed a switch and talked into another microphone.

"This is Dolphin. We have a positive on the client. Number sixteen on your dance card."

A very tired Frank Brown felt a rush of adrenaline jolt his body as he looked at the message. He'd spent most of the night on a plane from Washington to Los Angeles. For almost six hours he'd sat there, alone in the private aircraft, trying to develop a plan that would work.

His mind had been a jumble of conflicting thoughts. The very worst thing that could possibly happen had happened. Well, not the worst, but there was a strong possibility that the worst *would* happen. Especially if the President held fast to his present position.

He'd been given his instructions. An impossible task. Totally impossible.

And now, they had their first break. A crazy fluke. Two . . . no . . . three crazy flukes. All leading to one strong possibility. One of the twelve bombs was located in a house in West Hollywood occupied by "thirty-four." Abdul Ben-Azzuz. The brother of Hana Azzuz. One of Nadi Amur's closest associates.

What now?

The Los Angeles CIA unit, along with certain members of the FBI, were part of a large joint task force responsible for locating twelve nuclear devices hidden somewhere in the United States. One was probably buried in Washington! And yet the government was making no move to get to a safe place. In a situation like this, they were supposed to get the hell to Colorado Springs, stash themselves inside the mountain, so they could run the country if something happened.

But they were all pretending it wasn't happening! And the task force was to take no action until all the twelve bombs were located. The operation was to be carried out in such a manner as to arouse no notice from anyone! No press, no local police, no one!

Everyone was to be done in total secrecy. It had specifically been stated that should the operation be revealed, the country might be destroyed.

He almost laughed out loud. Nothing to it!

The cat had almost been let out of the bad already. A full day hadn't even passed and they were scrambling to invent crazy stories to block out the truth. The CIA had been successful in finding two cooperative Arabs to assist in the wild story about an extortion scheme. The FBI was manufacturing all sorts of evidence to back up the story. It was remarkable. The CIA and the FBI were usually at odds with each other.

But the plan, conceived in Washington, seemed to be working so far. Selective leaks of certain information were helping in building a story that the press was eating up. The proof of the pudding would be the reaction of the media when the President held his news conference.

But that was only one crisis possibly averted. They had probably located one bomb. Aided by some incredible luck and some . . . almost spooky coincidences. Or . . . it could be another part of Amur's carefully constructed plan.

For a moment the deputy director felt a certain tightness in his chest. His breathing became labored, and then, just as quickly as it had come on . . . it went away. He knew what it was. It had happened before. He knew he was working too hard. That the stress was taking a heavy toll on his body. That he should see a doctor and get some treatment.

He shook his head and let his thoughts return to the problem at hand. He stood up and walked to the window. It was another beautiful September day in California. Palm trees swaying gently in the breeze. A million cars without a speck of rust winding their way through the smog.

He wondered how long that scene would remain.

A madman wandering around somewhere in the world with his hand figuratively on the button that could end it all. Intelligence agencies all over the world looking for him and failing in the effort. Bombs buried all over the country.

The administration making out like it was all a hoax. Some inside the administration still convinced that it *was* a hoax. Maybe they'd believe it when the country went up in smoke.

He'd read the reports. He'd read the message from Amur. It was no goddamn hoax. They all should realize that. Instead of spending their time posturing, they should figure out what the hell to do. But most of Congress hadn't even been advised of the facts. Taylor was worried about some of them losing their grip. Some of them might well flip out.

How in hell were they supposed to stop the bastard? He had them all by the balls. And he was enjoying every minute of it.

He'd had them running in circles for years. People had been warned time and time again that security had to be tightened. But nobody gave a shit anymore. Plutonium was stolen and people shrugged their shoulders. Other things were stolen and they shrugged again. Like it was a load of watches or something.

They'd found the place where the bombs were made, thanks to the deliberate actions of Amur. He'd wanted them to know. What about the house in West Hollywood? Did he want them to know that, too? The shrinks had said the man was nuts. Liable to do anything.

That was just it! The guy *was* crazy! They were treating this as though it were some exercise. Another scenario played out for some chrome-domes to analyze. This was the real thing! Unless they did what the asshole asked, he'd do it! He'd actually blow the country up!

At least the President seemed to understand the severity of the problem. But he refused to negotiate. Instead, he wanted the bombs found and he wanted Amur found. In the meantime, there would be no announcements about Israel. No attempts to talk Amur out of it. No efforts to delay the deadline. He was going to go on television and tell everybody it was all a mistake. That the press was messing with their heads as they usually did. Anything to sell papers and get people watching the tube. If you haven't heard a good story by noon, invent one, that was their motto.

But the President was still sitting in Washington. Even if he believed it, it didn't seem to matter. President Taylor. A joke! The man had never worked a day in his life! Born into money, buying his way into the Presidency . . . what the hell did he know about anything! War hero! Bullshit! His family probably paid the North Koreans to fly slow so he could shoot them down. How the hell could this clown make the proper decisions?

There were hundreds of people involved in the investigation. All of them were supposed to keep their mouths shut. All of them had been briefed on the madness that was Nadi Amur. All of them had been told that the man was crazy enough to blow up America if he got wind of their efforts. Hundreds of people were supposed to be discreet.

There was simply no fucking way.

He laughed out loud. The crazy bastard would kill them all, sure as hell. Having a heart attack now might be a blessing.

The intercom buzzed.

"Yes?"

"Sir, I have Agent Baxter on the scrambler from the plane. He's en route now and wishes to speak to you."

"Fine."

Brown flicked off the intercom and picked up the scrambler telephone.

"Baxter? Brown . . . whatddaya got?"

"Frank, I'll have a full report ready for you when I get there. Right now I have another problem."

Another problem. God!

Brown's voice was harsh and raspy. "I'm listening."

There was a small hesitation and then Baxter laid it out. "Frank, you remember the *Washington Globe* article a few months ago about the possibility of something like this happening?"

"Yeah, I remember. So what?"

"Well . . . the woman who wrote that article, name's Cynthia Green . . . she was in Medicine Hat, digging around. She's put a lot of it together, Frank. A lot of it."

Brown exploded. "Jesus H. Christ! Well, what have you done about it?"

"Well, I thought maybe we could give her a break. You know, she took a real shit-kicking over that. . . ."

"Give her a break! Are you crazy? I want that woman on ice! Where is she now?"

There was another hesitation and Baxter's voice sounded a bit exasperated. "Frank, settle down, will you? Look, why can't she be sworn to secrecy and allowed to act as a pool reporter? Once the crisis is over, she can tell it like it was. It might do everyone some good. Especially coming from her, and especially if everything works out. It'll be good P.R."

"Good P.R.? What if it doesn't work out?"

There was silence for a moment and then, "Frank, if it doesn't work out, you, me, and Cynthia Green will be all very dead. So who gives a shit?"

"No! No goddamn way! I don't want any media people in on anything! Not now, not ever! I want her on ice, and that's an order! Now where is she?"

"She's with me on the plane."

Brown breathed a sigh of relief. "Good. We'll take it from here. Where are you?"

"We're just north of Reno. Should be there in little over an hour. Look . . . Frank. . . ."

"No! End of discussion! Understand!"

There was silence again and then the line went dead.

David Baxter sat at the communications desk for a moment, then got up and went into the other compartment. Cynthia was sitting in one of the thickly upholstered seats, speaking into a small tape recorder. Baxter sat down quietly beside her. His hand gently touched hers. She stopped speaking and turned off the machine.

"What's up?"

166

She could tell by his eyes that something was wrong.

Baxter cleared his throat. He didn't look at her, but stared straight ahead.

"Cynthia," he said. "I'm afraid there's a problem."

"What problem?"

"You."

"Me?"

"You."

Her face was becoming red. "Explain, please."

"Well, I don't have the authority to authorize the kind of thing we talked about. You being a pool reporter and all. I just got off the phone after talking to the man who does have the authority and he won't go for it. I'm sorry."

Her anger was immediate. "You're sorry? That's it? What happens now?"

Baxter still couldn't look at her. He found it hard to speak. Cynthia didn't wait. She almost spit out the words. "Let me guess. I'm going to be thrown into some dungeon until all of this is over. That's it, isn't it? I know too much, so I'm dangerous. You bastards . . . you're doing it to me again! I can't believe it. You tried to destroy me once before and that wasn't good enough! Now you're out to finish the job. You lying bastards! We're supposed to be a democracy, for God's sake. And we rely on people like you to protect us! Protect what? How can you do this?"

Baxter tried to explain. "Look, you have to understand something. There's a real danger of panic here. This story is one that just has to be kept under wraps. We have to weigh the lives of thousands of people against your right to print whatever the hell you want. It doesn't balance out!"

She sneered at him. Her voice was filled with scorn. "Spoken like a true dictator. God! You people are so corrupt, it makes me sick! You can rationalize anything! Anything! Well, let me tell you something, Mr. Baxter. You better save all of us a lot of trouble and kill me right now. Because the first moment I have the chance, I'll tell the world what's happening. You can play every dirty trick in the book. You can destroy my reputation, my character, whatever. But somewhere out there, someone will believe me. God help us all!"

He tried to calm her down. She wasn't having any of it. Her voice was now cold, emotionless, flat. Filled with hate.

"I'd appreciate it if you'd move, or allow me to move. I'm about to puke, and I'd rather do it in private, if you don't mind."

Baxter glanced at her, got up, and walked back into the communications room. He sat at the desk and looked over the report he'd written. His eyes wouldn't focus properly and the letters seemed blurred. He silently swore to himself. Somehow, he'd make it up to her.

If any of them managed to live through it.

Chapter Twelve

President Brandon Taylor was, once again, sitting behind the big desk, listening to the debate going on among his top security people. This time, he had confined the discussion to the directors of the FBI, the CIA, and the NSA. Taylor found small meetings much more productive than large meetings, and in this particular case, he felt it would be premature to discuss the matter with the entire cabinet, fearing leaks. It was bad enough that hundreds of CIA and FBI people were already aware of the problem.

As a matter of fact, the hideous terror facing the country was known to very few people inside the government. President Taylor knew that this couldn't last, that the basic logistics of conducting an intensive investigation would require a much broader list of those with a need to know. And when the time came to discuss the actual demands being made, the lid could pop right off.

Already, the media people were practically screaming for answers, not wanting to wait until the scheduled news conference this evening. Tim had issued a statement to the effect that the country was not in any danger and that further details would be forthcoming this evening. But it hadn't helped much. Reporters had interviewed several scientists who claimed to *know* that it would be entirely possible for terrorists to construct a nuclear bomb. They had gone so far as to interview members of the previous administration who had confirmed that such a thing had been considered as highly likely back then.

Even Amur's name had come up. Several times. It wasn't as though he was an unknown. In fact, his very notoriety had placed him on top of the list as the man who was most likely responsible for the continuing flap.

The President was listening to the conversation in the room with half an ear. The situation was so totally preposterous that he'd had difficulty grasping the reality of it ever since that first horrible moment. The words of Fred Briggs seemed to come at him from out of a fog.

". . . so we feel that we should send a team inside the house and have a look. We can determine quickly if there is, in fact, a bomb inside. And we're convinced we can get in and out without detection."

The three were looking at him, waiting. The President adjusted his glasses, cleared his throat, and asked, "Are you absolutely sure?"

The balding, overweight CIA director nodded. "Yes, we're sure, Mr. President. Within fifteen minutes we'll be able to determine the entire setup. Which satellite is involved, what frequencies are being used, where the bomb is located . . . even the method they intend to use to trigger the device. It could lead us to the other locations."

President Taylor sighed. "What about his radio signals? Your report shows that two messages have been intercepted from this Ben-Azzuz. Have there been any others?"

"Not that we know of. Neither have there been any responses. We've set up additional stations all over the country and there've been no messages on that frequency from anywhere."

The President rubbed his forehead. Then he said, "You realize what will happen if something goes wrong."

The CIA director nodded. "Yes, Mr. President. But, we really don't have many options. We need to determine exactly what the setup is. It's our only hope of even the remotest chance of learning whether we can successfully disarm the bomb." There was a hint of scorn in the voice that didn't escape the notice of Brandon Taylor.

The President finally managed to focus his attention on the three and looked from one face to the other. "I take it you still feel that I'm making a mistake."

FBI Director George Halman looked at the other two men and nodded. "I know Mr. Briggs disagrees, Mr. President, but . . . what we really need is time.

Somehow, we have to convince Amur, without going public, that we intend to go along with him, but that we need more time. I'm sure that given enough time we can locate the other bombs. But thirty days! I just don't think it's possible, given the constraints you've placed upon us. If Amur is convinced that we are taking the necessary steps to accede to his demands, he'll have no hesitation in extending the deadline. In fact, it's been a pattern with terrorists. They set deadlines and then extend them . . . as long as they think negotiations are bearing fruit."

Briggs shook his head. "George . . . Amur is different. In the first place, he's never threatened anything before. He just does it. In the second place, he's nuts. There's no way the bastard is going to be reasonable. And Amur knows . . . just as everyone else knows, that it's impossible for us to negotiate with him. We have nothing to negotiate. We simply can't do it. Period."

President Taylor shook his head. "Besides, George, do you really believe that Amur, after going to all of this trouble, is about to have his plan altered in any way? I'm afraid I can't accept that. The man is completely ruthless. I think he'd see it for what it is, a stalling tactic. We're going to make some small moves that might give him the impression that we're gearing up for negotiations, like the talk with Rashon, but other than that. . . ."

President Taylor poured some water into a glass and drank it. Then he slumped deeper into the leather chair and sighed. "Rashon will be arriving here this evening. I'll be meeting with him at Camp

David tonight. He has to be told. We have to make it appear that initial discussions are going on and that preliminary arrangements are being made." Then with a rueful grin, the President added, "I hope the prime minister's acting skills haven't diminished. He'll need them."

George Halman asked, "Sir, do you think it wise to reveal the true situation? Why not proceed as though you were really planning on doing what Amur is demanding? Then, Rashon wouldn't have to act at all."

Brandon Taylor gave the man a baleful stare. "Are you serious? Do you think for one minute that Rashon would believe that we would propose such a thing? He'd think we've lost our minds. Besides, we have a mutual treaty concerning terrorist acts. We're required to notify each other of any potential threats to either country. I'm bound by that treaty to notify Rashon. There's always the possibility that Amur will make Rashon aware of his plans. That's what makes this so incredibly difficult. Our friends and enemies alike will know, the moment we make any announcement, that something is seriously wrong. For us to propose that Israel turn over their country to a group of Palestinians led by Nadi Amur would be seen for what it truly is: an action taken because of an extortion we are unable to counter. An action that breaks every treaty ever written. An action that makes no sense. It's so blatant that the lowest form of media life would be able to guess what the true facts were. And what then . . . The speculation would be so rampant that the entire world would panic. They've been worried about just such a thing for years. The moment we make the announcement Amur is demanding, it's all over. Finished. No country can function in that kind of fear. Five billion people would simply hunker down and wait for Armageddon, immobile, frozen. . . ." His voice trailed off.

Fred Briggs stood up and paced the floor. His arms rose and then fell limply at his sides. "The President is right. Amur must be found. The bombs must be found. It's that simple."

"Surely Amur must realize the impact of his actions?" The almost plaintive question was posed by Ashton White, the National Security Agency director.

Briggs shook his head. "They say love is blind. Well, so is hate. The man has an obsession, and the dedication of a kamikazi. He can't see beyond the restoration of the Palestinian nation. That's his reason for being, and once that is achieved, whatever happens next is of little concern. He's a true psychopath. It probably never entered his mind that it would be impossible for us to agree. No matter what the stakes. The classic case of a man's placing himself in an untenable position. There's no way he can really win. All he can do is kill. No matter what we do, he loses . . . we all lose."

President Taylor slammed his hand on the table. The anger was evident in his eyes. "All right! Enough of the gloom and doom crap! We know what we have to do, so let's just get it done. In the meantime, I'll approve the search of the house in Los Angeles. But the men must be aware that there is absolutely no margin for error. If there is the

174

slightest chance . . . the mission must be aborted. This is no . . . game! I don't have to tell you!"

The room grew silent for a moment, and then the three men left, leaving the President alone with his thoughts.

He was fifty-eight years old. An attractive, vigorous fifty-eight. His body was lean and hard from the daily exercise workouts, his face a portrait of wisdom and strength, from the full head of wavy brown hair to the square jaw, seemingly chisled from some flesh-toned piece of rock.

Since he could remember, this was the job he'd always coveted. He'd entered politics at an early age, and his first elective office had been attained at the age of twenty-eight, the youngest congressman ever elected from his home state.

They had said his father's money had bought him the election, and of course it had. But no amount of money could have gotten a man elected if he had absolutely nothing to offer. And Taylor had plenty to offer.

At the age of eighteen, he'd volunteered for service in the Air Force at the onset of the Korean war. He'd started out as an enlisted man and after a year had garnered a slot in pilot's school. He'd managed to become an air ace at the tender age of twenty, his last kill coming just two months before the armistice and two weeks before his twenty-first birthday.

Coming home a war hero, he'd plunged himself into local politics, then state politics, and finally the national scene. As a twenty-eight-year-old member of Congress, and one of the richest young men in

America, he was one of the world's most eligible bachelors and seemed destined to sample each and every woman interested in changing that status before making his choice.

It was a choice that was finally made after his election to the Senate, at the ripe old age of thirty-five. Her name was Penelope Cummings, and she was a former beauty queen. It was said that the marriage was a natural, because Brandon had finally met a woman who could outlast him in bed. She was a beautiful, sensuous woman with a checkered past, which seemed to matter little to Taylor. Attempts to use both of their backgrounds against them in later election campaigns backfired badly. They were, after all, married to each other. There was no hint of unfaithfulness after the marriage, and what people did before they got married was their own business.

They were a beautiful, charming, gregarious couple. And they aged most gracefully. To the point that when Brandon Taylor finally made his long-expected bid for the presidency, his election was almost automatic. Except it didn't work out that way. Instead of the presidency, he ended up with the vice-presidency. And the beautiful Penelope was still at his side, as were their three handsome children.

He'd entered college upon his return from Korea and had graduated summa cum laude. He'd been first in his class in law school. He'd turned away from a cinch career in business, managing his father's conglomerate. He'd never lost an election. He'd married one of the most beautiful women in America after bedding at least fifty of the best. It was to his everlasting credit that not a single one of them had ever spoken out against him, or tried to make a dollar from the experience. For years, magazines had pursued many of them, offering great clods of money for just one little article. "My night of bliss with Brandon Taylor." None of them had uttered a work in public, or, it would appear, in private.

Such was the power of Brandon Taylor.

He had money, position, power, good looks, good health, a family that loved him . . . and now, after the death of President Collins, he was finally the President of the most powerful nation on earth. He had it all.

Including a fearful responsibility, which he'd never really understood until now. He'd looked to his chosen subordinates for strength . . . for some glimmer of hope. For the very first time he really *needed* help. And he wasn't getting any. They were as confused as he. They were looking to *him* for help. Looking to him for leadership. It was on his shoulders. They could advise, they could suggest, but it was the President who had to make the ultimate decision. The President who had to handle the situation. The President who had to bear the blame should there be a mistake in judgment. He'd been President for less than a year. He'd loved every minute of it . . . until the day the message arrived.

Now, for the very first time in his life, Brandon Taylor wondered about his ability to handle the situation. For the first time, he felt as Harry Truman had felt. Like the moon, the stars, and all of the planets had fallen on him.

177

Until now, he'd had confidence that he could handle whatever was thrown at him.

If what was in the message was the truth, then the city of Washington was included in the list of cities that faced obliteration. But why should the message be true? Why would Nadi Amur tell them where the bombs really were? Or whether there were twelve or twenty?

It was possible there were twenty. If the bombs were smaller than described, there could be as many as fifty. Fifty!

The country could be destroyed in a single instant on the whim of a single insane person, beyond the reach of reason, or money, or retribution.

Brandon Taylor had come a long way. And never once had he been truly afraid.

And now he was.

Now he was terrified.

The press conference had been moved up an hour, because of the continuing pressure from the media. A seemingly calm and confident Brandon Taylor strode to the podium, smiled, and began his remarks.

"Good evening. I'm sure all of you have had an interesting day."

There was a ripple of nervous laughter throughout the room. The smile remained on the President's face.

"Let me say at the very outset, that this country is in no danger from attack by any terrorist group. As you know, a small quantity of plutonium was discovered in a building in Canada, along with some equipment suspected of being used for the production of nuclear devices. This has turned out to be part of a cleverly conceived plan initiated by a small group of terrorists attempting to extort money from the United States. The men responsible for this wanton act have been identified, captured and interrogated. They were picked up by a special multinational counterterrorist organization that was formed three years ago, funded by seven countries, including the United States, and that operates out of secret European and Middle—Eastern locations."

There was a surprised gasp that was clearly audible.

The President continued, his voice even and controlled. "We recognized, after the suicide attack in Lebanon, that the nations of the free world must unite and work together to wipe out the scourge of terrorism. This secret organization is but one weapon in the arsenal that is being used in the fight. And . . . it will remain a secret organization.

"I can tell you this: We know that no bomb was constructed in Canada. We know that it was simply an ingenious ruse to make it appear that a bomb had been constructed. The equipment has been recovered and analyzed. The terrorists have confessed and their stories have been checked. There was no bomb. It was a hoax. An attempt to extort money. An attempt that failed."

The President removed a sheet covering a graphic that had been set up beside the podium. The graphic held the enlarged photographs of three men. The President pointed to one of them.

"This man is Khalif Abab, a known terrorist. He was once a member of the PLO and left in anger when Arafat decided to leave Lebanon. From there, he went to join Nadi Amur's organization, but left after some disagreements. He finally formed his own group, comprised of dissidents and cast-offs, who were more interested in pursuing personal greed than in any particular cause. They enlisted the aid of this man." He pointed to another of the photographs. "An American-born son of Iranian parents, Abdul Khomalcha, who with the help of the third man, identified as Khalami Farsal, another Iranian, engineered the robbery of a shipment of plutonium that occurred in Mississippi two years ago."

The President paused for a moment and then continued. "These three men were the ringleaders. There were others. With the help of two engineers and some money from various Libyan groups, they were able to construct equipment that appeared to be authentic. Equipment to produce nuclear devices. The equipment is incapable of doing so. The captured men have confessed, and the multinational counterterrorist organization is now rounding up everyone involved in this incredible undertaking.

"Now, I know you are going to want lots of details. We've prepared a press kit that will give you everything we can. for security reasons, I am unable to tell you anything other than what is being released. I can, however, reiterate that the country is in no danger, the threat is over, and the people involved are either in custody or will be shortly.

"There will be other terrorist attempts to frighten us. There will probably be other terrorist attempts to attack us. This we know. But the work of the

180

counterterrorist organization is expanding, inroads are being made each and every day, and none of us will rest until all of these organizations are wiped from the face of the earth.

"To be candid, a decision has been made by the United States and six of its allies. Terrorism cannot be allowed to exist. The world cannot live in fear, nor can it live in a police-state atmosphere. Terrorism, left unchecked, is more deadly than a serious contagious disease. It will be attacked as a disease would be attacked, using whatever means necessary to eradicate the infection. There will be no rest until all such groups have been eliminated.

"Now . . . if you have some questions?"

The room erupted.

Questions were hurled at the President like spears, but he deflected them deftly, his manner gracious, his demeanor calm, his answers couched in careful, measured language. He refused to expand his remarks, refused to say whether or not the secret counterterrorist group had a name, refused even to name the six other countries involved.

He was adamant. The group could function only with complete secrecy. That it would have. The terrorist organizations operating throughout the world would learn of its operations the hard way. Without warning.

It was an impressive performance by Brandon Taylor.

And it was all a lie.

And there were some in the audience who were convinced it was a lie. Frank Bertram was among them.

He'd worked with Cynthia Green on the story she'd done six months ago. He'd carefully reviewed her work. She'd researched the hell out of the story, spending almost a full month poring over every scrap of information available. The President had referred to one of the men supposedly captured as a "known terrorist." He sure wasn't known to Cynthia, or Frank.

The President had talked about a special multinational counterterrorist group. A secret organization. Not possible. The government wasn't capable of keeping such a secret. They'd tried and failed with the "Stealth" fighter. Six other countries involved? A secret? No way.

It was a coverup. And it truly frightened Frank Bertram. Because it confirmed his conviction that nuclear devices were in the hands of terrorists inside the United States.

And it confirmed another suspicion. Cynthia Green was missing. The photographer had been searching for her for hours, without success. A reporter for another newspaper had seen her getting into a car with a man who, from the description given, could have been David Baxter.

Since then, there hadn't been a word from Cynthia. That wasn't like her. She was a pro.

In Frank's mind, it all added up to one thing. Cynthia had talked to Baxter and had been taken somewhere because she knew too much. There was no other explanation. And because it was just another part of what looked like a big coverup, there was no one to turn to. Not the FBI, not anyone.

That sense of hopelessness was almost as frightening as the prospect of terrorists with nuclear bombs.

David Baxter sat in the chair, one leg crossed over the other, his fingers tightly gripping the arms of the chair. A very tired, older-looking Frank Brown was sitting behind a desk, his eyes glancing over David's report and his hand rubbing his chin.

His voice was raspy. The lips seemed slack, as though the man hadn't slept in some time. David had found himself in the same room with this man several times, and he had never seen him looking so upset. He looked much worse than he had just hours ago on the other side of the country.

The skin was sallow, the bloodshot eyes were sunk into his skull. His normally rigid body seemed affected by some illness that had sapped his strength. The shoulders were slumped, the spine bent slightly forward, and there was even a slight tremor in the left hand.

He leaned back in the chair and sighed. "Well, Baxter, there isn't much question but that the tannery really was used to produce bombs. You've seen it all firsthand . . . you've talked to the brains. Do you agree?"

David nodded. "Yes. The equipment recovered from the pond included some very hard-to-find items. I strongly doubt they would discard them simply to support a con job. They didn't need them anymore, so they dumped them. As for our discovering the setup, we were meant to. Amur wanted us to find the place so we'd be convinced he meant business. I'm sure of that. The man likes to throw a lot of curve balls at us. But sometimes he simply wants to get his message across. The two men who were identified . . . there's no reason they would have been seen unless Amur wanted it that way. The witnesses all agree that they saw the men the same week the place shut down. Now . . . those men must have been there for some time. If it was just an oversight, the men would have been noticed early on. But Amur made sure they weren't noticed. Only when he wanted us to know did they reveal their real faces."

Brown nodded, opened a file folder, and began rubbing his forehead as he went over some details. "Canada Customs says that the first shipment of wine came into Montreal onboard a Panamanian freighter named the *Little Star*. The ship is owned and operated by the Panama Star Shipping Company, a very legitimate outfit. The French have initiated their investigation on that, and so far have found nothing even remotely amiss. They're checking into the other shipments now, but it strikes me as a little strange that the first shipment was clean."

Baxter shrugged. "Maybe the wine shipment had nothing to do with the plutonium. The wine distribution business was just a cover, so maybe the plutonium came in some other way."

Brown pursed his lips. "Maybe. So far, there's nothing on either the wine company or the shipping company, but I can't shake this feeling that it's all connected, somehow. That the plutonium taken from the French freighter was somehow transferred to this Panamanian freighter and secreted inside the wine shipment. The *Little Star* just happened to be in the Mediteranean Sea the day the French freighter was attacked. A bit of a coincidence, don't you think?"

That piece of news was a shock. David nodded. "Just a bit. I can understand your concern. But Special Services people are good. If there was something, they would have found it, don't you think?

"Maybe."

It *did* seem strange. Why arrange for shipments of wine from France, and go to all of the trouble of setting up a distribution cover, if the wine shipments weren't being used to transfer the plutonium.

David got up and started pacing the floor. "There's no way that a submarine could meet with a freighter at sea without the entire crew knowing about it. No way. The Special Services guys are real pros . . . if they questioned all of the crew members . . . somebody would have to talk."

Brown shook his head. "Well, all but two of the people they've talked to were onboard the day of the submarine attack, and nobody saw anything."

David cursed. "Impossible! If that's true, then the wine shipment had nothing to do with the plutonium. And yet, it was consigned to Amur's people in Canada. It just doesn't make sense! Have our people talked to the Panamanians?"

"No. Not yet, at least. We're letting the French handle that end of it."

"Why?"

Brown rubbed his forehead. "President Taylor wants it that way. He says we need the cooperation

185

of all of the world's intelligence agencies, and he feels that the investigation should be parceled out. Since the wine shipments originated in France, that part of the investigation should be consigned to the French."

David shook his head. "That's crazy. The President has enough to do without personally directing this investigation. What does Briggs have to say?"

Brown hesitated, then looked away.

David didn't have to be told. He knew how that would go. The agency would obey orders for a while, but when the chips were down, they'd proceed as they saw fit.

David said. "I think we should do it now. And use the drug."

Brown shook his head.

"Why not?"

"Because the Special Services guys have their own methods that are almost as effective. Since they're involved, and since we don't want the world knowing about the drug, we've backed off."

David was livid. "Frank . . . this is no time to play politics. There's too much at stake! I have a lot of admiration for Special Services . . . as a matter of fact, one of their people is a friend of mind, but this is nuts. There has to be a connection! We need to talk to those people, use the drug . . . get at the truth."

Brown nodded. "I agree with you. But Briggs says no. At least, not at this point. We really do need the cooperation of every intelligence organization in the world. He feels that by double-checking their work, we'll make them look bad and that

186

cooperation will stop. You know the French. As for the drug, it's being reissued to the members of the task force." He paused, coughed, and a small smile formed on his lips. "Let's hope that this time its use is confined to the purposes for which the drug is intended."

David remembered the scandal. It was good fortune combined with some skillful administrative work that had kept it from becoming public. Someone with a malevolent sense of humor had spread a rumor that the new "truth drug" being made available to agents was also an excellent aphrodisiac. Its misuse had threatened to become widespread before the drug was withdrawn from use.

In the old days, if you wanted someone to talk, you kept them awake. For days, you refused to allow them to rest, to sleep, to dream. Eventually, they'd tell you anything.

But it wasn't always effective. Sometimes, they would lose their minds completely, and the information obtained would be practically useless. In other cases, it was the time factor. Three, four, even five days would pass before the information was gained. Too late. With the drug, interrogation became easy. It was quick and effective. They told you whatever you wanted to know.

And the word was getting out. Just the knowledge that a drug was available that was impossible to resist was sometimes enough to gain the necessary information. Especially when the side effects were known. Some were unaffected, but others became blind within two weeks.

The red eyes watched David carefully. "David . . .

187

are you sure this isn't a con? Really sure?"

There it was again. That almost plaintive hope that it was all a big mistake. The heartfelt wish that somehow, some way, this nightmare wasn't really happening.

Baxter didn't hesitate. "I'm sure it's no hoax. I'm positive. I've been on Amur's ass so long I can almost . . . almost understand how he thinks. I'm convinced that he's serious. I'm also convinced that he's enjoying all of this immensely. And . . . I'm convinced that he knows we're going after him."

The deputy director sat upright in his chair. "But the message said that. . . ."

"I know. But Amur wants to enjoy watching us chase after him. I don't believe for a minute that he'll detonate the bombs as soon as he finds out . . . and he will find out . . . that we're back on his trail. I think he expects that. I think he welcomes it. Another boost to his ego. If you look at the pattern, the trail he's left for us . . . a man who really wanted us to stay away wouldn't do what Amur is doing. I know he's crazy and unpredictable, but we don't have a choice here anyway. None at all. We have to find him."

Brown looked grim. He sighed and leaned forward in his chair, shuffling some papers, almost absentmindedly. "I'll have our people look over the records again. Maybe we can get the director to let us give the drug to the French . . . maybe. Somehow, their methods aren't as effective as they used to be. There's got to be a connection. There just has to be! In the meantime, you handle the house in West Hollywood. That one could be another

188

Medicine Hat. Might be a bomb . . . might not. With Amur, you never know."

David nodded and thought about Nadi Amur. The man worked within a system that had layer after layer of protection. Those people who formed the outer layer took their directions from people who lived in shadows. The next layer of people took their instructions from people they never met. And those members of the innermost layer, the only ones who might know where Amur was on any given day, were divided into separate cells, where only a single person, on rotation, would be the contact.

You could capture one of his people and use the drug. They would tell you everything they knew. But that information, unless coupled with countless other bits of information, was practically useless. And the innermost circle was never together. And Amur never spent more than three days in the same place.

An impossible situation.

David Baxter looked at the deputy director, a man who seemed already beaten. He wanted to reassure the man, but he couldn't. He could only say, "I'll look after it."

Frank Brown stood up and extended his hand. "Welcome back, Baxter. As of now, you're in charge, reporting to me. Good luck!"

David shook the hand, covered with cold sweat, turned, and then stopped.

"Frank, if I'm in charge of this end of the investigation, then I want to do it my way. And that means letting the reporter in on it."

"No! No fucking way!"

David whirled and stood in front of the desk, glaring down at the deputy director. His voice was angry, his face red, his arms chopping through the air as he made his case.

"Look . . . she'll agree to secrecy. She's a professional and every bit as concerned as we are. By getting her cooperation, we can ensure that this story is kept under wraps. But doing what you're doing is wrong. We'll either have to release her sometime or kill her. She's so goddamn angry right now, that releasing her is out of the question. And I certainly won't sit still for killing her. Neither will you. This is stupid! And unnecessary! Let me take the responsibility for it. If you don't think I can handle it, then maybe someone else should be in charge of the entire operation."

Brown was livid. His eyes bulged in their sockets, the veins around his temples stood out, and his hands formed fists. He wanted to tell David Baxter that no one could talk to him like that. He wanted to tell David Baxter that he was fired! That there was no place for his little-boy morality in the agency. That he was just one man, easily replaced, regardless of his experience.

But he didn't. He felt the pain again. Sharper this time, taking his breath away. And lasting longer, too. It frightened Frank Brown.

At this moment, all he wanted was to be alone. To deal with the pain on his own terms. He didn't want Baxter to see the fear in his eyes. So he let his fists unlock, took some shallow breaths so his chest didn't hurt so much, and nodded.

"OK. You handle it."

Baxter had been gone for almost five minutes before the pain went away, leaving Frank Brown bathed in sweat, light-headed, and feeling very close to death.

David Baxter headed for the motel where Cynthia Green was being held. He wondered how she'd react. Her distrust of him would make it difficult. Her anger would make it tougher still. Somehow, he had to get her to agree to kill the story before he let her go.

For a moment, he thought how wonderful it would be if he was a truck driver instead of a CIA agent. Married instead of divorced. Able to take a break from the stress, to kick back, play with the kids, and just enjoy an evening. But it was a fantasy.

There'd been other times when David Baxter had wished he didn't know so much. Wished he was just a simple man with a simple job, coming home from work into the arms of a loving wife and adoring children, happy to see him home. When his main worries were bills, a raise in pay, a bigger house, a new car. A cranky boss. . . .

This time the fantasy seemed to take form. As he headed for his car, he made a pledge to himself. When this was over, he'd get out. He was still young. The first marriage had been a mistake, but that didn't mean he couldn't find someone interested in sharing his life. A normal life. He'd go back to law. Shuffle papers. Make lots of money. Join the mainstream. He'd joined the CIA for some excitement.

Right now, he'd had enough excitement to last him a lifetime. Which, unless a few miracles appeared, might not be much longer.

He spat on the ground.

Spooks. That's what they called them. Members of the CIA. Spooks. A city full of people going about their lives totally oblivious to the frantic actions of a few people trying to save their lives. If they were successful, they'd probably never know. If they weren't. . . .

Chapter Thirteen

David Baxter parked his car and walked briskly toward the motel room. He knocked once, paused, and knocked once again. The door opened a crack and then fully.

She was sitting on the bed, her arms behind her head, staring at the ceiling, the face a mask of anger. She never moved her head an inch. The television set was on, the sound low, tuned to an all-news station. The two men assigned to guard her seemed antsy, happy to see someone who didn't look at them as though they were some unspeakable slime.

"OK. You guys take a break. Leave us for about half an hour."

They were more than happy to oblige.

David switched off the television set and took a seat in the cheap vinyl chair. She still hadn't moved a muscle. The ashtray beside the bed was filled to overflowing with butts and the air in the room reminded David of another place. In France. A thousand years ago.

She was still dressed in those fatigues, lying there, looking forlorn and abused, her hair strewn all over the blanket covering the pillows.

The dresser was marred with scrapes and cigarette burns, and David spotted the two small tape recorders, the tapes and the batteries. Obviously, the men had searched her and taken them away.

"Cynthia."

She continued to stare at the ceiling, ignoring him, her fury almost beyond control.

He spoke her name again.

No answer.

"It was wrong. This is wrong. I'm going to let you go."

That got her attention. She bolted upright in the bed and glared at him.

"More lies! As soon as I walk out that door, I'm a dead woman! You people are animals! If you're going to kill me, do it here!"

Baxter slowly reached inside his jacket and pulled out the Colt. He pulled back the slide, cocking the weapon and placing a round in the chamber. As he did so, Cynthia's eyes grew larger, her jaw dropped, and her body became rigid. David stood up and walked toward the bed. As he did so, her body pressed itself against the backboard, as if the action could ward off the bullet she was sure was coming.

Baxter turned the gun in his hand and handed it to her.

"Here. The gun is loaded and cocked. If you really think I'm going to kill you, then pull the trigger. On the other hand, you can wait and listen to what I have to say and then kill me."

She stared at him in shock. Baxter turned and went back to the chair and sat down. Cynthia Green was speechless, her expression almost comical as she sat there on the bed, the big gun in her shaking hands, her face reflecting the tortured effort to understand what was happening.

"Cynthia," he said, "I'm going to tell you everything. I'm breaking every rule in the book by doing this, but I want to trust you. For some reason, I have to trust you. If, after I've told you everything, you want to walk out of here and print what I've told you, I won't stop you. But, I'm gambling that you'll understand the dangers in that. In fact, I'm praying that you understand.

"After this is over . . . well . . . you'll have to make your own judgment."

She continued to stare at him as though he were mad.

He told her everything.

He told her about the bombs, all twelve of them. About the message. About their chances. And when he was finished, the gun had fallen to the bed and she had covered her face with her hands. Her entire body was shaking violently.

Baxter moved to the edge of the bed and took her in his arms. She flung her arms around his neck and buried her head in his chest, the sobs coming in short gasps.

"I'm sorry about the way you were treated," he said.

He could feel her head nodding.

The trembling and the sobbing stopped and she

pulled away from him slowly, turning her head and looking for a tissue. He reached into his pocket, pulled out a handkerchief, and handed it to her.

She turned away to blow her nose and then looked at him, her eyes full of uncertainty. "I . . . understand . . . now. I don't . . . know what to do. I have a job to do. You do, too. I just. . . ."

He took her hands in his and looked into her green eyes. For some reason, he felt uneasy. It wasn't the situation, the terror . . . it was something else. Something that couldn't be. Not now.

His voice was soft, almost pleading. "Cynthia, don't you see? This entire country could be destroyed. There's a good chance that Amur intends to break the news himself. He's probably going to send a copy of that message to every newspaper and television station in the country. It might be part of his plan. The man is fully aware of the impact that would have. He'd relish seeing us in total panic. He'd love watching us go crazy before he finally pulls the pin. We don't have much going for us, but if you let the word out, it'll make our chances even slimmer. We need time! Help me!"

She hesitated, and then her arms were around his neck and her moist lips were on his, pressing, searching, causing a rush of passion to surge within him, almost with a life of its own.

He could feel her heart pounding . . . or was it his?

Or was it the door?

The two agents were back.

Pounding on the door.

Damn!

David and Cynthia looked sheepishly at each other and then David got up and opened the door. It was them all right.

"It's OK. Mizz Green has agreed to cooperate with us. We won't need to keep her under wraps any longer."

The two men looked first at David and then at Cynthia, sitting demurely on the bed.

"Brown said. . . ."

David held up his hand. "Forget what Brown said. I'm telling you that I'll take care of this. Now, report to Wilson. We've got an operation to attend to in about one hour."

They looked at each other, shrugged, and turned away. David closed the door and put the chain on. Then he returned to the bed.

The look in Cynthia's eyes was anything but hate. "I better let my paper know I'm OK. They'll be worried."

Baxter took her in his arms. "Later. Let them worry just a bit longer."

The house had been carefully examined for almost two days. Every listening device, every sensor, every intelligence-gathering gadget had been used in an effort to determine the best way to get in, get the information, and get out.

The data had been gone over carefully, and now, the time was at hand.

It was three in the morning.

The two men approached from the alley in back. They'd carefully examined the original blueprints of the house. They'd looked over the spectrographic photos of the inside, which outlined every piece of furniture and its location.

They'd walked through a layout a hundred times.

They knew where the man was. They knew he was sleeping. They knew he was alone. They were going in.

They would use a small gas cannister to make sure he slept. Should there be a sound, he wouldn't hear it.

They were equipped with special goggles and special flashlights that would allow them to see inside. They were to take photographs of the layout. They were to determine how the bomb was connected to the satellite receiving dish. They were to try to find out as much as possible in thirty minutes.

They must not fail.

Almost a block away, a large truck was parked at a service station, from which the front of the house could be observed. In back, the normal garbage bin had been replaced by a blue-painted steel bin, which held three additional men, along with a host of electronic gear.

The two men entered the house with ease and immediately spotted the infrared alarm system. Carefully, they slipped under the beams and stopped, their monitoring equipment checking for any noise-activated devices that might lie in their path. There were none. They checked for temperature-variance detectors. There were two. One near the rear entrance and one near the front entrance.

They stopped and pulled from their backpacks

two mini air-conditioning units. For a few moments they took readings of the room temperature, then set the instruments and placed them in position. That would allow the men to walk past the detectors without triggering the alarms.

They checked for vibration detectors. There were none. The men allowed themselves a small smile. Even Amur's people were aware that the ground in California was constantly in motion. Sensitive vibration detectors would be triggered three or four times a day.

Soundlessly, they made their way to the bedroom. Abdul Ben-Azzuz lay naked on top of the bed, breathing deeply. One of the men twisted the nozzle of the small gas cannister and held it close to the nose of the sleeping man. They waited for almost a full minute and then one of the men poked Azzuz in the chest. There was no response. He poked him again. Harder. No response.

They proceeded with their mission.

First they used the laser flashlight to detect fingerprint impressions on the furniture. They then took pieces of adhesive tape and lifted several of the prints. Abdul Ben-Azzuz's fingerprints were on file. They could be checked. Then they photographed every inch of the place. They activated another small piece of equipment and charted the exact location of the bomb, buried in concrete right under the living room carpet.

They traced the wiring in the house and marked it on their blueprint. Then they carefully gathered up their equipment, slipped back under the infrared beams, and left through the back door.

In seconds, they were inside the big truck parked at the service station, now on its way to a special lab some three miles away. Some of the film was already being processed as the big truck moved through the almost empty streets.

The men slumped in metal chairs bolted to the floor and stripped off their black coveralls. They felt a release of tension, and yet . . . something was very wrong. They'd both noticed it inside the house.

One of the men looked at David Baxter and shook his head. "It doesn't make sense, sir."

A weary Baxter waved his hand at the man. "What? What doesn't make sense?"

"The bomb. It's there all right. But it isn't hooked up to the satellite dish. It's hooked up to a simple push-button that sits right in the bed. Azzuz's hand was on it as he slept! It's just like the call bell in a hospital. Shit! If the guy has a fucking nightmare he could push it and it's all over!"

David stared at him with eyes that seemed not to focus. There was urgency in his voice. "What's with the dish?"

The young man shook his head. "It's just like any other. It's hooked up to a TV set in the living room. It's no different than any other dish. The box is an unaltered receiver with the normal number of channels. The dish is properly aligned and can be aimed at the normal satellites. There seems to be no variation. There's nothing connecting the receiver to the bomb, either directly or indirectly. The only way the bomb can be triggered is if Azzuz pushes the button."

"Are you sure?"

The young man hesitated and then nodded his head. "I think the photos will back me up."

David rubbed his eyes and stared at the wall. "The cord. Tell me about the cord."

"It looks just like a regular AC extension cord. Goes along with the wall and under the carpet. No plug-ins or batteries that I could see. We'd have to examine the bomb itself to determine whether it's an open circuit or a closed circuit."

It was so simple. And yet so difficult. They could disarm the bomb by intercepting the circuit from the button to the bomb. But they had to know . . . closed circuit or open circuit. The wrong choice would detonate two megatons of nuclear destruction.

David asked, "What the hell is the satellite setup for, then?"

The young man shrugged and said, "Maybe Amur's gonna send a television message to his people. Maybe he wants to tell them personally when to push the button. Maybe it's an ego trip of some sort."

Baxter sat bolt upright and stared at the man. Then his face broke into a grin and he slapped his knee.

"Of course!" he exclaimed. "That's it exactly! Fenson, you're a genius. An absolute genius! That's it! That's our chance!"

The tall man with the crooked nose seemed to have been charged with a shot of energy from the depths of his soul. He reached for the telephone on the wall of the truck and punched some buttons. "This is Baxter. Give me the deputy director!"

There was a pause and then Frank Brown was on the line. "Frank, we've got a break. A real break!"

As he explained it all, he noticed a black substance on the shoes of the two men who had been inside the house. It was on the soles and mostly covered with dirt, but clearly, they had stepped in something. While he talked to Brown, David motioned to the men to take off their shoes and hand them to him.

They did, and he got a closer look. There wasn't much of it, just enough on the instep to tell him what it was. A light oil.

David looked at the two men and felt the frustration returning. Amur thought of everything. Now he'd know that they'd been there. It could have tragic consequences.

Chapter Fourteen

Brandon Taylor looked at his wife, resplendent in a blue silken peignoir, her long blond hair cascading down to slide along her shoulders. The electric-blue eyes that seemed charged with some special energy source. The skin that seemed luminescent, un-flawed, covering smoothed edges of bone in a face that, at forty-seven, still seemed perfect.

She'd given birth to three children and yet her body was toned and smoothly muscled, and not an ounce of flesh had been displaced from its location of twenty-one years ago. The full breasts had sagged not a millimeter, the stomach was as flat as it was the first day she had ever stood before a group of leering judges at some county beauty contest. Her legs were long and smooth. Evidence that here was a woman who took care of her body. Who spent long hours almost every single day working out. Who watched what she ate and drank. Who believed that a beautiful woman was forever cursed with the need to be beautiful. That those who appreciated the beauty would be the first to turn on her, like savages, at the first hint of fading.

She hadn't worn that particular peignoir in years. In fact, it had been months since they'd made love.

When they'd married, there'd been a clear understanding. Brandon Taylor was a man who loved all women. Penny would be first among equals. She would be privy to the elite in Washington society. She would receive all of the advantages that wealth and power could provide. Someday, he could even be President, and she knew that it wasn't a fantasy.

But she must understand that Brandon Taylor would continue to sample women, like a connoisseur. Power was an aphrodisiac, and Brandon Taylor was a junkie. A sex junkie. He knew it, he didn't try to fight it, and he had the intelligence and means to cater to his needs without destroying his career. She had to understand that this strange part of him could never change.

She'd agreed, partly because she loved him, partly because she wanted the prestige and power, but mainly because she thought she could change him. She thought that she'd be able to fill his sexual needs.

But she was wrong. It wasn't that the other women were better lovers, it was just that they were *different*! And that was what he craved, for reasons she'd never understand.

He'd been kind and attentive, and aside from the weirdness of it all, a fairly good husband and father. She'd hoped that this voraciousness would eventually weaken, and it did . . . but only mildly.

Twenty-one years.

They slept in separate bedrooms, something he'd arranged the first day they moved into the White House. Because of his position, he wasn't as free to move about as he'd been as a senator. So the women had to be brought here. At least he had the decency to perform his rituals away from his own bedroom, away from the door that separated the two rooms, away from her ears.

There was a night when he came to her, and for the first time, she'd told him she just didn't feel like it. He hadn't chastised her, never complained, nor had his attitude toward her changed outwardly. Except for one thing.

He just never came to her again.

Now, as she stood framed in the doorway, the light in her room casting an ethereal back-lighting on her silhouetted body, it was all forgotten.

He smiled at her. "You look lovely, Penny. I was just getting ready for bed. Is there something you wanted?"

She glided smoothly over to the bed and sat on the edge. He had already removed his clothes and taken a shower. He never wore pajamas, and he was sitting on the bed, a glass of brandy in his hand.

She reached over to touch his hand. "Nothing special. I watched you today, and yesterday. It's the first time I've seen you look really upset about anything in all the time I've known you. It's all over your face. You've always been able to hide your emotions. You're the most controlled person I've ever encountered in my life. But, for the last two days . . . there's something wrong, isn't there?"

He laughed and took a sip of the brandy. "No,

my love. There's nothing wrong. Not at all. I've just been working harder than I normally do. This . . . being President . . . is a lot different than I imagined it would be. I thought I knew that, but I guess I didn't."

She could feel the coldness in his hand. See the fear in his eyes. They were both new experiences. She moved closer. "Brandon, I know our marriage has been a little . . . unusual. But I do love you. I care about you. More than the men who surround you. More then the women who make love to you because . . . of your needs and theirs. You may not be the most romantic man on earth, but you were honest with me. You've always been honest with me. I'm the one person on this earth who cares about you more than any other. Talk to me! Tell me what it is! Let me help you."

She moved across the bed and placed herself at his side, her hand resting on his flat stomach, her fingers playing with the abundance of hair.

He was staring at the ceiling, his eyes unfocused, his breathing shallow.

Her voice softened as her lips rested on his ear. "I love you. What is it? Tell me what's bothering you."

He didn't move. He just sat there and stared at the ceiling. And then, in a voice that seemed to come from some remote depth, he said, "Penny . . . I've been such a shit. How could you possibly love me after what I've been all these years?"

She stroked his forehead. "You're not a shit. You told me what I was letting myself in for. I came into this marriage with my eyes wide open. You just happen to be the horniest person on the face of the earth. Aside from that, you're a pretty good guy. And I do love you. Still. Always have, always will."

Penny pressed again. "The press conference. You said that everything was fine. That the whole thing was just an extortion scheme. That's not the way it is, is it?"

He looked away without answering.

She pulled his face in front of her and stared directly into his eyes. "Brandon . . . listen to me. I'm your wife! I know that doesn't mean much to you in the traditional sense. I've accepted that for all these years, and I'm still here. Doesn't that tell you something? Surely you must realize that there are other men with money. Perhaps not the power, but I was never into power like you are. Don't you realize that I'm your one real friend? The one real friend you have in all the world? Let me in . . . let me help you. You've closed me out during most of our entire life together. Maybe you've never really needed me. But you need me now. I can see it in your eyes. Tell me!"

She'd never seen him like this. Uncertain, unsure, the confidence melting away like ice cream in the sunlight. For the first time ever, he appeared vulnerable. It triggered a desire within her she hadn't felt in years.

He remained silent, but his gaze flicked from one of her eyes to the other. His hands were formed into fists and his entire body seemed rigid, unyielding. Then, in one sudden movement, he reached out and pulled her to him, placing her head under his chin, his ice-cold hands pressing against her back.

His voice was like a tortured wail. "Oh God! I never thought it would come to this . . . sweet Jesus! I'm so scared I can hardly see straight! It's all bullshit, Penny. All of it! The terrorists have the bomb . . . God! They've got twelve of them! Planted all over the country."

He lifted his head up and stared into her eyes. "They've made demands, Penny! Demands that we can't possibly meet. I met with the Israeli prime minister after the press conference. I had to tell him. The man went bananas! They plan to launch an all-out attack against every terrorist group head-quarters they know about. He wouldn't listen to me! I tried to tell him that Amur would blow the whole country up if they did that, and you know what he said?"

She asked him softly, her voice almost a purr. "What did he say?"

"He said the only possible way to handle this was to launch an all-out attack on every terrorist strong-hold known and suspected. He even wanted us to drop nuclear weapons and wipe out half of the Middle East. He said their intelligence could almost guarantee that one of the strikes would get Amur. Perhaps millions of innocent people would die, but, in his words, it would put an end to the threat from terrorists once and for all. Can you imagine?"

Penny nodded and let him talk.

"He's almost as crazy as Amur! Jesus Christ! This can't be happening!"

She took him in her arms and rested his head on her breasts, stroking his hair gently, as though he were a little child. In a way, he was. Like all men.

208

They all played little games, as children and adults alike. As adults the games were deadlier, but they were games nonetheless. It had always been and always would be. She remembered the words of Juvenal: "We are now suffering the evils of a long peace. Luxury, more deadly than war, broods over the city, and avenges a conquered world."

It had been faulty thinking then and it was faulty thinking now. Man hadn't learned a thing in two thousand years.

She continued to keep her voice soft and low. "When did Rashon say he would attack the terrorists?"

The words from her husband were halting, muffled by her body. "He . . . said he'd hold off for one week. It would take that . . . long to set it all up, anyway. I practically begged him to reconsider . . . they were right . . . Briggs, the others . . . they warned me . . . not to tell him. I should have listened to them. It was a mistake."

"Where is he now?"

"Still at Camp David. I came back here because he's not supposed to be there. I wanted . . . to make things look normal. He's agreed to talk again tomorrow . . . but. . . ."

She pulled his head up and held it in her hands, her blue eyes staring straight into his. She could smell the fear in him, like an after-shave kept too long. "Now you listen to me, Brandon Taylor. You have the courage required to face up to any challenge. And you have at your fingertips the most sophisticated people and equipment ever placed on earth. Most important, you have the wisdom to

209

make the proper judgments, make the correct decisions. This country couldn't be in better hands. I believe in you . . . not just because I love you, but because I know you better than anyone. All you need is some help. Someone you can really talk to. Someone you can be yourself with. Someone who loves you. And that's me. I'm no politician, but I'm all you've got. I'm the only person in this world who really gives a damn about you. So, let me help you. At least, let me be a sounding board for your ideas. Let me play devil's advocate. It will help you in your thinking."

His arms encircled her and he held her tightly. She could feel his head nodding in agreement.

Frank Brown was seated at the conference desk, surrounded by five fellow agency men and three FBI men assigned to the joint task force.

For three hours, they had been reviewing the information garnered from the raid on the house in West Hollywood, as well as every infinitesimal shred of background material acquired over many years.

It was almost noon, and although he'd been able to steal a few precious hours of sleep, he still felt totally exhausted. In one hour, he had to give a report to the director. The preliminary reports had already been communicated, but the final recommendations were due soon, and Frank Brown was trying to gain a consensus among the members of the team.

His voice betrayed his extreme tiredness. ". . . OK, let's go over it one more time, and then we'll make our recommendations. Parkins, go over it again, all of it."

Parkins, a veteran FBI agent assigned to the task force, looked over his notes and read them off. "The building is owned by an outfit called Victor Investments, Inc. Nothing there. The place was rented to an Agmar Khamil two months ago. Khamil answered a classified ad placed by Farnsworth Realty, took the place on a one-year lease. Paid the first and last month's rent, plus a six-month security deposit in cash. The Social Security number he gave was a fake.

"The photograph identified by the cop was shown to Mr. David North, the real estate agent, and he positively identified the man as Khamil. He tried to check the guy's credit, but there are no records. That's why they wanted six months' rent as a security deposit. Khamil had no objection.

"Khamil rented all of the furniture from Cooper Furniture Rentals. A national chain. Again, he paid cash. Since they couldn't do a credit check, he paid a two-thousand-dollar deposit, also cash. Highly unusual. Also high-profile. Which doesn't fit the normal pattern with Amur's people.

"He made a deal with the rental outfit to pick up and deliver six crates that he had in storage at Shefield Moving and Storage. The crates had been shipped by Khamil from Havre, Montana. Commercial carrier. We've talked to the people at Shefield and Cooper and everything seems kosher there.

"We're checking with every moving company and commercial carrier in the country for similar ship-

211

ments within the last three months, but so far . . . nothing. Neighbors confirm seeing the crates delivered with the furniture.

"He purchased the satellite dish from Jackson Electronics, who also did the installation. They warned him that the city ordinance was on the agenda, but he didn't care. Again, he paid cash. Three thousand five hundred. They have also identified the photo.

"He paid a cash deposit to the telephone company, the gas company, and the electric company. Showed up in person. All have ID'd the photo. The telephone number is 546-7883. Unlisted. There have been no long distance calls, no access charges.

"We have nothing on the security system and assume he installed it himself. Nobody remembers selling anything like it to any Arab. As for the concrete . . . it was purchased from National. Six eighty-pound bags. Paid cash and picked it up himself. Nothing on any vehicle. He appears not to own one, so he might have had help. No cab company remembers anything about picking up cement. All of the rental outfits have checked their records and come up dry.

"None of the neighbors have ever seen the guy come or go, except for moving-in day. Not even when he was out buying this stuff. We assume he came and went through the back. We can't find anyone who has seen anyone else come or go.

"The outline of the bomb is in the living room under the carpet. It's well shielded and emits no Gamma, X-rays, or anything else. The satellite system appears not to be modified, and the bomb appears to be triggered manually.

"Everyone we've talked to is sure the man is Khamil, however, we have him listed as Azzuz. The prints match those of Azzuz. So the name Khamil is a phony. We have nothing on anyone named Khamil, nor does the NSA, who has been keeping track of potential terrorists for some time.

"The only radio transmissions we know of have been the two listed."

He stopped and shrugged. "Two other points. The photos show the man has a telescope in his bedroom. The only view he has is a very narrow field of vision, about eight degrees, of the Verdugo mountains, aside from a small portion of sky. We found a flashlight in one of the drawers. It's possible he's communicating this way. We have a crew checking out the mountain now."

He'd finished with his notes. David Baxter took it from there. "OK . . . some questions. The man seems to be living there alone. He must go out once in a while for groceries. He answered the door when the cop paid a visit to tell him about the dish.

"The bomb is connected to a simple push-button. Why would they take a chance like that? Suppose the cop knocked on his door again and as soon as he answered it, we nailed him. Doesn't that seem a bit stupid?"

Ronald Wilson tried to answer the question. "Well, there could be a number of reasons. In the first place, October sixth is the big day. So, they may not be too concerned at this time. In the second place, because Azzuz left such a hot trail for us, they may be using him as a decoy . . . to see if

213

we're on to them. The message warned against taking any action. If we pick up Azzuz, Amur will find out and the other bombs go off. They must have some way of communicating on a regular basis. Maybe at night, with that flashlight. And then . . . there's always the chance that there is no bomb. That Azzuz is strictly a red herring. Once we cap Azzuz . . . Amur knows, but . . . we don't have the real bomb."

David rubbed his chin and cursed. "Well, one thing's for sure. They know we were inside."

Frank Brown shook his head. "You can't be sure of that, Baxter. There could be some other explanation for that oil. Maybe they don't know."

David shook his head. "They know!"

Brown was adamant. "Then how come we're still here? Amur threatened to blow up the country if we made any moves."

David shook his head. "I can't answer that. But I feel it in my gut. He knows! He's toying with us, having a ball with the knowledge and the power."

The room became silent for a moment. Then Ronald Wilson carried on. "The outside layout of the bomb matches the blueprints forwarded in the message. But, unless you dug that sucker up and really examined it, you'd have no way of knowing whether or not it's real. It seems to be well shielded. We couldn't get any readings at all. But if I had to make a guess, I'd say that it's real."

"According to the way the thing is set up, the man hits the button and blows himself up with the bomb. Azzuz is one of Amur's closest associates, and he's the brother of Hana Azzuz, who's also real

214

tight with the sumbitch. I'm a little surprised that it's him. I can see Azzuz not being too crazy about going up in smoke. Some of the others would consider it an honor."

David scratched his head. That was a good point. One would have thought that the inner circle would want to survive any explosions. He mulled it over in his mind for a moment. There were so many things that didn't make sense.

He set the thought aside for the moment. "Once we find out whether or not that really is a bomb, we'll be more able to make a proper judgment. We have to go in again. Dig underneath the house. Have a good look at that thing and disarm it."

They all looked at him. Then Frank Brown grimaced. "Too risky, Baxter . . . much too risky. If we screwed up once, we'll probably screw up again. The bastards are clever. The bomb could have a hundred damn booby traps. We can't take the chance! We have to work it from the other side. Get to Amur!"

David's voice was like a growl. "Get to Amur! Jesus Christ! We've been trying for years!"

Again, there was silence in the room. Wilson tried to break the tension with some other information. "We'll have to keep an eye on Azzuz for a few more days to see if anyone contacts him. The bugs are in place and we'll know every move he makes. We'll be keeping an eye on the window with our own telescope up in the mountains to see if we can pick up anything. We've got crews checking out every satellite dish in fifteen cities, going over records of home ownership and talking with landlords. We're also checking all sales of satellite dishes

215

within the last six months. And cross-checking in-stallations with recent apartment or home rentals, or even home purchases. The message said that the twelve biggest cities were targeted, but that can be confusing, as well. Another one of his little games. Depending on what sources he used, the twelve cities could actually be any of twenty cities. Where did he get his information? An old census, or a new one? Metropolitan areas or just the basic city? The guy plays every trick in the book. Who knows where Amur gets his info?"

Baxter held up his hand.

"The NSA has a file on almost every Arab in this country, but these guys all came in from Canada, so that won't help us much . . . unless . . . tell the crews we want the addresses of every home occu-pied by anyone that looks even remotely Arab, whether they have a satellite dish or not. Then, run those names through NSA, and if any of them don't match, we have a possible."

Brown looked at Baxter quizzically. "I thought we were after people with satellite dishes?"

Baxter ran a hand over his skull as he answered. "True. But we have to explore the possibility that this whole thing with satellite dishes is another of Amur's blind alleys."

He paused and then started talking again, more thinking out loud than anything else.

"There are several things that disturb me. One is this business of Azzuz . . . Khamil . . . running around making all kinds of business deals with cash. People remember those things. It looks like Amur being obvious again. I can't shake this feeling that he's setting us up. Maybe he's got some way of knowing if we touch that bomb. Maybe . . . just touching it sets it off. In Amur's mind, there could be a certain justice in that.

"In view of the fact that he made sure the people in Canada were recognized, it's possible that he planned on Khamil's being recognized. That scares the hell out me. Really, it does. The trail is too obvious. He used a regular shipping company to ship the bomb from Montana to L.A. But so far, this is the only location where he's used that method. It's as though he was deliberately leading us right to it. Sure, the cop was the first man who recognized Azzuz. But think about it. He put in a satellite dish knowing he'd have to move it within a limited time frame. The crates were large and would naturally bring attention. And the radio transmissions . . . if he has another method of communication, why use a radio at all?

"It stinks. The more I think about it, the more I'm afraid that each city has a completely different setup. And Amur wanted us to find this one, just like he wanted us to find the tannery."

Then he turned to Frank Brown and sighed. "Another thing. What about transmission systems? Up-links? If the satellite receivers are supposed to receive some message, then there has to be equipment somewhere to transmit it. We need to check out every single transmission system sold over the last five years."

Frank Brown protested. "For Christ's sake, we don't have that kind of time!"

Baxter shook his head. "We better find the time.

We have to expand the teams. We have to take the wraps off. They don't need to know the whole story, but there's no point in mincing around. Amur knows we're searching! He hasn't pulled the trigger yet! That has to mean something."

Wilson was on his feet. "David's right, sir. We have to do it. And we have to dig underneath the house and get at the bomb, without Azzuz ever knowing. If it's real, we can disarm it. If it's not real, then we'll have an answer."

Brown didn't respond at first. Then he looked around the room and his shoulders sagged. "All of you have looked over the profile. The man is crazy. Who the hell knows what's really going on in his mind."

Frank Brown's face was beginning to look pasty. He seemed to be having some difficulty breathing. His voice seemed almost timid as he said, "You understand? This is no ordinary deal . . . we mess this up and millions die. Millions! The whole country would go ape-shit. Los Angeles would be destroyed! We can't take the chance!"

David Baxter tried to keep his voice controlled as he spoke to that issue. "Frank . . . we can't sit here and do nothing! The bastard knows that we've discovered the Los Angeles location. . . . he's liable to have them push the button at any minute! We've got to move in and have a look at the thing!"

Frank Brown rubbed his forehead. A tremendous headache was making its way across his skull. He looked at the faces of the men. He could see the frustration in their eyes, feel their sense of helplessness. They were all going around in circles, like dogs chasing their own tails.

It was understandable. They'd faced many serious situations in their combined careers, but nothing could ever prepare them for something as insane as this. It was hard to grasp the reality of it. Minds inculcated with situations and solutions suddenly confronted with a situation that seemed without a solution. Like trying to nail water to a wall.

It was making them all sick.

And he felt that pain in his chest again.

Frank Brown continued to rub his forehead. Never in his life had he dealt with such an insufferable problem. He tried to will the pain in his chest away. "The message said that the bombs were connected to satellite receiving dishes. That detonation would be made through a signal that could be sent from almost anywhere. That's not true. Some person has to push the button."

Wilson nodded, and continued. "Yes . . . but in fact, the concept is the same. A signal is received and a human pushes the button instead of a remote-controlled electronic device. The difference is symbolic, I think. The shrinks are working on that angle, so I haven't a clue, but we do know that Amur is an egomaniac. While it's entirely possible that he intends to send a message via television, for some reason we have yet to understand, there is nothing to indicate that the bomb is anything less than depicted in the design drawings . . . or, for that matter, a fake."

David shook his head. "I don't think it's the same at all. The difference is very significant. I think Amur plans to beam a message to these people . . .

a message that also blocks out the major networks. Think of it! Fifty million Americans sitting in front of the tube and Amur comes on and says, 'Guess what, folks . . . I'm telling my guys to push the button now!' Don't forget . . . the man is totally insane. To do it by remote control would lessen the meaning for him. He's got to order the actual button-pushing personally. That's his ultimate kick. And that's our key to stopping him. But . . . and it's a big but, if he's letting us in on his plan by leading us to this location, there's got to be something more."

Frank Brown shook his head. "All right . . . we have to cut this off. Can we get at that bomb, find out if it's real or fake . . . without blowing up Los Angeles? That's what I want to know. That's what Briggs wants to know. Is it possible?"

The room grew quiet. Then David, in a voice filled with uncertainty, said, "Frank . . . we don't have much choice."

No one else spoke. Such a terrible decision to have to make. The weight of it was on everyone's shoulders. The almost palpable silence was broken by the shrillness of the telephone ringing. Brown picked it up, listened for a moment, and his face became whiter still. Then he dropped the phone and clutched at his throat. The excruciating pain was immediately obvious. Something was happening. Brown's hands went from his throat to his chest, and he looked around the room in utter surprise before his eyeballs went up into his head and he pitched forward facedown on the big table.

"Jesus Christ!" someone yelled.

Everyone sprang into action. Two men placed him on the floor and began resuscitation procedures. Baxter grabbed the phone.

"Call the paramedics . . . Frank's having a heart attack!" He hung up the phone and within a minute it rang again. He picked it up. The paramedics were on their way. "What was the message you gave Brown?" David asked.

He listened and then replaced the receiver. Brown was getting mouth-to-mouth and outside heart massage. The skin hadn't turn blue so it seemed to be working. Ronald Wilson tugged at his arm. "David . . . what was so terrible that it did this?"

Baxter didn't trust himself to look the man in the eye. He kept his gaze on the men working on Frank Brown.

"Israeli is planning an all-out offensive against Syria. Everything they've got, save for nuclear weapons. But they could be included. The raid could begin at any moment. Taylor's still talking with Rashon, but the bastard is stubborn. Taylor is beside himself."

Wilson sat down and buried his head in his hands.

"Jesus H. Christ!"

Through the window, David could hear the wail of the ambulance. The paramedics would be here in minutes. Perhaps they could save Frank Brown and perhaps they couldn't.

Baxter looked at the man lying on the floor. He'd devoted almost his entire life to the agency. To his country. Over the years, he'd taken a lot of heat for actions that had seemed stupid. Some the man had agreed with, some he hadn't. But it was such a rotten business. Everybody wanted the country protected, but they wanted it done within a certain moral standard.

They just didn't understand. There were no rules. There were just situations. Situations that had to be handled. Some of them impossible. Like this one.

The man might be dying. And if he was, he might be one of the lucky ones.

Chapter Fifteen

The smoke was becoming thick in the conference room of the *Washington Globe*. The rules stated that there was to be no smoking in the room, because some of the reporters smoked and others didn't, but the tension of the last two conferences was so strong that even Jessica, the resident protector of everyone's lungs, failed to complain. Or maybe Jessica hadn't complained because Alice Tremont, the publisher, had joined the group, sitting silently, smoking cigarette after cigarette in that long gold holder she favored.

There were ten of them altogether. The managing editor, Frank Bertram, the national editor, John Forsythe, the international editor, Henry Givens, six reporters, and Alice Tremont.

Frank Bertram was chairing this important meeting. They were going over the facts gleaned from hundreds of personal and telephone interviews. Information drawn from their own extensive files, longtime sources, wire service reports, other news organizations, and competitive newspapers.

Bertram grunted and leaned back in his chair. "All right, let's go over it one more time. Bill, you start . . ."

Bill Pensky, one of the reporters, cleared his throat and read from the notes in front of him. "Well . . . we have a real serious situation here. No question about it. First, Dr. Gibbons did a stress analysis on the President's remarks and he says the man is lying. Prime Minister Rashon is still at Camp David. Tim Burke has said nothing other than that the meeting was called because of rumors of an attack against Israel by Syria. It should be noted that the White House has made no mention of the meeting at all until United Broadcasting broke the story of Rashon's visit.

"But while the Israeli armed forces are on full alert, Rashon is still here. And we've learned that the armed forces went on alert *after* he arrived here, which shoots a hole through Tim's statement. John, I'm sure, has more on that.

"As for our own armed forces, nothing has changed. The Delta group hasn't even been placed on alert, near as we can tell. However, aside from Camp David, there have been a lot of meetings at odd hours at the White House. And some normally extroverted politicians are taking very unusual steps to avoid us. In fact, three of them have checked into Bethesda. That's really strange.

"My normal sources of information have dried up, and I've noticed that there's a real sense of impending doom on the hill. A lot of people are *very* uptight. Oh . . . another thing. President Taylor has taken his wife to Camp David. That's something he's never done before, when it's been business. And this is definitely business. All in all, I'd say something very big indeed is afoot."

Bertram turned his attention to John Forsythe. "John?"

Forsythe tapped a pencil on the table as he talked in that flat monotone of his. "Well, Cynthia has certainly thrown us a curve. I can't understand why she hasn't given us a goddamn thing. It was you she talked to, Frank. What the hell is going on?"

Bertram had known it wouldn't be long before the subject of Cynthia Green came up. He was ready for it.

"She's on the inside. That's all I can tell you. It's a rather unusual situation. We'll just have to let her play it her way. Right now . . . she can't tell us anything."

Forsythe almost smirked. "Tell me . . . is she working for us or the CIA? You sent her after this Baxter character, and unless I miss my guess, she made contact. Then, we get nothing. That sucks, Frank. She can't have it both ways."

A bit of color was coming into Bertram's cheeks. "With all due respect, John, Cynthia knows what she's doing. As I have already said, she's unable to tell us anything, but I think it's safe to make a couple of assumptions.

"I'm sure she did meet Baxter. As all of you know, Cynthia has a style that might be termed confrontational. She was armed with some information that might have given the CIA fits. It's possible they're keeping her on ice. Now, we could get

225

exercised about this, and normally I would, but Cynthia specifically asked that we not.

"She asked how my daughter was, and as all of you know, that means that she's working free and clear and in no danger. Obviously, whatever is going on is delicate, and I'm sure we'll know it all as soon as Cynthia is in a position to tell us. It would seem to confirm, however, that whatever she's dug up is extremely sensitive. I think we can take that as further confirmation that, as Bill says, something very big is afoot. In the meantime, we'll just have to work around her."

Forsythe was not to be denied. "I've gone over a copy of the file you sent along with her. It looks to me like we're being snowed by the White House. There's nothing in her file regarding the so-called terrorists the President mentioned. There's no reason in the world Israel would be in such a state of alert if this was simply an extortion scam. The very fact that Cynthia called you from L.A. *after* she met with the CIA people would be a strong indication to me that she fell into something and has decided to keep her mouth shut. That's not what she's being paid for. She's supposed to be a reporter. If she's so damn free and clear, then where the hell's the story? Those decisions are made by editors, not reporters! What I can't understand is your calmness in the face of it. Surely, you can see what's happening."

The redness in Bertram's face was beginning to turn crimson. His voice started getting louder. "Look, John. . . ."

Alice Tremont tapped her cigarette holder on the

table. All eyes immediately turned toward her. "Gentlemen, could we leave Cynthia Green for the moment and get *on* with it. I want to know what we're going to publish in this newspaper. You two can settle your differences another time and in another place."

Forsythe nodded, smiled thinly, and resumed. "Of course, Mrs. Tremont. My apologies. It's just. . . ."

"Get *on* with it!"

Forsythe cleared his throat and referred to his own notes. "From what I've been able to determine from other sources, the equipment found in the pond was certainly used to produce at least one nuclear device. Perhaps more than one. The men identified by the President show up nowhere in any files we've got, nor do they appear in any pictures in the morgue. Nobody ever heard of these characters before.

"The Canadians, after saying that a bomb *was* produced in the tannery, now say that they were mistaken, that the whole thing was a hoax, supporting the White House position. It's interesting to note that this flip-flop occurred after this Baxter had a talk with a . . . Robert Tines, a member of the Canadian government.

"I've had telephone conversations with three people who were instrumental in Cynthia's earlier piece, and they all reconfirmed their earlier thoughts. That enough plutonium has been stolen over the years to produce any number of nuclear bombs. In fact, over the last twenty-five years, at least a ton of the stuff has turned up missing from Hanford, Washington alone. There are other quantities missing from facilities in Ohio and Georgia, as well. Since it takes about fifty pounds to make a bomb of any consequence, there's more than enough missing to make anyone's hair stand on end.

"We know that Amur has accumulated large quantities of cash. We also know that the raid on Libya in 1986 included an attack on a so-called secret facility in Tripoli, suspected of being a bomb factory. It's fairly certain that nothing was found, although that information is still classified.

"We have confirmation that the navy diving bell DS-4 was used in the Mediterranean Sea, searching the bottom, at the exact last known position where the French freighter *Armand Lavertue* went down three years ago. It's common knowledge that the French make shipments of plutonium to Japan on ships such as these, despite all of the warnings, and we can reasonably assume that the ship contained plutonium. There's no other valid reason why the U.S. Navy would be searching the wreck.

"On the whole, I think that the Canadian building was a bomb factory, that bombs were in fact produced there, and that the White House story is nothing but a smoke screen. There're really only three questions that seem important. How many bombs were produced . . . where are they now . . . and what does Amur plan to do with them?"

Forsythe was surprised at the calmness in his voice. He'd just uttered the most heart-stopping words he'd ever voiced and done it rather matter-of-factly. Maybe it was a dream he was having. A nightmare. He'd wake up and this crazy vision would be all over.

228

They were all staring at him.

Bertram asked, "What about the plutonium found in Canada? What's the explanation for that? A mistake? An accident?"

Forsythe shook his head. "Anything but. All of the Amur experts I've talked to say the same thing. The man likes to see people sweat. He enjoys creating fear in the hearts of his enemies. He's cocky, because he's managed to remain at large for years, even though a worldwide manhunt has been ongoing. The theory is that he deliberately left the plutonium there to back up whatever threat he is making. He wanted us to know he really has a bomb. Or bombs. No . . . the so-called extortion thing isn't the threat. If we look at what's going on in Israel, I'd guess that the threat involves Israel directly. I'd further guess that Amur has threatened to explode a nuclear device somewhere in this country unless Israel does something. Knowing Amur, we can all assume what that is."

He stopped and lit a cigarette. His mouth felt dry. All of a sudden, it wasn't a dream anymore. Frank Bertram turned to Jessica Chase. "Jessica?"

Jessica, a reporter with a penchant for high fashion, looked more like a woman who covered the rag trade, not hard news. Her hair was carefully piled on top of her head, the expensive, imported dress was offset with real pearls, and as usual, she spoke with her chin high in the air. "Yes . . . well, the Israelis are certainly in a bit of a lather. They've clamped the security lid down so hard inside Israel that all troops are confined to base. There are no calls in or out of any government agencies. No one is talking. The embassy here is closed down. The people are there, but they aren't seeing anyone, or answering phone calls. Airports throughout Israel are closed and the border has been sealed. Other than troops, no one is being allowed through. Tourists and foreign press people have been advised to remain in their hotels.

"Israeli embassies throughout the rest of the world are following the same pattern. There's not even the remotest effort to maintain normal routines. They're preparing for something very big and they don't seem to care who knows it. No public statements have been made, normal sources are completely in the dark, and we can't find out anything. It's total isolation. It's as though they were preparing for . . . total war.

"As for the President's remarks about a special secret multinational counterterrorist organization, that seems to be pure, unadulterated fantasy. I've tried to talk to some former intelligence people, but they've disappeared. Bernard Marks, at Harvard, didn't show up yesterday, and nobody knows where he is. Three former CIA directors are missing, two former FBI assistant directors are missing, and seven experts on the Middle East are also missing."

A small smile came over her face. "I *do* have my sources, however, and they say it's impossible. There's simply no way that seven countries could cooperate in that fashion and keep it a secret. As for the missing people, it seems clear that the White House, or even the CIA for that matter, has had these people picked up and kept incommunicado, for obvious reasons. It's the biggest coverup I've ever seen, and it's so clumsy and poorly conceived, anyone can see that it was fashioned in one terrible hurry. Frankly, I sense that our dear President seems to be functioning under a sense of panic. It worries me. It also makes me agree with the general consensus of opinion, that something very, very serious is taking place here.

"I think it's clear what's happened to Cynthia. If the White House is going to hide former government officials, they certainly aren't going to hesitate to keep Cynthia from telling us what she's discovered. Although Cynthia is an excellent reporter, she is, after all, still quite young. It's possible she gave Frank the OK signal while under the impression that she was free to come and go as she pleased, when in fact she is not. My inclination would be to raise a terrible fuss until she's back, safely, at her desk. This simply cannot be allowed to pass."

Frank Bertram glared at her. "Thank you for your input. If you don't mind. . . ."

Once again, Alice Tremont leaned forward and tapped her cigarette holder on the table. The publisher and majority owner of the newspaper was in her sixties, but looked much younger. Ever since the death of the only man she'd ever loved, she'd run the newspaper. Some said she ran it better than he ever had. She was a strong force, considered tough but fair. A cliché to be sure, but there was no other way to describe her management style. She was feared by some, admired by others, and respected by almost all of her employees.

As for her peers, she was known throughout the country as an uncompromising publisher who felt all politicians should be kept at a distance. She rarely held parties, nor did she attend them, leaving the gathering of inside information to her staff. Unlike others in her field, she resisted the temptation to hobnob with those in power, and the *Globe*'s editorial policy reflected her nonpartisan political stance.

In Washington, she was considered an intensely private person. Little did they know that she had contributed millions of dollars to various charitable causes through trusts that bore no record of her name. Nor did they know that for two years she had lived with a secret that would have stunned even the most jaded Washington power broker.

Her voice was even and controlled. Almost a monotone, like John Forsythe's. Her lips hardly moved when she spoke, a feature that many found disconcerting. It was as though she were practicing ventriloquism. Her eyes rarely gave away her true feelings. Some said that the day her husband died was the day her eyes died.

"I don't mean to interrupt," she droned. "but I would like to make a suggestion. It seems to me that what we have here is a story that is, perhaps, the biggest we've ever encountered. My suggestion is quite simple. I'd like you to take the next sixty minutes and consider, if you will, what will happen in this country if we print it."

That was all she said. She looked around the room, then stood up and left, closing the door very quietly behind her.

No one in the room could remember her ever having made such a statement before. They were in the newspaper business. They were supposed to print the news. All of the news, good and bad, although the bad news seemed to get the attention more often than not.

They looked at each other, expressions of confusion on all of their faces. If they didn't print it, other newspapers would, so what was the difference? Granted, they did have some details that the others didn't have as yet, but what were they supposed to do? Ignore them?

Frank Bertram broke the uneasy silence. He got up from his chair and said, "I'll have a talk with her. While I'm gone, keep at it."

He left the room and took the elevator up to the eighth floor. The door to her office was open and she was sitting at her desk sipping a drink, something totally out of character for her. She never drank at work.

He walked slowly into the expansive, elegantly decorated office and wordlessly poured one for himself from the crystal decanter. Then he turned to face her. "What is it, Alice? This isn't like you."

She flashed a weak smile and said, "Close the door, will you, Frank?"

He walked over and closed the door, then took a seat across from the desk.

Alice Tremont looked quite sad. She took another sip of her drink. "You knew Ballard quite well, didn't you Frank?"

He nodded. "Yes. He was a fine publisher. A fine man. I considered it a privilege to work for him. As I do working for you."

She let the compliment pass without comment.

233

"Did he ever tell you about his greatest fear?"

Frank thought for a moment and then said, "No . . . I never considered Ballard as a man with any fear whatsoever."

She smiled wanly. "All men have fears, Frank. They just manage to hide them in different ways. Ballard's greatest fear was that a nuclear war would destroy the earth. He reasoned that it would happen by accident or design. In the case of an accident, he felt that it was most likely that man would place too much trust in machines. Allow the machines to make decisions . . . allow a little piece of silicone to be the final arbitrator.

"In the case of design, he felt it was only a matter of time before a group of insane men would gain access to nuclear weapons, either through theft of the actual weapons themselves, or through theft of enough materials to produce their own. He really believed that. And I believe it."

She looked at him with those dead eyes and continued. "I think the time has come, Frank. I think it's all over. I think that man has finally made the ultimate miscalculation, thinking he could control something so powerful it should never have been entrusted to him in the first place."

She sipped her drink while Frank remained quiet, letting her talk it out.

Her face became red as the anger mounted. "We are so arrogant! We go through life despoiling our environment, creating new and more deadly weapons, developing a culture that consumes more than it replenishes, assuming all along that something . . . somehow . . . will take care of our future problems. And we're always so shocked when it all goes wrong. Always so surprised. It happens over and over, and we never learn. We adjust, but in inches, when miles are called for."

She stopped and lit another cigarette.

"I think what we have here is the very thing that Ballard feared. I think a group of terrorists, probably those led by Nadi Amur, have managed to steal or produce nuclear weapons. I think they're being used to intimidate the United States. And knowing the firm position that all administrations have taken over the years, I think it's going to end in disaster. I don't want to be the bearer of this kind of news. It's . . . it reminds me of Sophocles:

'How dreadful knowledge of the truth can be
When there's no help in truth.' "

Her body stiffened. "I simply can't do it, Frank! I can't publish a story that will throw our readers into a flat panic! Even if it's true! And don't talk to me about responsibility! Does a doctor have a responsibility to tell a terminal patient that he's dying? No! I can't . . . I won't print a story, even if it's true . . . that could have the devastating effect this one could."

She seemed out of breath.

Frank Bertram walked over to her and placed his arm around her shoulders. His voice was calm. "I understand how you feel."

She seemed surprised. "You do?"

He nodded. "Of course. In the first place, what we have is a lot of circumstantial stuff . . . not real, hard evidence. It all points to one thing, but you know as well as I that stories have been misplaced before. In the second place, assuming that we knew exactly what is going on, we would have to assume that the government knows, as well. Obviously, they're doing whatever they can. To shoot their legs out from under them would be an act of . . . treason. This thing has developed so quickly that they haven't really had a chance to react. They're probably moving in so many directions, they're just keeping their fingers crossed that the story doesn't get out."

He paused to scratch his head. "I think you've hit the nail on the head. I think we're in a lot of trouble."

He patted her shoulder. "God, it's really frightening. But . . . you mustn't give up. You know it's only a matter of time before other newspapers have what we have. They'll print it. The television people will broadcast it. Hell, they're already stoking the fires. We can't pretend it isn't happening, but we can be supportive of the administration's position. We can play down the terror and play up the successful interventions in the past. We can slant . . . God, I hate to use that word . . . the story in such a way as to make it appear that everything that can be done is being done. And we can print the truth. That there is no hard evidence to support the contention that the worst is about to happen."

Alice Tremont looked at him with those dead eyes. "I think I'd rather shut down the paper."

Bertram practically dropped his glass. "What!"

She repeated it. "I'd rather shut down the paper. I

236

won't print a story that I believe is true when it will certainly cause unbelievable harm to this country. And I won't print a story that I know is false. No matter what the higher purpose."

He stared at her in disbelief. "Alice . . . you can't be serious! What good will that do? If the only voices heard are the voices of doom, what will you have accomplished? Nothing!"

His face took on the look of a stern parent's. "Look, you pay *me* to make these kinds of decisions. So, let me do my job. I don't think you've lost confidence in my ability."

She shook her head.

"Fine. Then leave it to me. I understand your depression. But let me handle it. You know very well that shutting down this paper to avoid a story is . . . preposterous. It isn't the answer. Trust me! We can give them lots of reasons to hope. The President spoke of a special counterintelligence force. According to our experts, he was lying, but the machines . . . could be wrong. Maybe the stress was caused by the problem and not the fact that he was lying. There are obviously many people all over the world who are hard at work on the problem. It's also possible that the entire thing is a hoax. We don't really know. So, while we print what we do know, we can tell our readers the many reasons why they should have faith. If God really wants to end life on earth, I suspect he'd choose someone other than Nadi Amur to be His instrument."

There was small smile from Alice Tremont. "I'm sorry, Frank. I don't want this story printed. It's not a question of your ability at all. It's a question of . . . I can't really express it. The evidence is circumstantial, as you've said. But I've studied the exploits of this Amur for some time. He's the embodiment of evil. A man who is truly in league with the devil, who's only desire is to cause harm to other human beings. By some stroke of ill fortune, and some incredible incompetence on the part of a lot of well-meaning people, the man has the power to destroy this country. I'm sure, as you are, that those we've entrusted to lead us, as thoroughly incompetent as *they* are, are doing everything they can. I don't know that it will be enough. I'm afraid I've run out of faith in our ability to cope with such a horror. You must not print this story as a normal news story. I want you to play it bland. Very bland. And I want to approve the copy before we go to press. I realize what an insult this is, and I wouldn't blame you if you walked out of here in a huff, but I'm asking for your support. I know this goes against everything you believe in. I know it goes against everything I believe in. But that's what I want. Will you give an old woman her last request?"

Frank Bertram looked at her. Under any other circumstances, he would have resigned on the spot. But the expression in those dead eyes, pleading, almost begging, held him fast. He stood there for a moment, saying nothing, then slowly nodded.

He put his glass down, reached for her hand, kissed it, and left the room without another word.

She watched him leave the room and close the door behind him. Then she picked up the telephone, the private line, and dialed a number. The

238

voice on the other end answered with one word. "Yes?"

"This is Alice Tremont. Is he available for just a moment?"

"Hold on."

She waited for a few moments and then the familiar voice was on the line. "Yes, Alice."

"Brandon . . . we're very close to the story. Very close. I'm sure it's just a matter of time before others have it. I've been able to slow things down here, but I don't think you can stop it now. It's going to come out."

He seemed perturbed, the voice filled with sadness. "I know. We can feel it here. We're . . . working hard, Alice. Very hard. We're running out of time. I can't tell you how much I appreciate your help. Pray for us, Alice. Pray for all of us."

"I will. I'll wait to hear from you. Under the circumstances, I'll consider our appointment tomorrow night cancelled."

There was a pause, and then, "Yes . . . although I do want to talk to you about that. Penny and I . . . well, I don't want to discuss this on the telephone. We'll get together as soon as this is over, which . . . I hope . . . will be shortly. I don't think any of us can take much more."

She winced. It was true. "Brandon . . . why are you still in Washington? You should go to Colorado, or even out of the country. . . ."

He cut her off. "Alice . . . we've had several discussions about that. Aside from the disruption, the panic it would cause, we've all agreed . . . if Washington blows up, we'd rather go with it. We

239

don't want to be alive to see the holocaust. A coward's answer, to be sure . . . but that's how we feel. I've got to go now . . . but I'll be in touch soon. Thanks for calling."

She hung up the phone and lit another cigarette. She watched the smoke curl lazily toward the ceiling and realized that no matter what happened, her secret love affair with the President of the United States was over.

It was the voice.

She could tell by his voice.

The man was in love with his wife.

Nadi Amur sat at the small table, sipping some bottled water and waiting patiently for the arrival of Hana Azzuz. Mid-September was beautiful in Paris. It had been over a year since he'd last set foot in this, one of his favorite places, and he relished the two days he would spend here. Especially with Hana. She was a beautiful woman and wise in the ways of lovemaking. He'd missed that.

He continued to read the American papers. They were filled with stories about unusual activity in Washington and Israel. About strange meetings between the President and Rashon. About the press conference. Some were making thinly veiled hints that the President had been less than candid.

He almost laughed out loud at that one.

There was speculation that Israel was preparing to attack Syria. There was speculation that the United States was preparing to attack Libya. There was speculation that they would join together to

240

attack both countries.

Editorials spoke of madness. Of Presidents losing control of their own emotions, wanting to strike out in frustration. The American Congress was calling for a special bill requiring the President to seek approval before taking any action. Of course, that was against the Constitution, they said. But something must be done.

There were stories that said no bombs had been produced in Canada by any terrorist groups. Other stories contended that as many as fifty might have been produced. The latter stories had appeared in papers that were considered exploitive, so not much credence was being given them.

He saw his name mentioned several times. He saw the photograph that had been taken many years ago. It looked nothing like him, since the injury and subsequent corrective surgery performed in a Moscow hospital. He'd made sure no photographs were ever taken of his new face.

He almost laughed out loud again. They were starting to become concerned. The panic would not be long in coming. And they would bend to his will. And the will of Allah.

His nostrils became aware of a particularly unusual fragrance closeby. He turned and saw her standing behind him, dressed in a traditional Indian costume complete with a caste mark on her forehead. They looked a splendid couple, she in her flowing robes and he in his turban, full beard, and western-style suit.

She took a seat across from him and smiled. "It is good to see you, Nadi. You have read the

241

papers?"

He tapped a finger at them and smiled. "Yes. They are like rats, all scrambling to get away from the fire."

Her gaze fell to the table. "I have news. Bad news."

"Tell me."

"My brother. He has been discovered."

Amur sat up straight in the chair. "But . . . how? His message said only that he wanted to move."

Hana Azzuz waited as the waiter appeared, ordered some water, and then continued. "We just received a radio message. He doesn't know how they did it, but he knows they were inside the house. This morning he got up and checked the oil on the carpet. It revealed footprints. He never heard them come in, so he assumes he was gassed. But they were there. Nothing was disturbed, but there is activity on the street where none existed before. Service people. He thinks they will come again."

Amur was visibly upset. For a few moments he said nothing, then, "So be it. We made a mistake. One should never be in a hurry. We should have trucked the bomb in our own truck, as we did with the others." He sighed and leaned back in the chair. "What's done is done. They will soon find the other locations. We can't move them now. But. . . ."

Hana waited while he stroked his beard and thought about it. Then he smiled and looked into her eyes. "Tell me . . . of all the American cities, which do you like the least?"

She thought for a moment and then said, "New York."

He smiled. "Fine. A good choice. New York it will be." He stood up. "Now, before we return to our duties, I feel the need of your affection. I have taken a room not a block away."

She stared at him in awe. "New York . . . what about New York?"

The smile grew larger. When he spoke, the voice was filled with hatred. "New York will cease to exist. We will send a message to the American people and tell them what they must do. Then we will explode the bomb in New York. They will understand. There will be no more interference. No more searching. No more discoveries. Only death to America. They will understand."

He tugged at her arm. "Come. There is much to be done. But first. . . ."

She rose and gathered up her robe. Fifteen minutes later, they were locked together in an act of furious lovemaking, the Indian costumes strewn about the room, their naked bodies heaving and bucking in unison.

Chapter Sixteen

Peter Hudson was in a foul mood.

Once a week, he played poker at the club with the same group of high-stakes players, most of them wealthy industrialists like himself. Usually, he either won or, at the very least, broke even. Peter Hudson was an excellent poker player. He enjoyed the game, he enjoyed the conversation, and most of all, he enjoyed doing something that kept his mind off business.

Lately, that had become a growing concern. Hudson Electronics was one of the smaller firms in Silicone Valley, but it made enough money to keep Peter and Sharon living in the accepted Palo Alto style. At least it had until the last year, when the Japanese had started to make severe inroads into the mainstay of Hudson's business.

Peter Hudson manufactured television systems. Mobile up-links, transmitters, antenna systems, and everything that went with them.

For years, they'd incorporated Japanese equipment into their own line, but now the little bastards were providing complete systems at almost half the cost.

It couldn't continue like this.

Neither could this game.

This night, Peter was losing his shirt.

It was nuts. Benson had drawn to an inside straight and hit it! Brown had taken a big pot with four queens. Four queens! Only one of which was showing. Christ! Peter had gone for a bundle on that one. The guy had been sitting there, that stupid expression on his face, showing a queen of hearts, a three of clubs, a seven of diamonds, and an eight of hearts.

It was impossible! Peter had three kings, two of which were showing, and the idiot kept bumping!

And looking worried with every move.

The bastard!

When the cards were shown, his cackle had been heard out in the dining room. Five thousand dollars!

The man had ten million in the bank and tonight he was luckier than anyone deserved to be.

Peter lit a cigar and wondered when his customary luck would start to return. As the cards were being shuffled, two men entered the room and stood by the table. One white guy and one black guy. The black guy asked, "Which one of you is Peter Hudson?"

Hudson turned and asked, "Who wants to know?"

The black guy reached in his jacket and pulled out his credentials. "Mr. Hudson? Special Agent Binns . . . this is Agent Tucker. FBI. Could we have a few words with you?"

"FBI? What the hell you want with me?"

They both seemed impatient. Binns said, "Could we talk outside for a moment?"

Peter Hudson cursed, got up, and went with them out to the parking lot. "What's the problem?" he asked.

Tucker said, "We need a list of every customer who's purchased television transmitting systems from you over the last five years."

"Now? Can't this wait until morning?"

"I'm afraid not."

Hudson was incensed. If he went to the office now, it would take a half hour. Who knew how long these guys would be going through the files? Then a half hour to get back. He'd never get even.

"It'll have to wait."

Tucker's eyes were hard and cold. "Mr. Hudson, we have a court order. Now, if you don't cooperate, we'll have to bust down the door and mess up your place. What'll it be?"

"What's this all about?"

Binns took his arm as he answered, "It's a matter of national security, Mr. Hudson. We appreciate your help. Please, we haven't much time."

Cynthia Green stood at the hotel room window, smoking a cigarette and watching the planes take off and land at nearby Los Angeles International Airport.

For most of the night, she'd looked over several of the files that David Baxter had given her. It was so strange, she thought. So very strange.

The man was a CIA agent, a representative of the

247

one government organization she hated above all others. He'd actually kidnapped her, taken her to Los Angeles against her will, had her held prisoner in some godforsaken dump in Long Beach and then. . . .

Something had happened.

Something wonderful, amidst all of the terror.

Like a spring crocus, pushing its way through the snow and ice, searching for the sun, he'd reached for her . . . and found her.

He'd decided to trust her completely. Nothing to sign, no long harangue about secrets and duty and patriotism, or any of that bullshit. He'd simply told her everything.

It had terrified her.

And then he'd reached for her again. Perhaps because at that moment he needed some sort of reassurance of his own, or perhaps because of some deeper need, he'd held her close.

She'd wanted him to stop because she hadn't showered, her hair was a mess, her body was tired, and it was the most unromantic of settings.

But he'd lifted her up as though he could read her mind, carried her into the bathroom, and placed her under the shower, fully clothed.

He'd closed the curtain, and when it opened he was naked, stepping into the shower, turning on the water, and carefully removing her battered fatigues. Without a word, he soaped her body and his own, shampooed her hair and then his own.

And then he was carrying her back to the bed, the water dripping from both of their bodies, soaking the carpet and then the bed.

And all the time, his eyes had never left hers.

They were locked together, neither speaking, reaching for each other in some desperate struggle to escape, if only for a moment, the horrors of reality.

And then they had made love.

In that shabby room, now plunged into darkness, he had taken her away from all of it. As his lips caressed her skin, and his hands, surprisingly gentle, awakened feelings that seemed new to her, she'd let it all go.

They both had.

And it had been magic. There was no other word that fit. It had just been magic.

And then he'd moved her to a hotel near the airport, left her with some files to look over, and told her he'd return when he could.

And now, as still another airplane, its lights blinking green and red, touched down on the runway, she longed for his return. Not just because she wanted to be with him, but for another reason.

She'd found something.

Something in the files.

And then a niggling doubt crept into her mind. David Baxter was a handsome man. He was also a clever man. Perhaps a little too clever.

Maybe he was manipulating her.

The trick with the gun had been very dramatic. It had taken her by surprise. And then . . . he'd told her everything about the message, the bombs . . . all of it. The frantic efforts to stop Amur before he decided to kill millions of Americans. Baxter had held nothing back. Why? He was an experienced

CIA agent, and she was a reporter. He'd told her she was free to print it if she wanted to, but that by doing so she would give Amur what he wanted. An excuse to detonate the bombs.

At the very least, printing the story would create a panic. Even she had to agree with that.

She was in a box. Now she knew it all.

And that knowledge was a terrible thing. With it came the responsibility.

He'd counted on that.

Did that mean that the lovemaking had been manipulative as well? Was David Baxter *that* cool? That singleminded?

As she continued to stare out the window, she had the strong desire to pick up the phone and call Frank. The urge to tell *him* everything . . . let *him* make the decision. After all, that was what he got paid for. He was the editor, she was the reporter.

She turned away from the window and reached for the telephone. She looked at her watch. It was early in the morning in Washington. Frank would be at home.

She punched the buttons and waited.

A sleepy voice answered, "Hello . . . who is it?"

There was a pause. "Who is this?"

Cynthia hesitated for a moment and then hung up the phone.

Damn that David Baxter!

Manny Tobin couldn't believe it. As he switched on the light beside the bed, he looked at the clock. It was four in the morning.

Someone was ringing the front doorbell incessantly. And pounding on the door.

Four in the morning.

"Manny! Who is it?"

A typical question from Rose, lying there like a beached whale, the grease all over her face.

"How the hell do I know?"

"Call the police!"

Manny snorted, reached inside the night stand, and took out the .38. Call the police! He could handle it himself.

"Manny! Don't be a fool! Call the police!"

He put on the silk robe, shoved the gun into one of the large pockets, and held up his hand. "Rose," he said, "just relax. It's probably some drunk."

"In this neighborhood?"

"What? People don't get drunk in Coral Gables? Relax. I'll handle it."

The ringing and the pounding continued as Manny Tobin made his way to the front door, switching lights on as he went. With the gun now in his hand, the portly bald-headed man peered through the little glass circle in the door and called out, "Who is it?"

"Mr. Tobin? FBI. We need to talk to you right away. Please open the door."

There were two of them. Young, dressed in business suits. FBI. Maybe, maybe not. They were both holding their credentials up near the little window where he could see them.

"Just a minute," he called.

"Mr. Tobin, this is an emergency!"

"I've got to get my glasses!"

Tobin went into the den and retrieved his glasses, returned to the door, and took another look. The credentials looked real, but how could he know?

"What do you want?"

The two men looked at each other in exasperation. One was a bit taller than the other and it was he who was doing the talking.

"Mr. Tobin. This is an emergency! We don't have time to mess around. Either open this door or we'll come through it. Please!"

"I have a gun!"

The tall one slapped his forehead. "All right! Call the FBI office. Ask them if two agents have been assigned to see you. Do it now!"

They looked angry. Manny rubbed his chin as he thought about it. They must be legit. They wouldn't have suggested he call. . . . .

Manny opened the door.

"Thank you, Mr. Tobin. I'm Agent Strong, and this is Special Agent Lisk."

The two men entered the house quickly. Strong did the talking.

"Mr. Tobin, according to Hudson Electronics, you purchased four complete mobile up-link transmitting stations five months ago. Where are they now?"

Manny remembered the sale immediately. It was one of the biggest deals he'd ever put together.

"I imagine they're on some little island off South America."

"Say again?"

"I was just the broker on that deal. They were purchased by a rich English guy name of Henry

Tomkins. You probably heard of him. Lives in Hong Kong. Has interests all over the world. Owns half the apartments in San Francisco, they tell me."

"The equipment . . . where is it?"

"Like I told you. Tomkins owns an island . . . can you imagine? A whole island! Somewhere off the coast of South America. That's where he lives part of the time. Anyway, he wanted to be able to communicate with his offices all over the world, so he bought all of this stuff through me."

"Why you?"

"I don't know. Maybe taxes or something."

"Where exactly did you ship it?"

"To the island! Like I said."

"We need to know the name of the island and the method of shipment."

Manny ran a hand over his skull. "I don't remember that!"

Agent Strong seemed impatient. "Mr. Tobin, would you come with us please! We'll take you to your office and bring you back."

"Can I get dressed first?"

"We don't have time, sir. Mr. Lisk will stay and explain it to your wife."

"What's the hell's this all about?"

The agent didn't answer. Instead, he pulled Manny Tobin by the arm out of the house and into the hot, sultry south Florida air.

FBI Agent Harold Simms couldn't believe it. It was too easy. Much too easy.

A beat-up old house within sight of the White

House, the satellite receiving dish sitting on the roof.

The neighbors had said the man had moved in three months ago. He was an Arab, they said. Hardly ever came out of the house. They didn't even know his name.

When he'd moved in, a truck had delivered a bunch of crates in the middle of the night. It had seemed suspicious, so somebody had called the cops. But the cops had said everything was OK, and left.

Simms had checked with the D.C. police and read the report. The man's name was Sakkim, he had a green card and a Social Security card. He'd just moved to Washington from Montana and he was a writer. The crates were full of word-processing equipment. He showed them the receipts.

The reason he was moving in the middle of the night was because some friends were helping him and the truck had had mechanical difficulty. He was sorry for the disturbance.

The cops had done nothing. They hadn't checked the ID at all! Just given it back to him and let it go at that.

Simms had run the numbers through the FBI computer. They were phony. Both the green card and the Social Security card. An Arab terrorist had set up shop eighteen blocks from the White House, talked to the cops, and been let go.

Simms didn't know what the flap was. All he knew was that he was supposed to report any Arab unaccounted for, with or without a satellite dish.

Well, he sure as hell had one. Somebody's ass was

going to be in big trouble.

David Baxter was back in the office after visiting with Frank Brown. The deputy director had just undergone a triple bypass operation and was still in intensive care. But the prognosis was good. He'd be away from the job for some time, but with the proper rest and diet, and avoidance of stress, he was expected to make a full recovery.

David had talked with the doctor, and when the word "stress" was mentioned, had practically laughed in the man's face. If Frank Brown had to avoid stress in order to live, his career was over. In the long run, it might not matter a hell of a lot.

It was almost midnight. A full report had been forwarded to Langley and the Los Angeles task force was awaiting further instructions.

He could understand the indecision. Things were beginning to fall into place. An army of agents, both FBI and CIA, augmented by local police, none of whom had been given the whole story, had fanned out all over the country.

They had checked the owners of every satellite dish in twenty major centers. They had pinpointed the location of every Arabic-looking person in America. They had run computers programmed with special systems.

And they had struck pay dirt.

They'd found and confirmed the locations of six of the bombs and it would be simply a matter of hours before the rest were located. They had already identified two of the six men looking after the bombs as members of Amur's inner circle. They'd come up empty on the other four.

They'd also found the truck that had been used to transport the bombs from Medicine Hat across farmers' fields into Montana. They'd found the tracks in the fields and had taken testimony from the farmers who'd heard sounds in the middle of the night. Some had reported the incidents, and customs officials had filed their own reports, but the normal bureaucratic machinery, coupled with the need to keep a low profile, had slowed the transfer of information.

It appeared that all of the bombs had been trucked to a small warehouse in Havre, Montana, where they had been transferred to another truck that had delivered them to the various cities. All but one. The bombs had been shipped one at a time, over a period of three months. The last bomb had been shipped by commercial carrier.

The truck used in the States had yet to be found.

The tracing of purchasers of satellite dishes had proved to be the key to finding the bomb locations.

Each of the bomb sites were similar. A small, rundown house, rented by a nondescript Arab within the last few months, always paying cash. It was strange. One would have thought they would want to keep a low profile. And in some ways they did, but in other ways they seemed unconcerned about discovery. Each house had a large satellite receiver located somewhere on the property.

So . . . in a matter of hours, they'd know where all of the bombs were located. There were several options available as to how to proceed from there.

None of which held much promise. All of which were fraught with extreme danger.

An intercepted message had confirmed Baxter's fear that the covert inspection of Azzuz's place had been discovered. Azzuz had used the radio for the third time, sending a long message advising Amur that his home had been searched and asking for instructions.

It made David's blood run cold.

Now Amur knew that *they* knew.

Amur had warned them that he would detonate all of the bombs if they tried to find them. Now he knew that they'd found them. He was insane.

He might just do it.

Frank Brown had told David that they were to abort the mission if there was any chance that their entry might be discovered. That had come right from the President, he'd said.

David had gone over everything. There simply was no choice. They had to get in and have a look. They had to know. He'd been sure they could pull it off.

He'd been wrong.

Very wrong.

A mistake that could end the lives of millions of Americans.

But it really hadn't mattered that much in the long run. The search for the other bombs had involved so many people that the media were making strong noises. They *knew* something was going on. They wanted answers and they weren't getting any. President Taylor was sticking to his story, saying only that the investigation was a follow-up on the capture of the terrorists responsible for the hoax in Canada. "Just making sure it never happens again." Quote. Unquote.

And still the President sat in Washington. Not eighteen blocks from one of the devices. Two megatons of nuclear devastation that would level Washington in a millisecond.

It was impossible. Totally impossible! And yet it was true. There could no longer be any doubt. Even with the media closing in on the story like barracuda after a wounded skin diver, swarming around the White House, chasing hapless politicians down streets, practically beating down the doors of their homes, the man clung to his story.

The panic was mounting.

And Amur was laughing his head off.

David slammed his hand on the desk and turned to one of the FBI men looking over some data.

"Amur's the key, dammit! We've got to find Amur!"

The startled FBI agent looked at David and said, "Take it easy, Mr. Baxter."

David started pacing the floor.

What now?

They would know where the bombs were located. But then what? They had to find Amur. And then what?

It was clear that the bombs were protected with any number of traps to foil attempts to disarm them. That was the reason Amur was so careless about his method of transporting and positioning them. He didn't care if they were discovered or not.

In fact, it was highly conceivable that he didn't

care if *he* was discovered or not. He was leaving such a big trail, mocking them, secure in the knowledge that there was little they could do to prevent the biggest disaster in the history of the world.

David looked at his watch. It was almost morning. His body ached from the unrelenting pressure. His head hurt from the never-ending brain exercises.

The only respite he'd had in the last few days had been some stolen moments with Cynthia Green.

Cynthia. . . .

It had been just hours ago, but it seemed like years.

He needed a rest. Just a few hours. He turned to the FBI man and said, "I'll be at the Marriott by the airport. Room 1256. I need about three hours of sleep. Call me if anything happens."

The FBI man nodded and Baxter dragged his exhausted body out of the office.

The distance to the hotel was short and the traffic light. He made it in ten minutes.

She seemed angry with him.

"What's the matter?" he asked.

She stared at him with those green eyes, as though trying to read his mind. Then the look of anger softened and she held him close. "Nothing . . . nothing's the matter."

She stepped back and looked at him once more. He looked whipped. "You look like you just went fifteen rounds with Cooney."

"I feel like it. You go over the files?"

"Yes."

"See anything?"

"Yes, but we'll talk about it later. You need some

259

sleep."

"Cynthia . . . I may have a lifetime to sleep. Give!"

He lay on the bed and she started to tell him what she'd found. After the first three sentences, she noticed his eyes starting to close, so she slowed down her speech pattern. She allowed her voice to get softer and softer, until it was apparent that the man was out like a light. He never felt the lips that gently touched his forehead.

She watched him sleeping, the eyes darting inside the closed eyelids, the arms twitching, the head moving from side to side, for almost two hours. And then she woke him.

He rubbed his reddened eyes and went into the bathroom to throw some water on his face. When he came out, he was angry.

"You let me sleep!"

"You're a man, not a machine! Sue me!"

He looked at her sheepishly. "What did I miss?"

As he said it, he turned on the television set, keeping the sound off.

"Well," Cynthia answered, "I've looked over some of your files and it seems to me that. . . ."

"Go on. . . ."

"David, I'm a reporter, not a detective."

"Same thing."

"No, it's not. I'm out of line here."

"Spare me the modesty! I've looked over those reports a hundred times. I'm missing something. We're all missing something. I need a fresh mind . . . one that isn't confused by the way we do things. Come on!"

She hesitated and then plunged ahead. "There's only one thing that strikes me as odd. A lot of investigation was done by the French. They checked into the freighter hijacking, the wine shipments, and the Panamanian outfit that owned the freighter carrying the wine to Canada. All three investigations were headed by one man. A man named Pierre Query."

"So?"

"Well, like I said, I don't know how you operate, but doesn't that seem a bit odd?"

"No. Pierre's one of their top. . . ."

Then he stopped talking and started thinking. It *was* odd. What was odder still was the fact that Pierre had let Amur slip from his fingers three years ago. He'd failed to prevent the death of Michele Dumont. He'd. . . .

David's attention was captured by something he was seeing on the television set. They had broken for a commercial, and as David watched it, something triggered in his brain. It was an ad for a soft drink, and instead of the normal spokesperson, there was a strange-looking graphic, an odd, computer-generated image of a man talking about the merits of the soft drink. The image was clearly inhuman, but. . . .

Baxter was overwhelmed with an idea. It came on him like a shock of electricity. As the news resumed, he thought about the commercial and Pierre Query and. . . .

He picked up the telephone and punched the buttons.

"This is Baxter. Call Briggs and tell him I'm on

my way to Washington."

David hung up the phone and turned to Cynthia. "Get packed. We're outta here!"

"Why did you do that?"

"What?"

"Tell that man to call Briggs. Why didn't you call him yourself?"

David was in a hurry. As he threw her things into her bag, he answered the question. "Two reasons. One, all of our conversations with Briggs go through a scrambler phone. Two, if I talk to him, he'll tell me to stay here. I don't want to give him the chance."

Chapter Seventeen

As the State Department jet headed east toward Washington, David Baxter tested his idea on Cynthia Green. As was often his habit, he thought out loud, saying whatever came into his head no matter how silly it sounded. The bounce-back would usually spark other thoughts, and after a while, the idea would take positive form.

This idea was following that same pattern. Cynthia was nodding her head slowly. "It could work. But . . . you're taking a terrible chance."

Baxter was well aware of that. "I know," he said softly, "but I can't get rid of this feeling that we're out of time. That . . . unless we act soon, we'll never have another chance."

He kissed her lightly on the lips and then headed into the other compartment to make some phone calls. He was gone almost an hour. When he came back, that tired look had returned to his face and some of the sparkle had gone out of the eyes. He took her hand in his and sighed.

"Well?" she asked.

"We're going to meet a doctor when we land, a shrink, one of the team that developed the profile on Amur, and then we see where we go from there. I'll have to run this thing by Briggs. It's such a long shot . . . I just don't know."

"What about Query?"

David looked away. His voice was almost inaudible. "They're looking into it."

Fred Briggs sat in the thickly upholstered chair across from the President and gritted his teeth. He'd been getting an earful ever since he'd made his final report regarding the situation in Los Angeles, including the fact that there was now no question but that Amur was aware of the entry into the house.

The President was still steaming. His voice was harsh, his manner arrogant, his disdain unhidden. "I told you there was no margin for error. None! Now, you tell me that the son of a bitch knows we've been in the Los Angeles house. He may well detonate every damn bomb he's got! The message made that perfectly clear. I just don't understand it. Your people are supposed to be experts. Professionals. And yet one man has been able to elude you for years. And a simple little exercise like breaking and entering becomes impossible. The whole country is at risk! Can't you assholes do anything right?"

Briggs hung his head. It seemed they couldn't.

President Taylor slammed his hand on the desk and practically screamed at the director of the CIA.

"Do you realize what you've done? Now that Amur knows we're on to him, the only possible thing we can do is go along with him. Tonight I'm meeting with the top media people in the country, and I have to tell them the whole thing! I have to let Amur know I'm giving up! I don't have any other choice!"

Fred Briggs's anger almost matched the President's. "The hell you don't . . . sir. You can send a team into every location and immobolize the occupant. Now! Right now! before Amur loses his mind completely and blows us all the hell up. *That's* your only choice!"

The President sneered at him. "Really. My only choice, you say? *You* couldn't even get into a house undetected. There are twelve bombs sitting in twelve houses with twelve crazy terrorists holding twelve buttons in their hands. Waiting. Just waiting for the chance to push the button. And you think you can send teams in to stop them? You're crazier than Amur! The man knows! He'll be waiting for us. Even the element of surprise is gone!"

He got up and paced the floor while he talked. "No . . . I've got to make it appear . . . publicly . . . that we're going along. Somehow, I've got to make him believe it."

Briggs cursed. "Sir, you know that won't work. The world will know you're being coerced. What with the speculation already running rampant, they'll put two and two together and you'll have such a complete shutdown . . . total panic. Christ! You can't do it! You know that! And what about Rashon? The moment you make that announcement, Rashon will attack. Then what?"

The President stopped pacing and stared at the CIA man. Rashon . . . in the heat of the moment he'd almost forgotten about Rashon.

Last night they'd been at an impasse, until Penny's angry outburst turned the tide. Brandon Taylor had stood there, thunderstruck, as she lashed out at the small man from the small country.

Perhaps it was because she was beautiful, perhaps simply because she was a woman. But the man had sat there and taken it . . . at first in shock and then, gradually, actually listening to the words, understanding what was being said, knowing that she spoke from the heart, not as the wife of the President, but as a human being.

She'd spoken in controlled anger, in a voice filled with scorn. "You people! For years, this country has stood by you. Championed your cause. Even when you were wrong, the people of the United States have been loyal friends. And you've been wrong many times. Now, this country is in trouble. If those bombs are detonated, the whole world is in trouble. The President has asked for your support and what does he get? A slap in the face. A complete rejection. No compromise. You *know* what to do. You're *sure* your actions are the right actions. Attack Syria. Attack Libya. You know the terrorists are there. You're sure! And whether you're right or wrong, half of the United States is destroyed by a madman who will probably laugh himself silly while he does it."

She paced the floor as she continued her tirade. "What's the hurry? We still have time . . . the bombs are here, not in Israel. Why not give the President a chance to prevent this disaster from happening?"

President Taylor had almost smiled at that moment. She was pacing the floor just as he did when he was angry. Even the expression on her face reminded him of himself. It was as though she was his alter ego, saying what he wanted to say. Except it seemed stronger, coming from her. "You may well be right," she continued, "This country may be so screwed up that we can't prevent it from happening at all. But if that's true, we will be punished for our weaknesses. Then you can attack whomever you wish. But to practically guarantee that Amur will strike us down, because of your stubborn desire for vengeance, without letting us have every opportunity to stop it, is a cruel act unworthy of a country that we have befriended for so many years. You owe it to us. Damn your policy! Damn your politics! The question as to who is right is not yours to judge. You owe us the chance to be wrong. You owe us! If you take this action now, you might destroy this country. In any case, you will have destroyed the relationship that now exists.

"Amur can be stopped. He *must* be stopped. But there will be other men like him. If you want to face a future that excludes the United States, you will have your wish."

Prime Minister Rashon sat in silence for some time. Everyone sat in silence and stared at the beautiful American First Lady, a woman who was perceived as a mindless decoration. A living accessory to the image of the handsome President, who went about the country involving herself in various "good works," lending her name and her time, but of course . . . everyone knew . . . it was just politics. Another image. Another photo opportunity.

For the first time, they saw a living, breathing human being. Who had suddenly come out of the background, who had made this unprecedented trip to Camp David, had been present at meetings considered most secret, sitting silently, calmly, until . . .

The Israeli prime minister stood up, went over to her, and hugged her to his tiny body. Then he turned and nodded to the President. "This is impossible. Absolutely impossible. But I will try. A week. I will do nothing for a week. As long as I'm still the prime minister."

He smiled ruefully. "That, I cannot guarantee. A problem you understand, I'm sure. I may very well face a vote of no-confidence from my own party. They are convinced of the merit of their plan."

It was remarkable. And later that night, when Brandon Taylor had held her close and found his strength returning as he felt the warmth of her body in the bed beside him, he thanked a God he thought he'd forgotten.

And the years seemed to wash away. He felt a passion he hadn't known before. And instantly realized what it was. He needed her. Not just her body, but all of her. Her mind, her love, her support. All of it. It was a terrible need, and she wanted to fill it. And he wanted her to fill it.

For the very first time, he felt lucky to have her.

Now, as he sat glaring at Fred Briggs, the President forced his mind back to the present. It was so unfair! Every move they made seemed to hasten the time when some lunatic would end their lives . . . and the lives of millions of Americans. It was as though fate was dictating an end to the great experiment. The image of the photograph of the smiling Arab standing by the bombs came back to him.

The bastards!

And then, for some unknown reason, even with events outside the room seemingly beyond control, he felt a strange calmness come over him that he couldn't explain. It didn't make sense at all.

The United States had never seen darker days. Probably never would again. If it managed to extricate itself from this nightmare, steps would be taken to ensure it never *could* happen again. All of the warnings would be heeded. Finally. Major decisions would be made. Security would be tightened to the point where the normal flow of commerce would be affected. As usual, the pendulum would swing wildly, as it did every time there was a threat. The people would demand stringent measures be taken. And they would be.

The anger was gone. There was no point. What was done was done. What was important now was to prevent disaster. He had to rely on his people. He had to.

The President turned to Briggs. "Fred . . . give me a few minutes. I want George and Hank in on this. If they concur with your conclusions, I'll . . . leave it in your hands."

The anger left Briggs as well. His voice was more even, almost sympathetic. "I . . . I was going to say, I'll do my best, but that won't do, will it?"

The President shook his head. "No . . . it won't. What we need is a miracle."

Fred Briggs nodded and started to leave the room. The President's intercom buzzed. FBI Director George Halman wanted to see the President. Most urgent.

President Taylor motioned to Fred Briggs to stay and asked that Halman be brought in.

The FBI director was almost beside himself as he entered the room. He seemed pleased that Briggs was there, which astonished Fred Briggs. The two had never seen eye to eye.

George Halman was a tall man, usually impassive, usually well groomed, the very model of a busy executive. As he stood beside the balding, overweight Fred Briggs, there seemed to be no question as to who had the smarts, but it was well known in Washington that Fred Briggs, while sartorially lacking, had a keen mind.

The natural interagency rivalry that had always existed between the FBI and the CIA had caused much conflict over the years. But these two men, at least for now, seemed to have put that aside. Nevertheless, they didn't like each other much.

Halman's voice betrayed his excitement. "Sir, we've got a very good lead on Amur!"

Both men looked at the FBI director in surprise. Halman turned to Briggs and said, "I've already passed the information along to your analysts, but I'm sure they'll concur." Then he opened a manilla folder and started to read from the enclosed notes.

"Remember the freighter that brought the wine to Montreal three years ago? Over the years, there

270

were several shipments of wine to that place in Canada, but the first shipment was on a ship of Panamanian registry, the *Little Star*. Other shipments were on other ships, but we always suspected that the first shipment contained the plutonium taken from the French freighter. As you know, we investigated everyone and found nothing. That is, until tonight."

Briggs and Taylor had practically stopped breathing. Halman's eyes widened as he continued. "The task force has been chasing the theory that Amur is somehow planning to use television satellites in his overall plan. It was suggested by one of Fred's people that we check into every piece of transmitting equipment that's been sold during the last five years. It's been a lot of work, but we've hit pay dirt.

"We've traced every single purchase, except one. Six months ago, Hudson Electronics sold four portable up-link units to a man named Henry Tomkins, who supposedly planned to use it on a remote island he owns off the coast of South America. Tomkins lives in Hong Kong and has interests all over the world. He's an Englishman and has close ties with the Chinese and us. In any case, he's been staying in Palm Springs for the last three months, being treated for a skin disease. We've just talked to him, and he's made a statement that he never ordered any television equipment from anyone."

He stopped to catch his breath. "Here's the kicker. The purchase was made through a broker in Miami. The broker shipped the equipment to Tomkins according to his special instructions, which required a specific ship. The shipment was put aboard the *Little Star* two months ago, for delivery to the island. Four complete tractor trailer units. A complete state-of-the-art television studio on wheels. The shipment left Miami, but the freighter never went near the island. As you know, the navy tracks every ship at sea, and this one headed straight to France, then Japan, then France, then Cairo, then France again.

"Now . . ." he looked at Briggs, "the task force has just confirmed that the television equipment was never off-loaded . . . anywhere." Then he turned to the President. "That means it's either still onboard or has been transferred to another ship at sea. I'm betting that it's still on board. I'd also be willing to bet that Amur is the one who really bought the stuff and that he's on that ship . . . getting ready to play out his next hand."

Brandon Taylor was stunned but recovered quickly. "George, that's good work. Very good work. Where is the ship now?"

"It left Marseilles yesterday, headed for Rio. The navy is tracking it."

The President turned to Briggs. "Fred, you checked that shipping line out . . . you said they were clean . . . what about that?'

Briggs cleared his throat and thrust his hands in his pockets. "Actually, we relied on the reports from the French. They could have overlooked something. If you remember, we didn't want to step on too many toes, so we didn't do our own investigation."

Brandon Taylor cursed. "That's a policy that is countermanded, as of this moment. What can you do?"

A faint smile played over the lips of the CIA man. "Well, first we can have a Blackbird take some pictures, and see whether or not those dishes are in position. As a matter of fact, with the cameras we have now, we might even be able to pick out Amur if he's on deck. Then, we can talk to the Panamanians ourselves. But this time, we'll do it . . . the old-fashioned way. If you don't mind."

The President shook his head. "I don't mind a bit. How long will it take you?"

Fred Briggs didn't hesitate. "Twelve hours."

The intercom buzzed. President Taylor answered it.

"Yes."

"Sir, I have Deputy Director Thorpe here with an urgent request to see Director Briggs."

"Send him in."

Thorpe entered the room, handed an envelope to Briggs, and then departed. Briggs studied the note and smiled.

Taylor asked, "What is it?"

"It's from one of my agents. David Baxter. He's on his way here. He's got an idea he wants to discuss, and he also suggests that we check into the activities of one of the French Special Services people. He says it's possible that the man is working for Amur."

President Taylor slapped his hands together. "Well, that certainly fits in with the Panamanian situation. George, how are we coming on the bomb placements?"

"We've got ten of them under surveillance. It

273

shouldn't be long before we have the other two."

"What then? Once we have the locations figured out, and if it turns out that Amur *is* onboard that freighter . . . what's our next step?"

The two agency directors looked at each other, and then Briggs said, "Well . . . you're against us rushing in. We'll have to go back to the drawing boards. I still think you need to make it look like we're going along with Amur. We need time!"

"Rashon . . . isn't there some way you can make him stand down this alert of his? That just tells Amur that we're getting ready to do something. And the press! Christ! If you could get Rashon to drop the alert, the press would accept the story that everything is cooling out. This way, they keep picking at it, like vultures. That just exposes everything we're doing. Amur is privy to all of this and might come totally unglued!"

President Taylor shook his head. "The Israeli alert is good in one sense. Amur knows we've discussed it with Rashon. That's something. He may think that after a time, it will all go his way."

The room grew silent and then President Taylor nodded. "OK, get to it. If Amur is on that ship, that's one thing. Finding a way to block his signal is another. Now that he knows we've located the bombs, he's liable to do anything. I have the feeling that the schedule is changing. That time is running out."

He paused, and then, in a voice that seemed more assured, said, "I'll make the decision, then. As soon as you have the information from Panama, I'll make my decision whether or not to take the chance and go in to have a look at the bomb. But I want the information from Panama in two hours, not twelve."

There was no argument.

As they left the room, Brandon Taylor looked toward the ceiling. He'd said they needed a miracle. Maybe they were getting one.

Less than an hour later, three men dressed in black coveralls entered the home of Ramon Ramiro, the president of Panama Star Shipping Company, gassed him, and removed him from the premises. They left a ransom note demanding four million American dollars for his return. They also left three dead security people in their wake.

Ramiro was taken to a small warehouse, tied to a bed, and given a shot of "the drug." Within thirty minutes, he told them everything.

The *Little Star* had been leased twice to a man who would supply his own crew. The first time, he'd paid a sum of three million American dollars, in cash. Ramiro was to reveal none of the details to anyone. He was to ensure that everything appeared normal, that false papers were prepared indicating that the ship was manned by employees of Panama Star Shipping, and to back up whatever records were supplied.

The second time had been three months ago. It was still on lease to the man. This time the fee was four million American dollars. Again the man had supplied his own crew. The same people.

The man had given his name as Muhammed

Farzi, and he'd said he was a Saudi prince. Ramiro hadn't asked questions and had taken the money, because he needed it.

When shown photographs, he recognized no one.

During the initial investigation three years before, he'd told the French investigators the story he'd been provided, and had shown them the false papers to back it up, because he'd been assured he would be killed if he failed to do so. He'd used almost half of the money to keep his own employees quiet, and they were still bleeding him dry. It hadn't been worth it.

They asked him about the French interrogation and he described it as routine. There was no rough stuff, just a polite asking and answering of questions. His interrogator was a short man, with a thin mustache. The man had been very pleasant and had told him not to worry. They showed him a picture of Pierre Query, and he identified the man in the photo as the man who had questioned him.

After some additional questioning, the men turned off the tape recorder used during the interview, untied the man, let him walk around for a while, and then shot him in the head.

They transcribed the interview into a computer, which converted it into code, then transmitted the entire interview, using a high-speed data transmission device that allowed the thirty-minute interview to be transmitted in less than forty seconds.

CIA communications received the transmission, put it back into plain language, and placed the interview, along with the past intelligence on Pierre Query's investigation, into a special folder, which was sent to the director's office.

At almost the same time, an SR-71 Blackbird, having been diverted from its regular reconnaissance over the Middle East, made a pass over the *Little Star*. The plane, flying at a height of seventy-five thousand feet, was not noticed by those on board the ship.

The cameras on the Blackbird took a series of photographs of the freighter, which were immediately converted into electronic signals, which were transmitted to a receiving station in Spain, and from there, via satellite, to CIA headquarters in Langley, Virginia.

The pictures were amazingly clear.

They showed four large dishes on the front deck of the freighter. They showed the tops of the heads of various people, none of whom were recognizable.

Fred Briggs looked over the material quickly. The name Muhammed Farzi meant nothing. The description of the man leasing the freighter didn't match that of Amur or any of his people. At least, not the known ones. But it was well known that Amur loved disguises. He'd used them successfully to avoid capture for over a decade.

The name Pierre Query leapt from the page like a bolt of lightning. Briggs jumped up and went over to the filing cabinet and pulled one of the folders out. He returned to his desk and speed-read the entire report.

It was starting to make sense.

Amur *was* using the ship. The up-links *were* still onboard.

The bastard was even more clever than they'd imagined. He'd managed to recruit a member of the French Special Services into his organization. A man who'd thrown a monkey wrench into the entire investigation.

He leaned back in his chair and stared at the ceiling. Where was he headed? Rio? What for?

Amur was obviously aware of the frantic searches being conducted by the world's intelligence forces. Even the Russians had been asked to assist in the search for Amur, without being told why. By now, they would have guessed.

Amur was also aware that his bomb locations had been discovered. He had to be aware.

A chill went down the spine of the director of the CIA. It was time to move. The President was right. Time *was* running out!

Chapter Eighteen

Pierre Query leaned against the trunk of the old oak tree and lit another cigarette. The rain was coming down harder now and he could hear the distant rumbling of approaching thunder. He glanced back at his home, lights ablaze in the deepening gloom, and felt a hot wetness on his cheeks that he knew to be his own tears.

The cigarette was out, ruined by the rain. He took it from his mouth and flung it to the ground.

As soon as he had read the initial report of the "kidnapping," in Panama, he'd known that it was just a matter of time. It was no kidnapping. The operation bore the mark of a CIA operation.

They were getting desperate now, killing whenever necessary in order to gain the information they sought. And who could blame them?

And when they found out about his involvement, they would kill him, as well. It wouldn't matter why he had done it, only that he'd done something unforgivable.

A bolt of lightning struck nearby, followed almost immediately by a loud crack of thunder. The storm was close now. Instinctively, he started to move away from the tree, stopped, and laughed. There was little point in moving from the danger. His life was over. In fact, his death sentence had been pronounced the moment he'd agreed to work with Amur, three years ago.

The voice on the telephone had said he had information, and Pierre had met him in a small cafe near the Arc de Triomphe. But it hadn't been information at all, it had been a message from Nadi Amur. A threat. Pierre was to do as he was asked or all eight of his children would be killed. There would be no escape. No way out. If Pierre failed to cooperate now or in the future, they would hunt his children down wherever they might be hidden and slaughter them like sheep.

At first, Pierre had doubted, but the man had given him information that only a close associate of Amur would know. And in his heart, he had known they would carry out their threat successfully.

So he had aided their cause, hoping against hope that others would be able to stop them. That his complicity would never be discovered. That it was all a bluff.

But it was not to be.

And when he'd read the report, just hours ago, he had known that the hunt for Amur was in full song, and that the horrible secret was secret no more.

He'd left the office and headed home. The children had met him at the door as they always did, and he'd wrestled with them for as long as he dared. Then he'd gone to his study and written a note to his dear wife and another to the director.

Finally, he'd held his wife close and told her that he needed to take a walk. To think, he'd said. But it wasn't to think. There was no point. There was no escape.

And now, as he stood in the midst of a thunderstorm, his small body wet and cold, he began to cry in earnest. It was so unfair! Life was so horribly unfair. He started to shiver from the cold and the wet and the sobbing and then. . . .

He could see the lights of the three cars approaching his house. They stopped and several men got out of the cars and started toward the front door.

There was no more time. He wanted it over before they talked to his beloved wife. It had to be now. The sound of a gunshot would bring them running. Perhaps, after they read the notes in his pocket, they would spare his family the disgrace.

He pulled out the gun and placed the barrel in his mouth. A quick prayer and then . . . he pulled the trigger.

As he fell to the ground, the gun fell from his one hand and the rosary from the other.

And the men came running.

Inside the communications room of the super-secret National Security Agency, a computer operator, one of many charged with the responsibility of reviewing the thousands of hours of data transmitted over the airwaves, looked at a printout and scratched his head.

He was doing a routine analysis of radio traffic. The regularly monitored data was handled immediately, such as communications from various foreign embassies to their home offices. That material was turned over to cryptologists who decoded the material and then forwarded it to the various interested parties.

His job was to review the unimportant material, just in case something had been overlooked. The traffic that was initiated by ham radio operators, or other traffic that was not initiated on a regular basis. All of it was given a quick look, and if nothing seemed amiss, stored for future reference.

As he looked over the printout, he knew he'd seen this particular message before. It hadn't made any sense, so he hadn't worried about it. But the regularity of the signal was, in itself, a sign that it *did* mean something.

He keyed the computer and punched in a code. It asked the computer to print data relating only to the one signal.

The printer chattered and the pattern emerged.

The young operator changed discs and then ran the program again. Once more, the printer banged away, and a long sheet of paper emerged similar to the first.

The operator looked at both pieces of paper and then tucked them under his arm. He left his post and headed for the office of one of his supervisors.

Within minutes, the information was on its way to Fred Briggs and George Halman. In this present crisis, information that normally took weeks to go from one agency to another was being delivered in minutes. The spirit of competition had turned into the spirit of cooperation. Though many within the various agencies were unaware of the official reason for the sudden policy shift, the rumors being circulated by the media seemed to point in only one direction.

Briggs had just finished reading the report from Panama when the material dug up from the young operator was placed on his desk. At first he barely glanced at it, and then his interest became intense.

According to the printout, at precisely fourteen minutes past every hour, a single number in Morse code was transmitted on the fifteen-meter band. The numbers changed with each transmission and were in random order. A run-through on the cryptographic analyzer had failed to determine any meaning. It was just a single number that constituted the entire message. And it had been going on for six weeks. A review of the tapes had confirmed it.

At the same time, another signal was being sent from various parts of the United States. The single letter "O" was being transmitted from twelve different cities on a regular pattern. Every six hours, each of twelve stations would transmit. That meant someone was receiving a message every half hour. The signals were being broadcast from New York, Los Angeles, Chicago, San Francisco, Philadelphia, Detroit, Boston, Houston, Dallas, Washington, Miami, and Cleveland.

The twelve biggest cities in the United States.

They would have missed it, except for the sharp-eyed awareness of a young communications expert.

What did it mean?

Was it connected to Amur?

It had to be. The twelve largest cities in the United States. Coincidence? Impossible! The original signal every hour was from Amur. If it stopped . . . it meant one thing. Detonate the bombs. The reports from the other stations were acknowledgments. If one of them missed, it meant discovery. Then Amur would. . . .

So there *was* a timetable!

But what was it?

Throughout the long flight from Los Angeles to Washington, David Baxter tried to rationalize away the guilt he felt. Even though it hadn't been entirely his decision, he'd played a large role in the abortive entry into the house. He'd been responsible for the fact that Amur now knew they had pinpointed one of the bomb locations.

He'd left Los Angeles because he'd felt compelled to talk with Briggs face to face. An idea had begun to take shape in his mind, an idea that needed to be presented in person not over some impersonal phone line. After he'd talked it over with the now-silent Cynthia, the idea continued to percolate inside his brain. The screw-up inside the Azzuz house had come as a bitter blow. They'd tried to think of everything, but had failed. There was a very good chance that any further attempts to get to the bombs would be met with disaster. The key was Amur! They had to get to Amur . . . Amur had to call it off. And if they couldn't get to Amur, they had to make it appear as though they had.

There was no possible way to avoid going in to disarm the bombs sooner or later. But it had to be under different circumstances. Where Amur was actually cooperating in the process. Or seemed to be cooperating.

They had to pull off the biggest con job in the history of the world. It was the only way.

They had learned some important facts. The bomb in Los Angeles was not connected directly to a satellite receiver. Amur planned to issue some sort of message . . . that was the reason for the satellite receivers. The egomaniac was going to become another Captain Midnight before he told his people to blow away the cities.

They had to move fast. David had read the psychological profile on Amur over and over. He was unstable. Liable to do anything. They couldn't delay. They had to make their move now. If they were successful, they could take their time and disarm the bombs properly.

They were all afraid. Afraid that Amur had some other trick up his sleeve they didn't know about. Afraid that moving in would somehow trigger the bombs. It was a very realistic fear. David Baxter was now convinced that Amur intended to blow them up anyway. No matter what. Even if the President agreed to the impossible demands. .

That was the plan.

Make the United States look like fools and then . . . destroy the country.

That was why Amur had made sure that the

plutonium was found in Medicine Hat. That was why the truck had been found. That was why Azzuz was nursemaiding the Los Angeles bomb.

They were all going to commit suicide.

Amur . . . twelve bombs. Twelve close associates. It was a suicide mission.

Because Amur knew there was no real chance he could possibly achieve his aims. He could destroy the United States. But by doing so, he would alienate some of his own brothers. Not the inner circle, but those outside. The ones who did business with the Americans. The Saudis, the Egyptians, even some Syrians. There was no place in the world where he would be safe. He'd be tracked by friends and enemies alike.

And as crazy as he was, he had to know that.

So it *was* a game. A man driven mad by hate, and clever enough to create a cadre who would follow him to the death.

The message, the demands . . . they meant nothing. This was simply a grandstand play by a man preparing to die. And making sure that he took America with him. Impossible . . . but there it was.

They were running out of time. Amur wasn't concerned about October 6. It was all going to happen much sooner than that. As the plane bored through the thin air at thirty-seven thousand feet, David nibbled away at the idea, eviscerated it, and glued it back together.

It could work. It *had* to work.

He pushed his feet against the floor, as though by doing so he might somehow make the airplane go faster. He caught himself doing it, and tried to

286

relax. He needed to conserve whatever energy he had left. He took several deep breaths and turned to Cynthia, lost in her own thoughts.

"Cynthia, when we get to Washington, I'd like you to go home and. . . ."

She wouldn't let him finish. "Forget it! I'm with you every step of the way. I'm not sitting at home waiting and wondering what the hell is going on!"

David's face grew taut. "You're going to have to! Look, there are several things. . . ."

She placed her hand over his mouth. "No! You can't do this to me! It's not the story anymore. I don't give a damn about that! If you make me stand aside now, I'm liable to lose my mind! Please, David. Let me come along. I won't get in your way. I won't . . . I might even be a help! I helped you back in Los Angeles, didn't I?"

He had to admit that she had.

In some desperate moment of need, he'd brought her into this, and now he was stuck with her. It was totally against the rules. As soon as Briggs found out, his career would be over.

And then he smiled to himself.

"OK. But at least do me this one small favor. When I talk to the director, they'll require you to wait in the lobby. You aren't cleared. Will you do that quietly? I'm in so much shit already, it really doesn't matter much, but. . . ."

She gripped his hand tightly. "Relax. I'll be good."

Dr. Walter Nesbit was waiting at the airport as

David had requested. Baxter had read three of the noted psychiatrist's books over the years and recognized him from the jacket picture. He stuck out his hand and introduced himself. "Dr. Nesbit, I'm David Baxter. Thank you for coming. This is Cynthia Green."

The doctor shook his hand warmly. "I'm pleased to meet you, Mr. Baxter, and you, Ms. Green. I'm afraid I'm still a little confused. I've already made my report . . . I don't know what other help I can be."

The man was in his sixties and looked it. He was a small man, slightly stooped, with long white hair that hung in clumps over a full, moon-shaped face. His mouth looked too small for the face, with lips that seemed almost nonexistent.

He was the archtypical academic, devoted to teaching, and learning, although not necessarily in that order. He had consulted to the agency many times when character studies were required. Even though the agency had their own doctors, the science of psychiatry was still, at best, an uncertain area.

David took the doctor by the arm. "You can be a great help. I want you to come with me to Langley. I need to talk to the director about an idea I have, and I want your opinion. It would be extremely helpful."

There was little hesitation. "Very well."

During the cab ride, David filled the man in. The doctor listened patiently and then looked at David, a hint of sadness in his eyes. "I wish I could tell you that your idea will work . . . but in truth . . .

there simply is no way of knowing. I've been able to study the man only at a distance. And then, only by his actions. Certainly there has been some interesting material provided by the University of Michigan, even interviews with former fellow students, but . . . it's not possible to predict how the man will react to any given situation. There are many mental disorders. Some are fairly easy to diagnose, others are extremely difficult. In the case of Amur, without hours and hours of testing and personal interviews, it would be impossible to attempt a diagnosis. A guess is all I could submit."

David looked at his notes. "And your guess is that the man has several disorders, not one."

Dr. Nesbit nodded. "Yes. The problem is that any of them by themselves can create unpredictability. Even so-called normal people are unpredictable in many situations. You take a person with multiple disorders and you're on uncharted ground. Although a tremendous amount of research has been done on the subject, there still is little real solid evidence that would allow a proper judgment to be made."

David rubbed his forehead. "But . . . you do think it's possible that he might explode the bombs at any time?"

The doctor nodded again. "Yes . . . in the case of Nadi Amur, the only absolute is the knowledge that he is capable of absolutely anything. The warnings, the messages, all of it, mean nothing. There is simply no way you can see into his mind. You can only act on what you know. What you have in your hands. There may be twelve bombs, there may be none. It's possible he wants to die . . . it's possible he wants to live. There is no way to know."

David asked the question that he wanted answered most. "And if the President agrees to the demands . . . that would mean nothing?"

The doctor hesitated and then slowly nodded his head. "I think I would agree with that. The demands mean nothing. Therefore . . . agreement means nothing."

By the time David Baxter arrived at the office of Fred Briggs with the doctor in tow, he'd formulated a plan that he was convinced would work. But before he had a chance to discuss it, he was subjected to a thorough chewing-out by the director.

"Baxter," Briggs shouted, taking no note of the astonished visitor, "you left L.A. without permission. You're supposed to be in charge of the task force there, and you show up here, a total dereliction of duty. Under normal circumstances, that would be an offense requiring the sternest possible measures, but under *these* circumstances, it almost amounts to . . . God! I just don't believe it. Now I find out that you've spilled everything to a reporter, for Christ's sake. You've actually brought her here! Have you lost your mind?"

David could feel the throb in the back of his neck come into full song. "Sir . . . we're running out of time . . . I couldn't give you everything in a report. I've been thinking about a plan that might work. . . ."

The director cut him off. "Really. I'm impressed!

290

Your handling of the entry into the Azzuz house was perfection. I can't wait to hear this one."

The voice was filled with sarcasm. David ignored it. His own voice was angry, urgent. "Look . . . you can do what you want. Shoot me if it makes you feel better, but I'll tell you this . . . Amur is going to blow the country up within days. I didn't feel like putting that in a written report. I've been talking to Dr. Nesbit here, and he concurs. We have to act now!"

"Act! And do what?"

David started to tell him the plan. "We have no idea where Amur is. But somehow, we have to. . . ."

"Correction! While you were flying out here, we located the bastard."

David stared at him, his jaw dropping. "What! When? How?"

The director sneered. "You aren't the only agent in the firm."

David exploded in rage. "Listen to me! We're on the same side here. After this is over, you can shit-can me. I don't care! But, for Christ's sake, let's quit the crap and work together for the moment. I may be out of line, but I've spent more time on Amur than anyone. I've studied the profiles for years. I've been after his ass for so long . . . I almost know him. At least better than anyone else in the agency. Don't close me out. You want my resignation, you got it. But before I leave, let me work on this thing."

They stared at each other for a moment and then the doctor stepped between them.

"Mr. Briggs . . . Baxter thinks that Amur is about to blow this country up within hours. I happen to agree with him. He also has a plan that has an excellent chance of working." He stopped and wiped his glasses. "Now I realize that everyone is under a great deal of pressure, but I'd suggest that we try to solve the problem at hand. The important problem. Your personal problems can be worked out later . . . if there is a later."

David asked, "Where's Amur?"

The director hesitated for a moment and then told him. "He's . . . well, we're not positive, but we're pretty sure he's on a Panamanian freighter, the *Little Star.*"

David lit up like a Christmas tree. He looked at the doctor and then back at Briggs. "Of course! The ship that brought the plutonium to Canada. Have you determined if there's any television broadcast equipment on board?"

Briggs's eyes widened and his face took on a look of astonishment. "Yes . . . how did you know? The ship has a complete mobile studio."

Baxter slapped his hands together. "That's it! He *is* going to do it. There's no question. He's going to make a broadcast and then blow up one . . . or all of the bombs. OK, I have a plan."

Briggs grimaced. "You didn't answer my question. How did you know about the TV stuff?"

"I've been studying the bastard's head. Along with Dr. Nesbit here. It fits. It all fits. The fact that there is broadcasting equipment on board that ship is the final clincher."

Briggs sighed. "What's the plan?"

David Baxter made his pitch.

As he went over every detail, he could see the expression on Fred Briggs's face change perceptibly. Where there had been anger and defeat, there was now hope . . . and fear.

Forty minutes later, David made the pitch again. This time, there was a larger audience. There was the CIA director, of course, FBI Director George Halman, and a presidential advisor, Henry Wilson. David had various notes in his hands, from ideas he'd scribbled down during the flight east, and he referred to them as he went along. His voice reflected the excitement he felt within.

". . . so we're all concerned about moving in, just in case any of the bombs are booby-trapped. And that's a legitimate concern. It has to be done carefully, after the threat of Amur has been removed. But . . . as Dr. Nesbit points out, the man is liable to do it at any moment. We simply can't wait any longer."

He stopped and cleared his throat. "We have to take a big chance . . . that Amur is actually on that ship. That the theory that he plans some sort of television broadcast is correct. If that's the case, then I think this can work. I talked to a man in L.A. who says that Jack Hodges in New York is the only man who might pull it off. I didn't fill the man in, just talked theory. But he says that all Jack would need is one minute, and then he can take it from there."

Briggs, for the first time in days, actually looked hopeful. "One minute. That's it?"

David nodded. "Right. He takes the one minute

293

of tape, works whatever miracles are required with the computer, and we've got Amur saying whatever we want. Except for a momentary interruption, you'd hardly notice."

Halman shook his head. "What if he only talks for ten seconds?"

David answered him quickly. "Then we lose. But Dr. Nesbit will back me up. The man is likely to want to take at least a minute to give his message. That's the whole point to this insanity. He wants to glory in his power. He wants to tell us what he's going to do to us, and then . . . he's going to do it."

Dr. Nesbit said, "There are no guarantees, you understand. I could be totally off the mark. But I don't think so. If you want, I can reassemble the group and give you a more complete recommendation."

Briggs waved him off. "We don't have the time."

Nesbit nodded. "As mad as the man is, and as unpredictable as he is, I would suggest that if, in fact, he plans to make some sort of address . . . it will be lengthy. Think of the speeches Castro makes. They can run for hours, and Castro is not insane. But he does have a well-developed ego. Amur's ego is immense! I feel confident that he plans to speak for a very long time. I'm sure of it!"

The room grew silent, and then Briggs stood up. "OK. Personally, I buy it. All of it. David . . . you go to New York and grab this Hodges guy. Get him set up. I'll talk to the President. . . ." He stopped and looked at his watch. "Shit!" He's giving a talk to some media types in about ten minutes. We've got to get to him before he makes his address."

He cursed again and then said, "I'll go over to the White House with George and Hank and we'll give him the picture. If he agrees, we'll do it. I want a call from you after you've talked to Hodges. He's got to be sure he can do it. In the meantime, we'll proceed as though it's a certainty."

David Baxter nodded and started to leave the room.

"Baxter!"

"Yessir."

"Take one of our planes. I'll phone New York and make sure Hodges is at the airport. Fly into La Guardia."

"Yessir."

"And the woman . . . are you sure she'll keep her mouth shut."

David paused and then shook his head. "No. I'm hoping that she does, but I don't really know."

Briggs groaned. "What the hell ever possessed you?"

David looked at the floor. "It was just . . . she was so angry, I was afraid she'd do something really stupid and get herself killed. . . ." He straightened up and looked Briggs in the eye. "I'm sorry. I know it was out of line. she hasn't done anything yet. I don't think she will."

Briggs just shook his head as David left the room and headed for the elevator. The pounding of his heart was almost frightening.

Chapter Nineteen

Jack Hodges met David and Cynthia at La Guardia and listened carefully as the plan was explained to him. David talked nonstop all the way to the headquarters of United Broadcasting. By the time they got there, Hodges knew exactly what was wanted.

He took David into a control room and positioned him in front of a television camera. He turned on a large video-taping machine and told David to say something, anything . . . for one minute.

David talked for a minute about the weather, baseball, the price of tea, and the various merits of sex at noon. Then Hodges motioned for David to join him at the console, with its thousands of lights and dials and switches and levers, looking like something out of a science fiction movie. The tape machine was still running and three computers were clacking away madly. David could see himself on the color monitor, still standing in front of the camera, his voice slightly muffled, but saying things other than what he had just voiced.

There was another man at the end of the console speaking into a microphone. It was his words that were coming from David's lips. His words, but the voice was David's, saying something about the price of coffee in Brazil and whether the size of women's brains were in inverse proportion to the size of their breasts.

Cynthia was making copious notes and underlined a memo to herself to research the connection between male chauvinism and stress. The country was on the verge of disaster and these people were making stupid jokes about women, oblivious of her presence.

The lip synchronization with the audio was a little off, and if you looked carefully, you could see that a portion of the picture, that part of the face where the lips were located, looked a little different. But only if you looked hard. And knew what was happening. The casual observer would never notice.

David stared at the monitor, stunned. Hodges was beaming.

David looked at him in awe. "How . . . ?"

Hodges grinned and lit a cigarette. "Ah . . . yes. How? Well . . . first the live tape is fed through a machine that converts the information on the magnetic tape into bytes, just like in a computer. Then we program this smaller computer to pick out only those bytes that we want to fool with. The small computer is connected to a voice synthesizer. The voice synthesizer has over sixteen thousand standard voices, which can be modified and made to sound almost exactly like any other voice. The computer picks the one that most closely matches the live voice, then automatically makes the adjustments needed. Then. . . ."

He stopped and seemed to notice Cynthia for the first time. He turned to David, concern written all over his face. "She CIA?"

"No."

"Then who the hell is she? She's making notes like a reporter, fer Chrissakes. This is supposed to be secret, isn't it?"

David nodded. "It is. Look, it's a little complicated and I don't have time to really explain. Trust me."

Hodges seemed unconvinced. David glared at Cynthia, his voice edged with impatience. "Cynthia . . . give us a break, will you? You're making everyone nervous. Could you put away the pen for a few minutes?"

"I'm sorry. It's just so fascinating, I wanted to. . . ."

Hodges interrupted her. "Do me a favor. Forget what you saw here. If the FCC ever gets wind of this, I'm in deep shit."

Cynthia nodded and put away the pen. Hodges continued to explain the system. "Like I said, it all gets fed into another computer, which takes the sound of the voice and matches the words being spoken to preprogrammed lip movements. The new, corrected image is reinserted back into a dupe of

299

the original tape and the whole thing is then fed back into the conversion machine, which puts it back on video tape. All we need is one minute and we can make anybody say anything. Only one problem."

David was still staring at the monitor. "What problem?"

"It's illegal as hell. The FCC would hang us by the nuts if they knew we had such a thing. We're only fooling around with it for kicks, but you can imagine what would happen if we really got to play. We could have the wildest presidential press conferences you ever saw."

David shook his head.

Hodges continued. "Most of the technology is off-the-shelf stuff. You see it in use every day. Chroma-key, for instance, where the weatherman is standing in front of this big map, except he really isn't. The map may be a hundred feet away, or in another room. All we're doing here is taking a portion of the picture, removing it from the image, changing it, and then putting it back in again. Only our way. The voice synthesizer is what would shake up the FCC if they knew. It's just a little too good."

David nodded. "It's fantastic! And a little scary. Imagine if the Russians had their grubby hands on this thing. They could show speeches by Taylor that had him saying all kinds of things. . . ."

Hodges's enthusiasm was dimmed slightly. "They'll have it within five years. There's been an embargo on certain types of computers headed for Russia, but they keep getting around that. In a few years, David, you'll see things on the tube that never happened. Actual news events, statements by known individuals, all of it fake. You won't know what the hell to believe."

"Well, that's not my problem right now. Right now, this thing could save a few million lives. Can you be ready to go on a moment's notice?"

"You bet. You give us the copy and we'll put it on the air. We'll have this terrorist asshole saying whatever you want him to say."

David asked, "And you can feed this to the other networks?"

"No sweat. We'll shoot it out to the satellite and they'll just pick up the feed. All we have to do is warn them and they simply push a button. If we have a conference call line open, we can time it to the very second. The only problem you'll have is overriding the original signal from the terrorist."

David looked grim. "We don't plan to override it. His signal will end and yours will start. We'll give you a countdown. But it could be any minute. I need you on alert from this moment on."

The portly Hodges grinned. "I ain't about to leave. If I need sleep or drop dead, there are three other guys right here who can do it all. We're ready right now. You just need to alert the other networks."

David nodded. "OK . . . I'll get the wheels going. We'll have someone call you within a few minutes with the script."

"OK . . . just remember. We need a full minute. It takes that long for the process to wind its way through the equipment. If the guy takes less time than that, we're outta luck."

David nodded. He thought: In more ways than one, friend.

Sitting in the small house in West Hollywood, Abdul Ben-Azzuz had seen the same news reports that everyone else had witnessed. He'd laughed at the President's claim that an extortion plot had been stopped in its tracks, then, as the news of the Israeli alert was broadcast, and the speculation continued that something else was going on, he began to get alarmed.

It seemed as though the Americans were ignoring Nadi's demands altogether. There were reports of meetings between the President and Rashon, meetings that were supposed to be secret, but were quickly discovered by a vigilant press. There was nothing to indicate that the demands were being met.

At first he couldn't believe it, and then he began to think that it was some sort of trick by the Americans. A trick he didn't understand, but a trick, nonetheless.

He considered sending another report, but discarded the idea. Nadi would know what was happening. He would make the appropriate response. The Americans had been warned not to attempt to interfere in any way. They had been warned!

And yet, they still had not announced any plans to force Israel to return the stolen lands. The stupid, stubborn Americans were going to let it happen.

He looked at his watch and moved into the

302

bedroom. In two minutes the signal would be given to maintain the vigil. He turned on the radio and set the dial to the proper frequency.

He waited.

One minute to go.

He had the feeling that this time there would be no signal, that Nadi would have lost his patience with these infidels. It meant that his life would be over in a matter of hours.

But he would accept that. He had prepared himself for it. In fact, he had reasoned all along that the Americans would never submit to the demands.

He waited.

There was no signal.

He checked his watch. It was working.

There was no question. The time had come.

He waited another minute and then moved back into the living room. He rolled back the carpet and lifted the cover from the one-square-foot hole in the concrete floor.

The timer had already been set. All that was left was to turn three switches.

He turned them one by one and watched as the digital display lit up. The bomb had been activated.

All that was left to do was wait. Wait to die.

He got down on his knees, bowed toward Mecca, and began to pray.

Nadi Amur sat in his cabin smoking American cigarettes and looking out the porthole. The seas were relatively calm, which was a blessing. It meant that the signals initiated by the four large dishes

303

aimed at satellites some twenty-two thousand three hundred miles up in space would hit their distant targets accurately. The dishes were placed on platforms equipped with gyros to keep the platforms positioned properly in seas with swells of up to five meters. These seas had swells of less than three.

His original idea had been to blow up one city at a time. After each explosion, he would demand, again, that the United States force Israel to surrender to him and his followers. He expected they would refuse at first. Then, he would destroy a city. He would demand anew. They would refuse again.

He'd calculated that after the third or fourth explosion, they would capitulate. The remaining bombs would stay in place. Assurance that agreements would be kept.

The plan had seemed foolproof. Even if the bombs were discovered, there was nothing they could do. If they tried to attack a location, the safeguards built into the bombs would detonate them automatically. If they tried to attack Nadi himself, the radio signals would cease and the bombs would be activated by those charged with that responsibility.

He picked up the report and looked it over again. It didn't make sense. They were refusing to obey his commands. He'd expected that. But he hadn't expected that they would report that there was but one bomb, which had been successfully disarmed. That was an insult. They were daring him!

The American press were printing a complete lie. There was no panic in America, and the people were going about their business as though nothing had happened.

He hadn't expected that.

He'd intended that the news of the discovery of the bomb factory in Canada would strike fear in the hearts of Americans. They would demand that their government obey Nadi Amur. Why should they have their comfortable lives interrupted because of some Zionists?

But they'd printed some lies about that and now they were broadcasting another lie. They were playing some stupid game with him.

It was then that he realized they would never give in. Never!

They hadn't heeded his warnings. They'd kept searching, digging . . . they'd followed the trail he'd left for them, but instead of accepting it as part of the warning, they'd simply used it to continue searching.

He'd wanted them to believe that he had the power. Obviously, they believed it, but didn't care. In their arrogance, they assumed they could stop him.

They couldn't.

They could kill him, but they couldn't stop him.

America would be destroyed.

Within a matter of hours.

The game was over. He wasn't enjoying this anymore. His plan had failed. They would never agree. So he had decided to eliminate one part of his plan and proceed to the end.

Instead of broadcasting a message of doom to the Americans and enjoying the spectacle of the resultant panic, he would make his broadcast, and instruct his men to trigger the bombs manually at the same time.

There was no reason to delay. No reason to play it out.

He had already give the order to stop the signals. The bombs had been activated. That was his insurance against a surprise attack on the ship. Even if they killed him before he had the chance to make the broadcast, the fate of the Americans was already sealed. The bombs would go off no matter what happened.

All twelve of them.

All at the same time.

Whether Nadi Amur lived or died.

The safeguards built into the bombs would prevent any attempts to disarm them in time.

All that remained now was to tell America why they were to be destroyed. He would make the broadcast and accept his fate, full in the knowledge that Allah's will would be served. Nadi Amur would die, but he would die with a smile on his lips. The world would always know he'd been there.

President Brandon Taylor sat at his desk, his hand clutching his wife's, and listened carefully as the tired men finished their presentation.

All of them had been at this too long. The unrelenting pressure had already put one man in the hospital and threatened to create other problems.

It was a nightmare that wouldn't stop. And in their exhausted state, the men presenting the plan seemed totally unsure of its chances of success.

Briggs, especially, seemed burned out. He'd stopped halfway through, out of breath, the perspiration pouring down his face, and asked George Halman to finish.

Halman, his eyes rimmed with red, his normally splendid clothes looking like he'd been on a three-week bender, carried on, his voice lacking in enthusiasm, his demeanor almost defeatist.

"The problem is," he said, "that we just don't know. We don't know anything for sure. But we're all agreed that it's the most logical explanation. And . . . we're all agreed that time *is* running out. If Amur is on that ship, and if he plans to make some sort of broadcast, it has to be one of two things. Either he plans to tell the American people that there are twelve bombs sitting in our major cities, or . . . he plans to tell his guys to push the buttons. Either way, he has to be stopped. And this crazy scheme of Briggs's boy is the only thing that has the remotest chance of working at all. If it fails, we have no alternative but to take the guardians of the bombs out and hope that none of them has a chance to push the button before we do."

Taylor listened carefully and nodded. "You're assuming that attacking the homes is too risky in and by itself?"

Halman nodded. "Yes. There are so many things that can go wrong. The button could be like a dead-man's switch on a subway car. The moment the guy dies, he releases his grip and the bomb is triggered."

"But the house in Los Angeles. The man wasn't holding the button."

"I know. But it could be a shift thing. You hold the button for a certain number of hours, then you turn a switch and you don't hold it for a number of hours. Amur has used both methods in the past with conventional explosives in aircraft. Suicide missions all. There's no way that Amur could know about a method of interrupting his remarks. Hell, *we* didn't even know that kind of technology existed. It could give us a chance."

President Taylor glanced at his wife. Penny nodded ever so slightly and he smiled at her. He leaned forward in his chair, rested his arms on the desk, and nodded himself.

"All right, gentlemen. That's it, then. I don't like it, but there it is. We have to go with it."

The moment he said it, he felt the strangest sensation come over him. As though the words had been uttered by someone other than himself. An image flashed through his mind. An image of an American general sitting in a room in wartime England in 1944. A man named Eisenhower . . . saying almost those same words about the decision to go ahead with the invasion of France.

The men quickly left the room to get the thing in motion. A technician entered and hooked up a speaker, which he placed on the President's desk. Then the President was alone with Penny Taylor.

He sighed as she kissed him on the forehead. "Penny," he said, "without you . . . I would have crumbled like a soda biscuit. Whatever happens, I want you to know that I'll never forget the help you've given me. And I want you to know something else. If we survive this thing, I'm going to

308

resign and you and I are going to spend some time together. Just you and me. Some remote island somewhere . . . maybe that rich English fella's."

She shook her head. "Wrong, my love. If we survive this thing, we've got another job to do before you and I can think about ourselves."

He looked at her with uncomprehending eyes. "I don't understand."

She moved over to the sofa and sat down, beckoning him to come and sit beside her. "Brandon . . . the time has come for some serious discussions with the Russians, the Israelis, the Chinese, and the others. Somehow, some way, we've *got* to put an end to this nuclear threat. Nadi Amur is a terrorist, but he represents something else. He represents the idea that we've come too far, too fast. It's more than the human mind can handle. There'll be other Nadi Amurs. Scores of them. We have to find a way to stop all of this."

Brandon Taylor sat beside his wife on the sofa and leaned his head back on the headrest. "Do you really think that's possible?"

"Yes. There has to be a way. And you have to help find it."

He thought about that for a moment. But then his thoughts turned back to the present. The moment at hand. He thought about the decision that had just been made. The task force had submitted a final report. They were convinced Nadi Amur was about to detonate twelve nuclear bombs. Any minute. The United States would be dealt a blow from which it might never recover. All because of one man. One man, who had worked feverishly for over ten years to exploit every mistake ever made in the handling of materials and people. Who had found holes in the most stringent of security measures; who had used guile and violence to gain access to the deadliest of weapons.

Briggs had presented a plan that could possibly prevent such a disaster. It had been the only plan presented. There were other options, but none that seemed capable of working, in any case.

And Brandon Taylor had given the approval.

Now, all he could do was sit and wait. Nothing could begin until Nadi Amur started to broadcast his television message, if indeed that was his intention. There had been so many ifs and buts to this incredible act of terrorism that no one knew for sure.

But they'd made the decision. He'd made the decision. They were going to act. They were, in effect, going to gamble. Gamble with the lives of millions of Americans. And if he'd made the wrong decision, he'd die right along with them. There was some comfort in that.

He sighed and looked up into the blue eyes of Penny, in whom he'd found a new source of strength. "God help us. God help us all. . . ."

She kissed him on the forehead and gripped his hand even tighter. "He will, Brandon. . . . He will."

The red telephone on the President's desk rang. He picked it up, listened, and then replaced the handset.

Again he sighed, and with a voice filled with terrible foreboding, said, "Well, the radio signals from Amur have stopped."

310

Penny's hand flew to her mouth. "What does it mean?"

"I'm not sure . . . we're still here. But. . . ."

David Baxter and Cynthia Green had arrived at the NSA headquarters in Fort Meade, Maryland, not far from Washington. With their vast network of listening equipment, augmented by the CIA's equipment, the NSA communications center was being used as the prime center for the entire operation.

Baxter had been cleared for entry into the top secret facility and Cynthia had not. There was no way David could explain her presence. She was a reporter. Almost the enemy.

He considered giving up and was about to leave when Fred Briggs entered the lobby. He looked at David and glared at Cynthia. Then the glare broke into a smile and he shook her hand.

"I understand you've been a big help to us."

She seemed shocked. "I don't know about that. . . ."

Briggs waved her off. "Look . . . I'm sure you realize the terrible spot we're in. Can we count on you to keep your mouth shut about all of this . . . until . . . well, you know what I mean."

She smiled at him, her green eyes wide. "I know what you mean. . . . I also know what terrible pressure you're under. It's so . . . unbelievable . . . all of it. I'll cooperate. I know it might mean my job, but that's not very important right now."

Briggs smiled again, his tired face barely able to

register the movement. "Thanks."

Briggs turned, walked over to the reception desk, and spoke to the security people, then returned with a tag, which he affixed to the lapel on her jacket. "Maybe Baxter's right. Maybe after this is all over, someone will have to tell the story in a way that makes us look good. God knows, we could use the help."

David was astonished at the sudden turnaround. Briggs had chewed his behind out thoroughly, and then, the first time he laid eyes on the woman, all was forgiven. He looked at Cynthia in awe. Such power! She'd caused David Baxter to break all of the rules and now she had converted Fred Briggs. She was a dangerous woman.

Cynthia thanked Briggs and the three of them walked towards the elevator in silence.

Then Briggs said, "It looks like you've been right on the money, David."

Baxter could tell that something had happened. He waited for Briggs to mention it. Briggs ran a hand over his forehead and then rubbed both of his temples. "The signals from Amur have stopped."

David could feel the breath leave him. "When?"

"About an hour ago."

"God!"

Cynthia asked, "What does it mean?"

David answered her. "We've not sure . . . but it could mean that all of the bombs have been armed, the timers set, ready to explode at a certain time. Maybe minutes . . . maybe hours."

Baxter asked Briggs, "Have any of Amur's people left the houses?"

"No."

"Well . . . that really nails it down, doesn't it?"

"I'd say so."

They seemed afraid to look each other in the eye. Three different people, all connected by a common thought. Wondering if in the next moment, or an hour from now, or six hours from now, their lives would end before they even knew it.

Chapter Twenty

Fred Briggs ushered David and Cynthia into a small office equipped with a television set and a ceiling speaker that would allow them to listen in on the radio traffic.

To avoid a prying media, not to mention Nadi Amur himself, all radio traffic was being transmitted through scramblers, then descrambled before being sent through the various closed circuits.

"You two will have to wait in here. I'm sure you understand."

Baxter asked, "Isn't there something I can do?"

Briggs shook his head. "No. Everything is set. If you're right, something should happen within hours." He paused and then said, rather grimly, "On the other hand, if you're wrong, something should happen . . . except we'll never know."

He turned to leave. "Maybe you should take turns getting some sleep."

Cynthia thanked Briggs for letting her in the building and curled up in a chair. David paced the floor.

The reporter took out a cigarette from the pack, looked inside the pack, swore, and threw the empty pack into a waste basket. She stared at the unlit cigarette for a moment and then laid it on a table.

"My last one. I'll save it. If I start to freak, try and find a cigarette machine will you?"

"What?"

"David . . . please stop pacing and sit down. I want to talk to you."

He blinked, sighed, and took a seat across from her.

"What's on your mind?"

"You."

"Me?"

"Yes, you. Do you mind telling me a few things about yourself? I've never slept with anyone I didn't know before. I'd kinda like to know a little bit about you, if only for the sake of propriety."

He looked at her with a bemused grin. "It's a tad late for that, don't you think?"

"Humor me."

"What do you want to know?"

"Everything."

He sighed and leaned back in the chair. "Nothing too exciting, really. I was born in Newport Beach, went to college at UCLA, majored in languages, then went to law school, got married, got divorced, and joined the CIA."

"That's it?"

"Just about."

"What about your parents? Are they still alive? Do you have any brothers or sisters?"

316

His eyes seemed stricken with a sharp pain that quickly disappeared. "My parents were killed in a car crash many years ago. I had a sister . . . but she was . . . killed a couple of years ago. What about you?"

"Me? Oh, let's see . . . I graduated from Oberlin with a journalism degree, worked as a reporter for a couple of small papers, then hooked on with the *Globe*. I was married for three years to a man who . . . well anyway, I'm divorced. My dad's gone but my mother is still alive. She lives in Maine with an aunt."

He seemed uncomfortable.

"What is it?" she asked.

He ran a hand across his forehead, the tiredness having taken its toll, and then said, "It's about Los Angeles. We were both worn out, and maybe it wouldn't have happened under different circumstances . . . but I want you to know . . . I'm not one for one-night stands. When this is over. . . ."

"Are you trying to tell me that you're attracted to me?"

Her eyes seemed to be daring him. The sparkle that had been gone for so many hours was now back, making them gleam.

"Yes . . . I am attracted to you."

"I see."

He looked hurt. He'd been hoping for a different response.

She looked away for a moment and then turned to face him. "I'll tell you what *I* plan to do when this is over. First, I'm going home to my apartment and sleep for about three days. Then, I'm going to

317

soak in a hot tub for at least a full day. After that, I'm going to a spa for two days and get the works. Then, I'm going to shop for some new clothes. After that, I'm going to drown myself in cheap perfume, put on some racy lingerie, light some candles, pick up the phone, and call you."

He was smiling again. "And then?"

"As soon as you get there, I'm going to screw your brains out."

He laughed. "Pick another part of me. I'd like it to last a little while."

They waited. While Fred Briggs and the others spent their time in the main communications center, David and Cynthia waited in the little room, taking turns catching some sleep.

While they waited, things were rapidly taking shape. The U.S. Navy submarine *Spicer* was in position, tracking the *Little Star* as it passed Gibraltar and entered the Atlantic Ocean.

Twelve teams of nuclear weapons experts waited near twelve homes, awaiting instructions to move in.

The radio signals from Nadi Amur had stopped. It was assumed that the lack of signals was in itself a message. As the day wore on, fears that a terrible gamble was about to be proven wrong mounted.

Perhaps Amur wouldn't make his expected announcement. Perhaps he would simply detonate the bombs. His past history had been one of killing first and then making pronouncements. Perhaps this would be the case now, as well.

They had put into motion a plan, first hatched in the fertile mind of David Baxter, who now slept, his subconscious mind squirting horrible things throughout his brain.

One of the images was of his old friend, Pierre Query. Query was clearly a member of Amur's inner circle. Query had faked most of the interrogation of the Panamanian shipping officials. For over a year, the Frenchman had provided false leads, withheld important information, aided the world's most ruthless terrorist, for reasons no one would ever understand.

Except that David understood. At least, he though he understood. There was only one possible explanation for Pierre's actions.

The information that Pierre was part of Amur's team had not been passed to anyone, including the French. There would be time for that later.

In the communications center, Fred Briggs listened nervously as the radio traffic continued. His mind reflected on the anguish on Brandon Taylor's face a few hours earlier as he was confronted with yet another horrible decision that had to be made. Briggs could almost feel the pain the President had felt, as the man had sat there, clutching the hand of his wife, almost unable to speak as Briggs laid it out.

"Sir . . . we have twelve teams in position. One in each city. If this scheme works and we are able to enter the homes freely, there are still certain problems. We need to decide beforehand . . . certain priorities."

President Taylor had seemed angry. "What priorities? What the hell are you talking about?"

"Sir . . . we are fairly certain that all of the bombs are the same. And we're sure that all of the bombs are booby-trapped. It's possible that the only people who would be able to tell us anything about the booby traps are dead. The Canadians have found some bodies near the site that are impossible to identify. We think they were the engineers. Normally, Amur kills his people when he doesn't need them anymore."

"I see . . . but what does that have to do with priorities? What priorities?"

Briggs was almost afraid to tell him. "Sir . . . it's very possible that one of the bombs may . . . go off. We'll proceed with the disarming procedure one step at a time. Each step will be monitored by each group, so that if something . . . goes wrong, the same mistake won't be made over and over again. We need to establish an . . . order of priority. In other words, which city we can afford to lose first . . . and then second. . . ."

For a moment, it looked as though the President might be physically ill. He sat there, staring at Briggs with unblinking eyes, the blood draining from his face, beads of perspiration popping up on his forehead and his upper lip.

"I don't . . . have any . . . idea."

Briggs pulled out a sheet of paper. "Sir, studies have been done . . . part of the exercises . . . we have some recommendations."

He handed the sheet of paper to the President,

who looked at it with eyes that threatened to fill with tears. Taylor nodded and returned the paper to Briggs. "Yes. . . ."

For whatever reason, the city of Cleveland was the first name on the list.

That had been three hours ago. And Briggs could see that same sick look on the face of many of the men as they all waited.

And waited. . . .

Listening to the radio traffic, the decoded messages, and watching the four television monitors mounted on the wall.

And then. . . .

At exactly 6:33 p.m., the waiting came to an end. The regular evening news broadcasts from New York on all four networks were interrupted. As was normally the case, the 6:30 feed was going out to the various affiliates, some of whom were rebroadcasting live, others taping for broadcast later. As a result, not all viewers in the eastern time zone were aware of the interruption, because it was the feed that was interrupted. As for viewers in the western time zones, they were oblivious of the entire thing.

The faces and stories being broadcast were replaced by the visage of a handsome olive-skinned man in his early forties, with deep creases in his face and seemingly perfect teeth. He sat at a small desk, inside some nondescript and unknown studio, wearing flowing white robes and smiling into the camera. His voice held barely the trace of an accent and his manner seemed unhurried, pleasant, like someone's uncle about to tell a bedtime story. Except the story he was about to tell was a nightmare.

"Good evening, ladies and gentlemen. I apologize for this intrusion into your homes, but unfortunately, your government has forced my hand. My name is Nadi Amur. You have probably heard about me. As you can see, I am very much alive. Just in case you think this might be a tape recording, let me assure you that it isn't . . . by giving you some of today's baseball scores."

In the National Security Agency's communications center, sixteen people immediately sprang into action. Telephone lines had been kept open to the Pentagon, United Broadcasting, the White House, the CIA, and the FBI, among others.

At United Broadcasting, Jack Hodges snapped three switches and the computers started clattering immediately. A signal went out to the U.S. Navy submarine *Spicer* and radar coordinates were fed into a computer. The *Spicer* was in position, at periscope depth, thirty nautical miles from the *Little Star*.

Cynthia Green sat stunned for a moment, then reached over and shook the sleeping David Baxter.

"David! It's started! It's started!"

For the briefest of moments, Baxter thought it was a continuation of the nightmare he was having, and then his pounding heart brought home the fact that the *real* nightmare was in front of him, on the television set.

From the speaker in the ceiling, the voice of the shooting officer on the *Spicer* could be clearly heard, from his station thousands of miles away, as he barked his instructions. "Twenty seconds!"

Commander Richard Booth acknowledged.

Nadi Amur continued his speech. "In the National League, the New York Mets lost to the Dodgers by a score of six to three. The winning pitcher was Fernando Valquez, the losing pitcher Roger Warden."

Across most of the eastern United States, people were puzzled but not yet concerned. For some unexplainable reason, a man who looked like some Arab was giving baseball scores. Most had missed his opening statement and were trying to figure out what was going on.

Jack Hodges, perspiration pouring down his face in the air-conditioned room inside the United Broadcasting studios, barked into the microphone in front of him. "We're rolling. Twenty-five seconds so far."

The shooting officer of the submarine *Spicer* yelled, "Ten seconds!"

Nadi Amur continued. "In the American League, the Boston Red Sox defeated the New York Yankees by a score of two to one.. The winning pitcher . . . well, I think you can see that I speak the truth. I am alive and well. Unfortunately, you Americans are about to face death."

"Fire One!"

The long, slender missile leaped from the submarine, trailing a plume of white smoke, headed toward the heavens, and then leaned over sharply as it followed the instructions implanted in its electronic brain.

Jack Hodges yelled into the telephone. "Thirty-five seconds!"

Nadi Amur smiled and leaned forward, his lips

almost touching the microphone in front of him. "On September sixth, I sent a message to your President. A very important message. It included a demand. A demand that has gone unheeded. You will be forced to suffer the consequences of that error in judgment."

Jack Hodges yelled into the microphone. "Forty-five seconds!"

The missile reached its programmed apogee and started a gentle arc back toward the sea.

Nadi Amur sighed and continued. "The Palestinian nation was seized illegally and turned over to the Zionists. For many years, we have fought to have this land returned to us, its rightful owners. Because of our never-ending struggle, we have been called terrorists . . . but it is the United States and Israel who are the terrorists. Our demands were simple."

Jack Hodges listened as the countdown continued. A voice could be heard in the ceiling speaker saying, "Six, five, four, three, two, one . . . zero." Hodges flipped three switches and pointed at a man at the end of the console. The man started talking.

The missile had hit its target perfectly. A nuclear missile, its normal yield reduced to the equivalent of a hundred tons of TNT, had created a temporary hole in the sea almost six hundred meters in diameter. The *Little Star* had been vaporized, along with millions of the ocean's inhabitants, into a cloud of gas and smoke and vapor that continued to rise into the air.

Caused by this relatively tiny device, a minor tidal wave rippled out from the impact point at almost the speed of sound, a wave that would rattle the diving submarine *Spicer* as it crash-dived to a safer position below the roiling ocean.

On television screens, the image of the strange man disappeared for a moment, and then, less than a second later, it reappeared. His voice seemed a little softer, but other than that, nothing had changed.

"We demanded that the United States force Israel to give our lands back to us. The United States has refused to do so. Reluctantly, I have come to the conclusion that they will never agree to such a thing. I have placed men in cities within the United States. Men armed with weapons of tremendous power. The power to destroy America. For a time, I considered using this power to force the terrorist America to. . . ."

Inside the studios of United Broadcasting, the tape continued to roll, the man at the end of the console continued to speak into the microphone, and fifty million Americans continued to wonder what the hell the man in the robe was trying to say.

". . . . stop supporting the illegal taking of our homeland. However, I have searched my soul and asked Allah for guidance. Allah has given me the answer. And the answer is not more death and destruction. The answer is wisdom and understanding. America will die eventually. It will die by its own hand. A hand soaked with the blood of innocent victims of its imperialistic policies. But it will not die by the hand of Nadi Amur. Allah has decreed that I commit no violent act. Therefore, I bow to the will of Allah. At this moment, I order

325

my men to vacate their positions and return to my headquarters. They will not be harmed. They are under the protection of Allah.

"But the United States must understand this: Allah is understanding. Allah is forgiving. Allah is patient. But He will not see injustice go unpunished. Unless the United States takes action to restore the Palestinian nation, Allah will strike with a fury that is beyond comprehension. Time is running out. My men will leave and return to my headquarters without taking action. Consider this a warning from Allah. There will be no further warnings. Good night."

Jack Hodges quickly flipped a series of switches and television screens across America went blank, then the images of various horrified newspeople appeared on the screens, sitting at their anchor desks, staring in disbelief at the studio monitors.

They were just starting to recover when pieces of paper were handed to them by completely disoriented staff members. Quickly, men and women paid large sums of money to deliver the news started to earn their keep.

At United Broadcasting, anchorman John Billings, who'd known nothing about the frantic machinations inside the control room, was as confused as those at the other networks. He tried to make the best of it.

"Well, ladies and gentlemen . . . it seems that our signal was interrupted by another of those nuts who likes to play around with electronic equipment. I have a note here that says . . . this is from the White House, apparently . . . no . . . OK, the note is not from the White House . . . it's a message from . . . wait a minute . . . yes. The President is about to make some comments on the broadcast that many of you have just seen. We're ready? All right. We now go directly to Washington and President Taylor."

Again, television screens across America went blank for a moment, and then the face of Brandon Taylor appeared, this time on almost every screen in America. Stations that had been taping the feed for later broadcast interrupted their programming to pick up the live feed.

President Taylor was seated in the Oval Office and looked calm.

"My fellow Americans. I'm sure many of you are wondering just what is going on. Well, I hope I can clear up the confusion." He paused and took a drink of water. "As you know, we reported to you that Nadi Amur had been responsible for the positioning of a nuclear device in Los Angeles. The device was disarmed. That statement was made as part of an agreement with Mr. Amur, an agreement that has been worked out after intensive negotiations with representatives of Mr. Amur's organization.

"As you know, it has been the long-standing policy of the United States not to negotiate with terrorist groups. That policy remains in place. However, because of the unusual circumstances surrounding Mr. Amur's acquisition of a nuclear device, we felt it advisable to try and reach some accord. Negotiations were begun secretly and agreement has been reached.

"Mr. Amur, as part of the agreement, has just made an address to some other groups loyal to his cause, requesting that they give themselves up and assist our people in disarming what, we are given to understand, are additional devices.

"Now, as Mr. Amur has stated, those people in his group who are in possession of nuclear devices have been ordered to turn themselves in to our security forces, who will provide safe passage for them . . . home."

As the President continued with his remarks, twelve teams of anxious men waited, secreted in positions surrounding the homes where the bombs were located, hoping against hope that this, the biggest con job ever perpetrated, would prove successful.

It had been determined that the first approach would be made in Los Angeles, because of the fact that Azzuz had already answered the door once, and would most likely do so again. The other teams would wait until they heard from Los Angeles before making a move.

Brian Carter, a member of the West Hollywood Police Department, the cop who had first encountered Azzuz, or Khamil, as he had then been known, had been enlisted to make the approach. Since he'd been there before, and since Khamil would probably recognize him, it was thought the least risky approach.

The nervous policeman walked slowly and carefully toward the front door. A few days ago he had approached this same door with a sense of boredom, a feeling of wasted effort. Now, with the knowledge that a bomb capable of destroying all of Los Angeles lay within the house, he could barely keep his knees from knocking.

He rapped lightly on the door and waited.

The wait seemed interminable. For a moment, Carter thought that the man wouldn't answer the door. Finally, the little man opened the door a crack and peered out at the young cop.

"Mr. Khamil . . . remember me, Brian Carter?"

The little man nodded. "Yes . . . what do you want?"

Carter could hardly speak. His voice seemed to go up and down the scale, oblivious of the commands from his brain.

"I . . . ah . . . I'm here on behalf . . . of the President. You heard the message from . . . Mr. Amur?"

Again, a nod.

"May I come in?"

There was a hesitation and then the door opened and Carter followed the Arab into the darkened house. The television set was on and Wilson could see the face of the President as he continued his address. Azzuz looked puzzled.

Carter said, "There are some men who would like to come in and disconnect the device. May I bring them in?"

The Arab stared at Carter and shook his head.

Carter felt his heart stop. "Why not?"

Azzuz ran a hand over his head and sighed. "The men may come in if they wish, but the device cannot be disarmed."

He looked at Carter with a face that was contorted with confusion. "That's what I don't understand. Nadi never even discussed the possibility of changing his mind. He is dedicated . . . to the idea that America must be destroyed. There is no way to stop the bomb. The timer has been set."

Carter felt the breath leave him. He could hardly utter the words. "Set? For when?"

Azzuz looked at his watch. "Tonight. In seven hours."

"Is it just this one . . . or all of them?"

"All of them. They are going to go off all at once. We received our instructions last night."

"How?"

"A radio signal. It stopped last night. That was our signal to activate the timers."

Brian Carter could feel his entire body shaking. "And you don't know how to disengage the timer?"

"No. We were never told. That's what I don't understand. Why Nadi would say what he did and not tell us. It doesn't make sense. Something is wrong. But if he was doing the broadcast with a gun at his head, he would have given us a code word. He didn't . . . so it was he . . . but it doesn't make sense."

Azzuz looked completely confused. Carter could feel his own heart pounding inside his chest at a dangerous rate. "Mr. Khamil . . . may these men come in?"

The little man sat down on the sofa and buried his head in his hands. "Yes . . . bring them in . . . I don't understand."

Carter fumbled with the small walkie-talkie and pushed the talk button. "This is Carter. You can

330

come in."

In minutes, the room was full of people, including Ronald Wilson. Wilson quickly administered "the drug" to Azzuz and waited for it to take effect.

Then he asked a series of questions. Within twenty minutes, the other eleven teams had the information. But it wasn't what they had hoped.

The bombs had been activated. Each bomb was the same. They were all real. They were all booby-trapped. Any attempt to deactivate them would set them off. And they were programmed to explode in less than seven hours.

The man who had designed the bombs was dead. Killed by Nadi Amur when his job was completed.

None of the guardians, the inner circle, knew anything about the workings of the bomb, only how to activate the trigger mechanism.

The word had gone to the teams in the other eleven cities. They approached the houses and captured the terrorists without difficulty. All were given "the drug." All gave the same information.

President Taylor, who had finished his television address and had been monitoring the radio traffic, gave the order. There would be no attempt to evacuate the cities. That would simply be impossible. Teams of experts were already in place. Because of the time factor, each team would work on deactivation independent of the others. But lines of communication would be set up connecting all twelve teams. Knowledge gained during each step would be shared. Each step would be charted. Each move would be broadcast before it was taken. In the event that one of the bombs went off, the other teams would know which move had caused the explosion.

It was all they could do.

And they would begin . . . now.

David Baxter leaned against the wall of the small office, listening to the messages as they went back and forth. He'd never felt so utterly helpless in his life.

In a way, he'd done his job well. He knew that. Nadi Amur had been found and killed. The bombs had been found and work was now beginning on deactivation. Part of him was sure that had it not been for his own actions, his own intuition, they might never have had even this opportunity to prevent disaster.

Another part of him was less sure. There had been those in the intelligence community, as well as in the administration, who had been convinced that some sort of negotiation with Amur might have defused the situation. That an effort to reach some sort of agreement with Amur would have resulted in the bombs' never being activated in the first place.

They had argued that time was needed. They had contended that the October 6 date was real and that Amur could be reached.

But David had studied the profiles, talked to doctors, become convinced that Amur, being totally mad, was not interested in anything except the destruction of the United States. He had sold that position to others and now it was too late. The die had been cast.

Right or wrong, there was nothing more he could do . . . but wait.

He looked at Cynthia sitting there in the chair, her hand at her mouth as she watched the television set and listened to the speaker in the ceiling. She was so very beautiful.

And, like himself, so very frightened.

He could hear the conversations between the various groups as they worked on the bombs.

"Just cleared through the concrete. The bomb is exactly as shown in the diagrams. The trigger activator shows six hours and three minutes. Checking now for obvious booby traps."

"Roger, we'll break through the concrete."

"Start with the hatch and work to the right of the CEDs."

"Roger."

Ten more locations acknowledged.

"The button is an open circuit. Removing button now."

"Roger."

"Button removed."

"Roger."

David picked up the phone and then pulled a note pad out of his pocket. He looked through it and then punched the buttons on the phone. In a moment, Jack Hodges was on the line.

"Jack, David Baxter. I just wanted to tell you what a great job you did."

"No sweat. Anytime, pal. It was kinda fun working with you guys. Maybe we can do it again, sometime. What happens now?"

"I don't know, Jack. You a religious man?"

333

"I haven't been for some time, but I am now. I'm praying in every religion I've ever heard of."

"Good. I'll talk to you soon. If this comes off, I'll come to New York and we'll get stupid drunk together. OK?"

"I'll hold you to that, pal."

David hung up the phone and went back to the chair, where he sat, immobile, as the work continued.

"This is Cleveland. The lead shield is probably wired to the casing. We're going to use the echogram now. Turning on echogram. . . ."

There was silence.

For perhaps thirty seconds, there was silence.

At first, David thought the speaker in the ceiling had fouled out, but as he moved closer to it, he could hear the sound of dead air.

And then, a seemingly disembodied voice was heard on the speaker.

"Oh . . . my God! My God! . . . This is . . . Air Force . . . Observer Three. The bomb in Cleveland . . . has just detonated. God! It's incredible! . . . The entire city is. . . ."

Chapter Twenty-one

The city of Cleveland had suffered the effects of a massive nuclear explosion. A gigantic dust cloud, the familiar mushroom shape now forming, was rising higher and higher into the air, being pushed southeast by the prevailing winds.

U.S. Air Force planes were in the air, confirming the explosion and tracking the cloud. They reported that initial tests indicated immense levels of radioactivity. National weather people quickly pinpointed an area stretching from Washington to New York City as being directly in the path of the cloud, and warnings were issued for everyone to head for cover. Basements, subways, even inside cars. Anything to get away from the deadly dust.

Throughout New York, Viginia, West Virginia, Pennsylvania, Maryland, Delaware, Ohio, and New Jersey, sirens wailed, all television and radio stations broadcast nothing but emergency warnings, and all police and fire stations were frantically trying to get the streets cleared.

Units of the army, marines, and the national guard swung into action to assist. Most of the northeastern section of the United States was in full, out-of-control panic. There were fears that as many might die in the panic as in the actual explosion.

As for the city of Cleveland, its central core was completely leveled. Almost every single thing within a six-mile radius of ground zero was completely destroyed. It appeared that the bomb had been detonated close to Cleveland Municipal Stadium. And outside the central core, the damage was incredible.

Fires were raging out of control in Shaker Heights, Maple Heights, Cleveland Heights, Lakewood, and as far away as South Euclid and North Olmstead. Initial estimates were that over eight hundred thousand people had died instantly, with the total death toll expected to top two million. An area of Lake Erie was actually boiling, and a tidal wave moving at five hundred miles per hour was crashing into lakeside cities. Detroit, Toledo, Erie, Buffalo were all awash with floodwaters. The Erie Canal had been destroyed. The blast had triggered an earthquake that had been felt from Chicago to New York City.

Within minutes of the explosion, the President spoke to the nation. His address was carried on every radio and television station in the country, and throughout most of the world.

He sat at his desk in the Oval Office, his face a

mask of horror, his eyes reflecting the terrible shock. His voice was halting, but he battled valiantly to exude some sort of confidence.

"My fellow Americans, it is with a heavy heart that I speak to you tonight. A monumental tragedy has been visited upon this great nation. A nuclear device, placed in the city of Cleveland by a group of terrorists . . . has exploded while attempts were being made to disarm the weapon. I have been advised that because of certain weather conditions, the radioactive cloud now moving over parts of Ohio and Pennsylvania is moving southeasterly at a height of twenty-seven thousand feet. A high pressure area, which has been covering the eastern part of the country for the last two days, is still in place. As a result, very little radioactive fallout is reaching the ground. I have been advised that very little is expected to reach the ground until the cloud is well out over the Atlantic Ocean. Therefore, I implore all of you to remain where you are, but take cover.

"The highways are already completely blocked. You are much safer if you stay in your homes, or place of business, keeping all doors and windows closed. Turn off all air-conditioning or heating systems and fill your bathtubs with water. Use whatever containers you can to accumulate water. It will not be contaminated at this time, but might be in a few days.

"All civil defense forces and the military are engaged in a program that will provide food and water to all of you. Medical supplies are on their way. The most massive rescue effort in the history of the world is, even as I speak, on its way to you. You have nothing to fear at this time.

"For those of you within fifty miles of the city of Cleveland, I urge you to disregard what I've just said and wait for the civil defense officials to assist you in evacuation. The evacuation must be done in an orderly fashion if it is to be effective.

"I have with me Dr. Walter Crone, who is an expert on the effects of radioactivity. He will now speak to you directly, and I urge you to follow his instructions to the letter. If you do so, many lives will be saved."

The cameras turned to Dr. Crone, who started giving instructions to all the people in the path of the radioactive cloud. President Taylor left the room and went to his private office, where he was joined by Penny and three of his closest advisors. They continued to listen to the radio traffic among those engaged in the effort to disarm the remaining bombs.

He took a seat beside his wife, who immediately grabbed his shaking hand and held it in hers.

"Brandon," she said, "you've got to pull yourself together. If you come apart now, this country is finished. It's taken a terrible blow, but it's still alive, still functioning. You're not just a man, my love, you're a symbol. The whole country looks to you for help. And you've got to give it. I know you blame yourself for this. But you mustn't. It isn't your fault. It's the fault of an insane group of men. You can't blame yourself."

He stared at her vacantly. "Penny . . . I was

338

wrong. It *is* my fault! Can't you see that! I should have tried to negotiate with Amur! I never gave it a chance! And now . . . all those people! God! And there are eleven more of them! Eleven more bombs! We'll never be able to do it! Don't you see that! The bastard has won! He's destroyed us! Just like he said he would!"

There was no consoling him. His head moved from side to side as if on a swivel. He looked as though he wanted to scream but the mouth just opened and closed silently. His eyeballs seemed to be spastic, jerking inside their sockets, unable to focus on any specific thing.

In his heart, all he wanted at this moment was the misery to end . . . his life to be over. The unbearable torture ended. Penny Taylor took his head in her arms and pressed it to her chest. She closed her eyes and uttered a silent prayer.

In the little room in the NSA building, David Baxter felt as though his lungs had ceased to function. His breathing was shallow and coming in short spurts. His heart was beating unmercifully and his hands felt ice cold.

Cynthia was gripping one of them so hard that it was numb. Her face was awash in tears.

It was impossible!

But it was happening.

The first of the bombs had gone off. The plan that David had been so excited about had been a failure. They had managed to kill Amur, get inside the houses, but the bastard had been ready for them.

339

The bombs had been booby-trapped with God only knew how many traps. It was impossible. They were running out of time.

Cleveland was gone. The other cities would be gone in a matter of minutes. Hours, at the most. And David Baxter would be dead, along with millions of Americans.

The country would be finished.

They had failed.

Failed.

With the stakes so incredibly high.

And there was nothing he could do, except wait for it to happen.

Maybe they should have tried something else. Maybe Amur might have listened. Maybe they should have just given in.

He tried to sort it out in his mind.

No . . . the man had been crazy. Nothing could have prevented it. He'd led them to the bombs because he'd wanted them found. He'd known all along what they would do. He'd counted on it. And even if they hadn't followed the expected procedure, he would have created another reason.

He'd won.

Cynthia tried to see through the silent tears but couldn't. Her hand held David's in a death grip. Ever since she'd become politically aware, while she was still in high school, she'd held the CIA in utter contempt. An attitude that had never wavered, until. . . she'd seen them at work. Frantically trying to prevent a mad terrorist from destroying the country. For the first time, she realized the horrors faced

· 340

by men who did what they did because they felt it was the only way.

There had been hundreds of situations that no one had ever heard about. In a way, they were like cops. Everybody hated cops . . . until they were stuck in the middle of nowhere, with a car that wouldn't go, the sounds of the night sending shivers up their spines . . . until a cop showed up . . . and sent the fears away.

She wiped the tears away and looked at David. He was sitting frozen in the chair, his face a deathly white, his chest heaving from the rapid breathing, his eyes dark and dead.

She wanted to say something. Something to comfort him. Something to make the pain go away. But her voice was still. The throat unable to do anything.

And in a hospital bed in Los Angeles, Frank Brown watched the television set in horror as President Taylor made his announcement and the civil defense system took over the airwaves, urging people to remain calm, not to panic . . . and he felt the pain in his chest change from the numbness following the operation to a sharp, breathtaking stab.

Mercifully, he lost consciousness immediately and monitor by the bed sent its message of death to the nurse's station.

In Alice Tremont's office in the *Washington Globe* building, Frank Bertram and Alice Tremont sat in chairs, nursing drinks and staring in horror at the television set.

Alice kept shaking her head and saying, over and over, "Ballard was right! This is just the beginning. Ballard was right!"

"How do you want this handled, Alice?"

"It doesn't matter anymore, Frank. Do what you want. It doesn't matter anymore. Can't you see? Ballard was right. All along!"

Frank Bertram quietly placed his drink on the table and left the room. Alice's longtime secretary was seated at her desk, crying uncontrollably. Frank grabbed her hand.

"Get on the phone now! Mrs. Tremont needs a doctor here right away."

The startled woman went through the roll-file and started dialing. Bertram returned to the office. She was still sitting there, staring at the television set. "You were right Ballard . . . you were right."

Inside the NSA communications center, a group of men and women sat silently, their bodies slumped, their faces drawn, as they concentrated on the communications between the other cities. The cities still alive.

For now.

"Turning on the Catscan now. . . ."

"Roger."

"No problem . . . we're getting a reading. We can

342

see the connections. There are three of them. The right front quadrant of the shield can be lifted three inches and the connection made. OK . . . we're lifting the right front quadrant now. . . ."

The was a deathly silence. Then, "Bingo! The right front quadrant is off."

"Nice going, Tommy!"

"OK, this is Miami. We're running the Catscan now. Same thing. Three connections on the right front quadrant."

"Roger."

The acknowledgments continued.

"This is Philly. There's a mercury switch on the casing of the left front quadrant. Make sure you don't move the bastard."

"Roger!"

"Let's not move too fast here. Everyone check in after every move. Identify yourselves."

"Miami, shield removed."

"Dallas, shield removed."

They all checked in and then someone said, "Three hours, four minutes."

In the White House, President Taylor seemed to have recovered slightly from the horrible shock. He stood up and paced the floor, his hands in his pockets.

Two men had come into the room, both close advisors to the President. They hadn't said a word, but for some reason each had felt this was where he wanted to be.

Taylor hadn't spoken a word to them, nor had he objected to their presence. Now, as he paced the floor, he talked to them both.

"If we get out of this alive, I want Bruniski in here. We have to end this . . . forever. The hell with the politics! We have to find a way!

"This has to be a message of some sort. A warning. Not from Amur . . . but from . . . God, maybe! I don't know . . . All I know is this! As long as we continue down this road we're on, we're forever at risk. We can't continue to live like this!"

The men nodded silently.

Penny Taylor walked over to her husband and put her arms around him and held him close. Then, together, they walked out of the Oval Office and into the press room. The President stood in front of a group of unusually quiet reporters and spoke, his voice even and controlled.

"Ladies and gentlemen, I'll continue to speak to the American people as this night wears on. I expect I'll be on the air every ten minutes or so. At the moment, the reports coming from Cleveland are not good. There are almost a million dead and many, many injured. Perhaps as many as five hundred thousand.

"The panic seems not to be abating, and we have some reports of panic in other parts of the country. The highways are a nightmare and riots have broken out in many of our major cities. We are doing everything we can to assure people, but as you can see, we're not meeting with much success.

"I would urge you to support the effort to bring

this situation under control. At the present time, the radio and television system is under the control of the civil defense people. It will remain like that for a few hours yet. But, once this is over, you'll have your airwaves back.

"I want you to consider carefully what you say as reporters and commentators. The most important thing you can do right now is to help in restoring calm. I beg you not to play up the negative aspects of what has just happened."

He started to move away from the podium as the questions were being screamed at him. He stopped, thought for a moment, and then returned to the podium.

"I'll be in from time to time to keep you updated. Tim will answer any questions you might have."

Then the President turned and left the room.

The radioactive cloud was now almost directly over Pittsburgh. It had been measured by special probes launched by U.S. Air Force aircraft, and the emissions at twenty-eight thousand feet were twenty-two hundred rems, dropping down to a hundred sixty rems at ground level. If the winds and high pressure system stayed constant, health problems could be minor on a short-term basis. However, it was well known that such a high dose could cause cancer in humans in later years.

A half hour later, the cloud had passed Pittsburgh, and the ground-level measurements were less than a hundred rems. Enough to cause nausea, but not enough to be fatal. The radioactive material within the cloud was dissipating, and it was determined that no evacuations of government people in Washington would be required, although cover was still called for.

A cordon was in the process of being placed around Cleveland, or what was left of Cleveland. In spite of the numbing shock of the disaster, an amazing amount of activity had been effected in a short five-hour time span.

Appeals went out nonstop for people to remain calm, but full-scale riots were raging in seven major cities, with large fires raging out of control in five cities.

On the highways in the states immediately southeast of Cleveland, injured and dead lay unattended on the pavement, among a mass of mangled steel. Every single highway and street was impassable. Vehicles of every description tried to find paths through farmland and forest, and the night was filled with the sounds of crashing metal and human screams.

In other parts of the world, people sat glued in front of television sets or radios as the reports kept coming . . . about the greatest disaster ever to strike America.

It was a carnage.

And still the teams worked on, now with less than two hours to go.

David Baxter and Cynthia Green remained in the little room that had become a prison of sorts, and listened quietly as the efforts continued.

346

The single cigarette that Cynthia had been saving still lay on the table, unsmoked. She hadn't had a cigarette all day, using the withdrawal symptoms as a way to force her mind off the terrible events of the day. It was a trick she'd used in other times of stress. She'd been known to place thumbtacks in her panty hose, at certain strategic places, as a way of keeping alert and attentive at functions where a display of total boredom was not in keeping with the festivities. People who had sat beside her at those functions thought she was a rather rigid personality. Subject to forced smiles.

She wanted a cigarette badly. In the absence of thumbtacks, that need helped to keep her in touch with reality.

They both listened as the litany continued.

"I can see the warhead connections now. There are three wires leading to the timer. Red, blue, and yellow. Let's all have them in front of us before we continue."

"Roger."

The other teams checked in.

"OK. We have a reading of twenty-four volts on the red lead. That check out with everyone?"

They acknowledged that it did.

"We have twelve volts on the blue lead."

The door to the small room opened and Fred Briggs walked in. He looked terrible.

They all looked terrible.

"I'm sorry, you two. We kinda forgot all about you. You need anything to eat?"

Both shook their heads.

"I've just been on the phone with the President. He asked me to pass along a message to both of you. Miss Green . . . the President has given permission for you to write this story as you see fit. Nothing is being classified. You're free to tell it any way you want."

Normally, Cynthia would have responded with glee. This time, her reaction was subdued to the point of indifference. "Well . . . thank you . . . I have some questions I'd like to ask."

"Go ahead."

"Well . . . when Amur made his . . . speech, he referred to men in cities . . . plural . . . armed with weapons of tremendous power. The President, in his follow-up remarks, made similar references. And yet, ever since that first broadcast, there's been no further reference to the other cities. Am I to understand that the people in those cities don't know what's going on? Why haven't the other cities been evacuated?"

Briggs glanced at David and then Cynthia. He seemed embarrassed. "Well," he said, "the fact is that reference was made to the other cities to alert Amur's men . . . to get them to surrender. The President's initial remarks were fed only to the stations that had seen Amur's remarks. We've refrained from making any other mention simply because no worthwhile purpose would be served."

"So the people in L.A. are unaware of the dangers?"

"That's right. There isn't anything we can do. To attempt an evacuation would create more harm than good."

"But . . . the people are in a panic!"

Briggs nodded. "I know. But it isn't nearly as bad as it could be. Amur's speech was seen live only in the East and some parts of the Midwest, except for his own men, who were seeing it directly from the satellite. The cities who saw the speech are the cities with a panic problem. In the rest of the country, they never saw the speech at all, and we won't allow it to be broadcast as news. Not until this is over, anyway. L.A., San Francisco, and the other big cities are totally unaware, and there is no panic whatsoever in those cities. In fact, everything has come to a complete halt. People are just sitting there watching television. It's . . . like the day Kennedy got shot. As for evacuation, you know as well as I do that the major cities are impossible to evacuate inside twenty-four hours. We don't have that kind of time."

Cynthia shook her head. "So . . . ignorance is bliss."

Briggs nodded. "In this case . . . yes." The director of the CIA paused and then said, "I know it sounds awful, but we've done a lot of studies on this subject. The steps we're taking here aren't frivolous. They're the result of some hardheaded thinking. Realistic appraisals of human reaction."

Cynthia withdrew and sat back in the chair, shaking her head. Briggs turned to the distraught Baxter. "David, the President asked me to tell you that he feels your plan was the only possible chance we have. No matter what happens, anything else would not have worked. We know that now. There's still a good chance that the rest of the cities will be saved. They've worked their way through half of the traps and things are moving more quickly than we'd expected they would. Clearly, some, if not all, of the rest of the cities will be saved. The President feels that you are primarily responsible for that. I concur. We all owe you a great deal."

David nodded slightly. "Well . . . I don't know. Maybe if we had. . . ."

Briggs cut him off. "David . . . we went over every possible angle. The bastard had it all worked out. If we hadn't interrupted his broadcast, we'd all be dead. The entire twelve cities would have gone up. If we had killed him before he made the speech, his guys would have blown up the bombs by hand. We're sure that the number sequences that were being broadcast were a code, giving the time of his speech. At first, cryptography couldn't get a handle on the number sequence, but they ran it again, using the time of six-thirty-three as a key. It worked. His men were expecting that speech. If it hadn't taken place, it would be all over. So you see, we would have been left with ashes. You saved a lot of lives, mister."

With that, the director walked over and hugged David Baxter, a most uncommon action.

He stepped back and said, "If you need anything, let me know."

And then he was gone.

And the teams worked on.

Cynthia was beaming. "Oh, David . . . I'm so

350

proud. I know what's happened is terrible . . . but at least. . . ."

David held up his hand. "Let's wait until this is over."

So they waited.

And listened.

And suddenly, the radio traffic was getting heavy. Several voices were talking, the mood shifting dramatically. The voices were the same ones that they'd been listening to for hours. But now, there was a sense of excitement in the voice of the point team leader. A feeling of hope.

"OK . . . I think this is the last one. Give me a minute, here . . . please God! YES! I've got it! The fucking thing is dead!"

The Philadelphia team removed the last of the thirteen booby traps that had been placed within the bomb, removed the warhead, and carefully placed it in a large drum. The bomb was disarmed.

Within fifteen minutes, the other ten bombs were disarmed.

The civil defense system went off the air and the networks went to work.

Inside the communications room there was jubilation, tempered by the continuing disaster of Cleveland.

But they still celebrated. It was horrible. Terrible. But it was over. And it could have been so much worse.

Cynthia Green finally lit the cigarette she'd been staring at most of the day and asked the telephone operator for an outside line. It was given without question.

"Washington Globe."

"Give me Frank Bertram."

"I'm sorry, that line is busy."

"Lady . . . this is Cynthia Green. At this moment, I am sitting in a room inside the National Security Agency building with the biggest story our newspaper will ever know. You've got five seconds to get Bertram on the telephone or I will personally come over there and kill you dead!"

"One moment please."

There was a short delay and then Frank was on the telephone.

"Cynthia? Where the hell are you?"

"Shut up, Frank. Turn on the tape recorder and don't say a word for the next half hour."

As she related the story, David Baxter watched her, her body and soul filled with spirit once again, like a battery that had been recharged.

She'd said she hated her job.

Sure she did.

Just like he hated his job.

He sighed. It was over. This time.

And no one was more aware of that fact than President Taylor. As exhausted as he was, his body incapable of producing any more adrenaline, he ordered that the Soviet ambassador be brought to the White House forthwith. It wasn't a request, it was a demand.

He looked at some of the telegrams that had poured into the White House from all over the world.

They were expressions of shock, sympathy, and support. Most were from heads of state. Most included offers of whatever help was needed.

So far, 127 countries had been heard from, with more coming in.

Now was the time.

It was just as Penny had said.

She was right.

Now was the time. There was a job to do.

Chapter Twenty-two

Three days later, David Baxter awoke in the fragrant bed of Cynthia Green. The sunlight was streaming in the partly open window, and the sound of birds could be heard as they busied themselves in the tree close by.

He rolled over and looked at the beautiful face of the woman who had entered his life so strangely. For the first time since he'd known her, she seemed at peace, her hair spread out on the yellow pillow slip, her breathing slow and even, her ample breasts rising and falling, the skin seemingly luminescent.

She was beautiful.

He slipped quietly out of the bed and went into the bathroom, grabbed a towel, wrapped it around his middle, and then headed for the kitchen.

By the time he returned to the bedroom with the coffee, she was awake, smiling at him and making no effort to replace the sheet that had fallen away during the night.

"Good morning," she said. "How are you feeling today?"

David grinned as he handed her a cup of coffee. "I feel a bit stupid."

"Stupid?"

"Yeah. All because of you."

"Me?"

"Yeah. You said. . . ."

She giggled. "I remember . . . I said I was going to screw your brains out."

"Right."

The smile left her face and she suddenly seemed sad again. David patted her hand. "Look . . . it's all over now."

She shook her head. "No, it isn't. In a few minutes, President Taylor is going to address the United Nations. He'll probably talk about the need for serious talks on nuclear disarmament, now that we all know the human race can't deal with such power. Everyone will nod their heads and push their pencils, meetings will be set up, and talks will begin. Then the horror will begin to fade, and the concerns will get around to other matters. After about a year of dancing around, they'll shelve the whole thing and get back to the job of making bigger and better bombs. Then some other nut with a cause will do it all over again . . . or some computer will hiccup and a thousand missiles will take to the sky and we can kiss our asses good-bye."

David shook his head. "You certainly are a cynic."

She picked up a copy of the *Globe* from the night

table and handed it to him. "See this! The paper reprinted the article I did six months ago. Sort of an I-told-you-so deal. They didn't pay attention then, David Baxter, and they won't pay attention now. Three million dead, eleven million injured, damages in the hundreds of billions of dollars . . . so far. God! The number of people that will die horribly in the months and years to come . . . not to mention the incredible damage done to people's hopes and dreams. What have they got to look forward to now? More of the same?"

She sat up in bed, talking with much animation, totally unconcerned with her nakedness.

"Right now, everyone's in shock. But we humans seem to be able to get over shock quickly. We'll manage to put this behind us and get on with the business of destroying the planet."

David shook his head. "You could be wrong about that. It's possible that this thing has shocked some important people more than you can imagine. It's possible some good may come of all the death, the destruction. . . . You know, the Soviets are very concerned. Chernobyl really scared the hell out of them, but Cleveland just knocked them on their cans. The fact that one crazy bastard was able to do that . . . one man! Christ! He might have succeeded in blasting all twelve cities off the map . . . it would have meant the end of America! It could happen to them, too!"

She shook her head. "You're a dreamer, Mr. CIA. Just like my ex-husband. I'd have thought, you being in the business you're in and all, that you'd see things as they really are. No . . . they'll never really believe that. They'll tighten up security all over the world, figuring that will do the trick. It won't. With all of our sophisticated systems, we still have bank robberies in this country. We still have husbands shooting wives over some stupid argument that the idiot can't even remember after he blows her away. And vice versa. Human beings have this arrogant attitude that they are thinkers, therefore superior. Name any issue . . . any issue! religion, politics, sex, whatever, and you'll get as many differing opinions as you'd ever want. We'll never put away our nuclear toys, because we think we can handle them. We have systems . . . Christ! Some systems . . . it's usually the human element that screws up. Usually—we like to blame it on the machines, but it's usually the human involvement. We can't handle the simplest things. Something as complex as worldwide nuclear disarmament is totally out of the picture. We never learn. Never will learn."

He was surprised by the depth of her negative feelings. "Cynthia . . . if everyone adopted that same attitude, we might as well throw in the towel. We've all got a right to be depressed, but. . . ."

She held up her hand. "I'm not depressed. I'm just a realist. Look at what's happened to Taylor. Already, there are people after his scalp, saying he messed it up. People out to grab votes in the next election, not caring one damn bit about anything but their own selfish interests. Who knows what decisions they would have made? It's so damn easy to sit back and criticize after the fact.

"David . . . this whole thing was a warning. A warning to the human race. We've come too far. Too fast. Our priorities are totally wrong. We've had other warnings in the past . . . some we listen to, most we ignore. If we ignore this one. . . ."

David looked at his watch. President Taylor was about to make his speech. He walked over to the television set and turned it on. Then he went back and lay down beside her, as Brandon Taylor, looking ten years older than he had a few weeks ago, began his remarks.

". . . States has received a severe blow. A blow that could have been fatal for the entire country, but for the efforts of a small group of dedicated men who risked their lives. Historically, it has always been thus. A small group of men risk their lives so that others might live. I speak to you today of the future. A future free of the horror of nuclear annihilation. Something that can be attained only. . . ."

Cynthia had switched the set off with her remote control. David looked at her, bewildered. "Don't you want to hear what the man has to say?"

She shook her head. "No. It's all bullshit. A small group of men risked their lives. . . . Hell, they risked *all* of our lives . . . they go up . . . we go up. It's just fantasy. I've had enough of that."

"You really are depressed!"

"No. Disappointed. I'm very disappointed, David Baxter."

He patted her arm. "I think you better turn that

thing back on. You're about to miss a very important speech."

She looked at him suspiciously. "You know something. What is it?"

"You'll have to listen to the President to find that out. But I can give you a hint. There was a meeting yesterday attended by the heads of thirteen countries. Including the Soviets. Very hush-hush. But today, it won't be.

"They've all agreed, Cynthia. Finally, they've all agreed. Politics is out the window, and survival of the human race is now the hot ticket. They're scared shitless, kid. They've agreed to eliminate nuclear weapons . . . all nuclear weapons . . . from the face of this earth. They've set up a special force . . . a multinational police force, to seek out and destroy any nuclear weapons in the hands of Third-World countries. They've agreed to force all countries to shut down reactors that use weapons-grade materials, or produce the stuff as a by-product.

"And they aren't wasting any time. The target is the end of the year. By then, they fully expect to have the schedule completed. Implementation is to take no longer than six months. It's really going to happen. They'll do it, Cynthia. They're really gonna do it."

She stared at him, shaking her head. "I don't believe it! For years, they've said that the Russians have such a superiority in conventional weapons systems that we can't afford to get rid of our nuclear arsenal."

"I know . . . but part of the deal is a balancing

of all troops and weapons systems. Even-steven."

"They did this in three days?"

"It looks that way."

She turned on the television set again.

"It's impossible! Those characters can't possibly come to such a agreement that quickly. Or carry it out! This is just some more bullshit!"

The smile left David's lips.

"Not this time, Cynthia. Not this time. They're really and truly terrified. It's much like you wrote in your article six months ago. Technology is moving ahead so fast, and we're beginning to rely on it so much, that they've really begun to understand the dangers. The confidence is gone. If one lunatic can do it, another lunatic can do it. They're finally beginning to realize that we're out of control. They're going to do it. Maybe twenty years down the road, they'll change their minds and start it all over again, but for now . . . they're really serious. They can all see with their own eyes the horrors that lie ahead. And they don't like what they see."

She grabbed his hand and held on. "I can't believe it. It seems too good to be true!"

They both watched as the President made his dramatic announcement, as Penny Taylor beamed, sitting in a chair just to the right and behind him. Beside her sat representatives from thirteen countries.

It was something. It was a start.

And after it was over, Cynthia asked David if he had any brains left.

He did.

And after *that* was over, she asked, "What about you, Mr. CIA man? Where are you off to?"

"I'm off to Paris to see my cousin. You know, the guy who works at the embassy? Then, I think I'll take a little vacation."

She couldn't help but laugh. "Your cousin, eh? God, you're an awful liar. Don't you ever tell the truth about anything?"

"Sometimes. Like . . . when I tell you that I'd like to take you with me to France. Have you ever been to France?"

She shook her head. "No. Besides, I don't have a passport."

He laughed out loud. "No passport! Well, that might be a problem for some people, but you have friends in high places, my love. Very high places."

She started to laugh, as well. She did have friends in high places. Higher than anything on earth.

The 747 landed at Orly, and Grant Talmage was there to meet them. It seemed as though years had passed, not weeks. David introduced Cynthia to Grant and they all walked out to the car. Grant was effusive. "I read your stories in the *Globe,* Miss Green. I must say, I can't remember the last time the CIA received a favorable review. Of course, you must remember that here in France, we're members of the State Department."

"I understand."

Grant started the car and pulled away from the curb. David noticed something instantly. The car smelled of perfume, not the normal reek of stale cigar smoke.

"You didn't!"

"Didn't what?"

"Quit smoking!"

Grant grinned. "Yeah, I did. How 'bout that?"

"I don't believe it. What brought this on?"

Grant smiled at him, opened his mouth wide, and pointed to the inflammation inside his mouth.

"What happened?"

Talmage grunted. "While I was listening to the chatter between the guys working on the bombs, I stuck a cigar in my mouth the wrong way. Twice! That did it."

David laughed. "Well, whatever it takes, I guess."

They drove in silence for a while, and then David asked, "Did you find out anything about Pierre's family?"

Grant sighed. "Yes . . . they'll be OK. The government cancelled his pension and the life insurance didn't pay off because of the suicide, but Mrs. Query has about thirty relatives, some of whom are doing real well. They're making sure she and the kids are looked after."

"Good. That's great. What would you do, Grant?"

"Do about what?"

"You know. If some assholes came to you and told you they'd kill every one of your kids unless you cooperated, what would you do?"

Grant shook his head. "I don't know. I really don't know. The man had eight of them, right?

Eight kids. And he was convinced that Amur was bluffing about the bomb, anyway. Sure, he knew that Amur had the plutonium, but he really didn't believe that the man was capable of producing a bomb. He thought it was a con. . . . Poor bastard. Even if he killed himself before working for Amur, he knew the man would still do it. That's what the note said, anyway . . . and I believe it. What would I do? In his shoes . . . probably the same thing. I guess that's why I never got married."

David snorted. "The reason you never married is because you're such an ugly bastard, nobody would have you."

Grant laughed. "Listen . . . you can't talk to me that way. I'm your boss! What are you doing back here, anyway? I'd figure you'd want to take a vacation after all of this."

"I intend to. But first, there's a small problem we have to clear up. I brought with me the results of the interrogations of some of Amur's people. We have some new information on 'the group.' Looks like they were concerned about Amur because they felt they couldn't control him, so they started peeling some of his people away. We've got a lead on where they are and what they're doing. Part of the plutonium taken from the *Armand Lavertue* three years ago ended up in their hands. That was the trade-off. They let him use the sub in return for some of the stuff."

Baxter sighed. As he heard himself say the words, it was like a nightmare being replayed in his mind. But this time, the nightmare had an ending. "Grant

. . . they're working on a bomb. You and I are heading to Tripoli and . . . get this . . . we're meeting with a group of Russians and some Syrians. Are you ready for that?"

Grant coughed. "I don't think so. What do we do when we get there?"

David grinned at him. "Nothing much. Just put 'the group' out of action. Permanently."

"Oh . . . well . . . that should be easy."

David laughed. "Well, it won't be as tough as you think. This is a whole new ball game, Grant. New rules, new players, new teams . . . it's weird. All we're doing is giving the briefing. The Russians and the Syrians are the ones who are going to do the job. It'll be easy for them. They have access . . . Christ! This is strange!"

Grant shook his head. "I can't see this love feast lasting very long."

"Maybe not . . . but we should enjoy it while we can."

Again, they grew silent. Both lost in thought. Both wondering the same thing. Was it really possible?

Cynthia broke the silence. "How long are you planning on being away?"

"Two days, tops. And then we'll have that vacation. I'll show you a Paris you won't believe. If I were you, love, I'd get as much rest as possible. You're going to need it."

Cynthia grinned. "Sure . . . promises, promises. By the way, there's something I've been meaning to ask you for some time. That gun you handed me

365

. . . back there in Los Angeles, was it . . . really loaded?"

David caught the strange look that Grant was aiming in his direction. He looked away and stared out the window. "No, it wasn't loaded. We're not allowed to carry loaded guns unless we're out of the country."

"So! You conned me! You bastard!"

Talmage grunted and asked, "Anybody got a cigar?"

ASHES
by William W. Johnstone

OUT OF THE ASHES (1137, $3.50)

Ben Raines hadn't looked forward to the War, but he knew it was coming. After the balloons went up, Ben was one of the survivors, fighting his way across the country, searching for his family, and leading a band of new pioneers attempting to bring American OUT OF THE ASHES.

FIRE IN THE ASHES (1310, $3.50)

It's 1999 and the world as we know it no longer exists. Ben Raines, leader of the Resistance, must regroup his rebels and prep them for bloody guerrilla war. But are they ready to face an even fiercer foe—the human mutants threatening to overpower the world!

ANARCHY IN THE ASHES (1387, $3.50)

Out of the smoldering nuclear wreckage of World War III, Ben Raines has emerged as the strong leader the Resistance needs. When Sam Hartline, the mercenary, joins forces with an invading army of Russians, Ben and his people raise a bloody banner of defiance to defend earth's last bastion of freedom.

BLOOD IN THE ASHES (1537, $3.50)

As Raines and his rugged band of followers search for land that has escaped radiation, the insidious group known as The Ninth Order rises up to destroy them. In a savage battle to the death, it is the fate of America itself that hangs in the balance!

ALONE IN THE ASHES (1721, $3.50)

In this hellish new world there are human animals and Ben Raines—famed soldier and survival expert—soon becomes their hunted prey. He desperately tries to stay one step ahead of death, but no one can survive ALONE IN THE ASHES.